LAST STAGE TO EL PASO

LAST STAGE TO EL PASO

•A RED RYAN WESTERN•

WILLIAM W. JOHNSTONE

AND J.A. JOHNSTONE

PINNACLE BOOKS
Kensington Publishing Corp.
www.kensingtonbooks.com

PINNACLE BOOKS are published by

Kensington Publishing Corp.
119 West 40th Street
New York, NY 10018

Copyright © 2022 by J. A. Johnstone

PUBLISHER'S NOTE
Following the death of William W. Johnstone, the Johnstone family is working with a carefully selected writer to organize and complete Mr. Johnstone's outlines and many unfinished manuscripts to create additional novels in all of his series like The Last Gunfighter, Mountain Man, and Eagles, among others. This novel was inspired by Mr. Johnstone's superb storytelling.

All Kensington titles, imprints, and distributed lines are available at special quantity discounts for bulk purchases for sales promotion, premiums, fund-raising, educational, or institutional use.

Special book excerpts or customized printings can also be created to fit specific needs. For details, write or phone the office of the Kensington Sales Manager: Attn.: Sales Department. Kensington Publishing Corp., 119 West 40th Street, New York, NY 10018. Phone: 1-800-221-2647.

PINNACLE BOOKS, the Pinnacle logo, and the WWJ steer head logo are Reg. U.S. Pat. & TM Off.

First Printing: January 2022

ISBN-13: 978-0-7860-4896-0
ISBN-13: 978-0-7860-4897-7 (eBook)

10 9 8 7 6 5 4 3 2 1

Printed in the United States of America

CHAPTER ONE

In the late summer of 1889, a six-horse team brought the Abbot and Morrison mail stage safely home to San Angelo . . . with two dead men in the box.

"How many does that make?" Captain Anton Decker said.

Long John Abbot looked miserable. Stunned. His bearded face ashen. "Six," he said. He shook his head. "I can't believe Phineas Doyle and Dewey Wilcox are dead. Just like that . . . dead."

"Believe it, they're all shot to pieces," Major Lewis Kane, the 10th Cavalry doctor, said. Gray-haired with a deeply lined face, he didn't appear too old to be a doctor but was well past his prime as an army officer. He climbed down from the box, shook his head, and added, "There's nothing I can do for them. They look like they've been dead for several hours."

Captain Decker, at twenty-seven, the youngest company commander in Fort Concho, was somewhat less than sympathetic. He badly wanted a name as an Indian fighter, but the Plains tribes were subdued and there was little glamour in fighting Apaches. "I'll report the incident to

Colonel Grierson but I'm sure he'll agree that this is a civilian matter," he said.

"The army could help me round up the road agents that are responsible for my six dead," Abbot said.

"As I said, I believe it's a strictly civilian matter," Decker said. "Perhaps if your stages were carrying army payrolls we would've taken an interest, but since they were not, it's unlikely Colonel Grierson will become involved, especially after the 10th Cavalry moved out and left us so undermanned."

"I'll talk to the county sheriff," Abbot said. "But he won't do anything."

"Try him. He might round up a posse or something."

Abbot laid bleak eyes on the soldier. "He'll sit in his chair with his feet on his desk, drink coffee, and give me sympathy, not a posse."

"That's just too bad," Decker said. He saluted smartly. "Your obedient servant, Mr. Abbot. Now, see to your dead."

"Two more, Long John," said Max Brewster, a small man dressed in buckskins, dwarfed by Abbot's six foot six and maybe a little more height. "On the El Paso run like the other four."

Brewster had once been a first-rate whip until the rheumatism in both hands done for him. Now he wore a plug hat and his stained and ragged buckskins and helped around the Abbot and Morrison stage depot. He favored a pipe that belched smoke that smelled bad.

"Phineas Doyle dead, murdered," Abbot said, shaking his head. "He was the best whip in Texas, bar none."

"And afore him, it was me," Brewster said. "Leastwise, that's what folks said."

"I ain't gonna dispute that, Max," Abbot said. He was a slightly round-shouldered man wearing a sweat-stained hat, a white collarless shirt, narrow suspenders, and black pants tucked into mule-ear boots. A man who never carried a gun, he now had a Remington tucked into his waistband, a sure sign that the death of his men had shaken him to the core.

"A gray stage," Max Brewster said after a while. He shook his head. "Now, that's unlucky. The Indians say like black, gray is no color at all and it can betoken loss and sadness. There are some Arapaho, and Utes as well, who would rather freeze to death than use a gray army blanket. It disturbs the hell out of them."

"So, what are the other drivers saying?" Abbot said.

"I just left the Alamo saloon and it's all folks are talking about," Brewster said. "They're saying three drivers and three messengers shot dead and not a bullet hole to be found anywhere in the stage is mighty strange. I reckon that's why they're calling the coach the Gray Ghost. Some say it's haunted and it was the restless spirit of Phineas Doyle that drove it back here to the depot."

"That's foolish talk," Abbot said. "It's a coach like any other."

"No, sir, it's a coach like no other," Brewster said. "It's a death trap, just ask Frank Gordon and Mack Blair, Steve Tanner and Lone Wolf Ellis Bryant, and now Phineas Doyle and Dewey Wilcox."

"They're all dead," Abbot said, irritated. "I can't ask them anything."

"And they're all dead because of the Gray Ghost,"

Brewster said. "Long John, it was your last stage to El Paso. You ain't never gonna find another driver or shotgun guard to work for you."

Abbot watched as the undertaker and his assistant lowered the bodies from the seat of the coach, bloody corpses with blue faces, open eyes staring into nothingness. Phineas Doyle's gray beard was stained with blood and there was a wound that looked like a blossoming rose smack in the middle of Dewey Wilcox's forehead.

The undertaker, a sprightly skeleton dressed in a broadcloth suit with narrow pants and a black top hat tied around with a wide taffeta ribbon, the ends hanging over his skinny shoulders, laid the corpses on a flat wagon and then said, his voice like a creaky gate, "Same as the other four deceased, Mr. Abbot?"

"Yeah, Silas, board coffins but clean them fellers up nice for viewing," Abbot said. "The womenfolk like that."

"I'll take care of it," Silas Woods said. His eyes moved from Long John to the stage. "Gray," he said. "Now, that's unusual, a gray stage."

"I know," Abbot said.

"Gray as graveyard mist," the undertaker said. "Why gray?"

"A canceled order," Abbot said. "I was told it was originally destined for a count in Transylvania, a country in eastern Europe somewhere. The coach is worth eighteen hundred dollars and I got it for fourteen hundred."

"You didn't get yourself a bargain," Woods said. He shook his head. "No, sir."

Abbot watched the undertaker's wagon leave, drawn by a black mule. His great beak of a nose under arched black eyebrows gave Long John the look of a perpetually surprised owl. He turned and said to Brewster, "If I can't find a driver, I'm out fourteen hundred dollars and out of business." He thought for a moment and said, "What about Buttons Muldoon?"

"He's working for Abe Patterson," Brewster said. "Muldoon's messenger is a young feller by the name of Red Ryan who's right handy with a gun and they say fear doesn't enter into his thinking. But I don't think those two will switch, and even if they did, they won't come cheap."

"All I can afford is cheap, the cheaper the better," Abbot said.

Brewster gave the man a long, speculative look and then said, "By the way, Abe Patterson is in town. He's over to his depot."

"What's that to me?" Abbot said.

Brewster smiled. "Long John, Patterson is made of money. Some folks say he's so rich he's got a half interest in the whole of creation."

"Made of money, huh?" Abbot said.

"Got a big, turreted mansion house up San Angelo way and a young, high-yeller wife to go along with it. A lively-stepping filly like that costs a man plenty and ol' Abe sure spends plenty on her."

Long John brightened. "Here . . . Max . . . you've given me an idea."

"I figured as much," Brewster said.

"Sure, Patterson is made of money. Like you said, everybody knows that. Hell, I can probably unload the stage. Abe won't pass up a bargain like that."

"How much, Long John?"

"How much what?"

"How much are you willing to take for the Gray Ghost?"

"I think maybe a thousand."

"Think again," Brewster said. "How much?"

"Nine hundred?" Abbot said, his face framing a question.

"Seven hundred and fifty and let him talk you down to seven hundred," Brewster said. "Abe will dicker and he's good at it."

"That's half what I paid for it," Abbot said. A thin whine.

Brewster smiled. "As the starving man said, *Half a pie is better than no pie at all*."

Abbot thought that through and said finally, "You think Abe will go for it?"

"Damn right he will," Brewster said. "A sharp businessman like Abe Patterson won't pass up a new Concord stage for seven hundred dollars."

"Maybe he doesn't know it's a bad luck coach," Abbot said.

"Long John, the whole town knows, and you can bet so does Abe," Brewster said. "But he ain't the superstitious type and to him a bargain, even if it's on the creepy side, is still a bargain."

"I could go into another business with seven hundred dollars," Abbot said. "I always figured I could prosper in hardware."

"There you go, Long John, selling pots and pans is just the thing for a man like you. Help you make your mark in the world."

"Right, I'll go do a little hoss trading with Abe."

"Good luck, and don't let him get you under seven hundred, mind," Brewster said.

* * *

Long John Abbot poured another splash of whiskey into Abe Patterson's glass. "Abe, seven-fifty, and I can go no lower than that without starving my wife and children," he said. "Have a cigar."

Abe Patterson took a cigar from the proffered box and said, "I hope the cigar is better than your whiskey. And that wouldn't be difficult."

"Two-cent Cubans," Abbot said. "Top-notch." He passed on commenting on the busthead that he bought by the jug.

Patterson took his time lighting his cigar and behind a curtain of blue smoke said, "I'm thinking about it, Long John. Giving it my most serious consideration."

"Red leather seating, Abe," Abbot said. "Now, that's class. I mean, that's big city."

"What about the sign on the doors?" Patterson said. "Some kind of fancy letter *D*."

"Ah, the coach was a canceled order from some count in Transylvania . . ."

"Where?"

"Transylvania. It's a country in eastern Europe. I guess the gent's name began with a *D*."

"Davy? Donny? Deacon?"

"Something like that, I guess," Abbot said. "Them foreigners have strange notions and stranger names."

"Seven hundred," Patterson said. "I will go no higher. Hard times, Long John, with the railroads expanding an' all, laying rails all over the place and taking a big chunk of my business. I just don't have as much capital to invest as I once did."

Abbot pretended to consider Abe's offer for a moment and then jumped to his feet.

"Done and done," he said. He extended his hand to

Patterson, a feisty little banty rooster a foot smaller than himself. Abe took Abbot's hand and said, "Have some of your men push or pull the thing to my depot as soon as the blood is washed off the driver's seat. Then come over yourself and I'll pay you."

"I'm glad you don't believe all that loose talk about the stage being haunted and all," Abbot said.

Abe Patterson smiled. "If I did, I'd tell you to hitch up a team and have Phineas Doyle drive it over."

CHAPTER TWO

"Phineas Doyle drove the stage back to the depot even though he was as dead as mutton," Patrick "Buttons" Muldoon said, his blue eyes as round as coins. "His ghost was standing over his shot-up body, the ribbons in his hands. Ol' Max Brewster says he seen that with his own two eyes and he says the coach was almost invisible, like a gray, graveyard mist."

"I don't believe it," Abe Patterson said.

"And Max says that letter *D* on the doors stands for death," Red Ryan said. "He says it must be a stage that carried the souls of the deceased and that's why Long John Abbot got it cheap."

"I don't believe it," Abe Patterson said.

"And, boss, you got it even cheaper, mind," Buttons said. He was dressed in a blue sailor coat decorated with two rows of silver buttons that gave him his name. He and Red Ryan had just arrived at the depot after a short mail run to Abilene and were mostly dust-free. "Boss, they call the stage the Gray Ghost and they say it's cursed," Buttons continued. "It's already been the death of six men and me and Red would make it eight."

"I don't believe it," Abe Patterson said.

Red Ryan said, "Max Brewster says that over to the Alamo saloon, Lonesome Edna Vincent, she's the redhead with the big . . ."

"I know who she is, and whatever she said, I don't believe it," Abe Patterson said.

"You haven't heard what I have to say yet," Red said. "Well, anyway, Max says that Edna says that she was asleep in her cot the very night the stage was delivered to Long John Abbot's depot. Then, when all the clocks in town chimed at the same time, saying that it was two in the morning, a loud and terrible scream woke her."

"I don't believe it," Abe Patterson said.

"Then Max says that Edna says she got up and looked out the window and then she heard the howls and wails of the damned coming from a gray coach. Max says that Edna says that the stage was rocking back and forth and seemed to be covered by an unholy blue fire. Max says that Edna says she got the fear of God in her and didn't get another wink of sleep all night."

Buttons said, arranging his features into an expression that passed for sincerity, "So, boss, after all them scary ha'ants you can savvy why me and Red can't drive the Gray Ghost. And now let us both thankee most wholeheartedly for your kindness, consideration, and understanding."

"I don't believe it," Abe Patterson said. "I don't believe that two grown men would set store by such nonsense. Road agents and maybe Apaches done for Long John's men, not a curse."

"But, boss . . ." Buttons said.

Patterson held up a silencing hand. "No buts. Here's

the situation. You already know, or maybe you don't, that the Apaches are out, a dozen renegades riding with the four half-breed Griffin brothers."

"I heard them Griffin breeds were hung by vigilantes up in the New Mexico Territory," Buttons said. "Didn't you hear that, Red?"

Red shook his head. "No, I can't say as I did. But folks don't tell me much."

"Seems that you heard wrong, Mr. Muldoon," Abe said. "A Texas Ranger by the name of Tom Wilson told me that five days ago the Griffins and the Apaches with them attacked a ranch house to the east of here, killed three men, and ran off with a couple of women. Wilson said he doubts that the women are still alive, but if they are, by now they'll be wishing they wasn't." Abe consulted his gold watch, snapped it shut, and said, "Ranger Wilson had more to tell. He told me no later than this morning that Powell left Fort Worth four days ago. Remember him? The local lawman wired that Powell has took to wearing an eye patch, and he swears that him and his boys are headed south."

"Or so the lawman says. Nobody's heard of Luke Powell in years," Red said.

Buttons said, "Who is he? I never heard of him until now. Maybe I was at sea at that time."

Red said, "It was before my time as a messenger, when I was still cowboying for Charlie Goodnight's JA Ranch up in the Panhandle, that Powell worked his protection racket, guaranteeing owners that their stages wouldn't be robbed if they paid up. He made some good money at it, too. But the last I heard he was an expensive hired assassin who squeezed cash or property from the marks to spare their lives. That way he got paid at both ends. But he suddenly dropped out of sight two or three years ago. Some say he fled abroad to escape the law, some say he found religion, so who knows what happened to him."

Abe waved his cigar and blue smoke curled in the air. "Maybe Luke Powell has returned to his old ways and he and his boys killed Doyle and Wilcox last night or this morning . . . or the Apaches did. The Apaches would do it for fun and Powell out of spite because the Abbot stage carries mail and never a strongbox. Well, I should say that it did carry mail. Long John told me he's quit the business and he's transferring the mail and his passengers to me."

"Powell was never known to be a road agent," Red said. "It's not his style."

Buttons snorted his disbelief. "Of course it wasn't Powell or Indians or anybody else. Everybody knows it was the Gray Ghost its own self that done for them six fellers."

"Mr. Muldoon, I don't wish to hear that again," Patterson said, frowning. "The coach is now with the Abe Patterson and Son Stage and Express Company and you will kindly refer to it as Number Seven. Do I make myself clear?"

"Why us?" Red Ryan said. "Boss, you've got other drivers and messengers."

"None of them as reliable as you and Mr. Muldoon," Patterson said. "That's the fact of the matter."

"And suppose we refuse?" Buttons said. His chin was set and stubborn and the buttons on his coat shone like newly minted silver dollars.

"Ah, if you refuse to work?" Abe rubbed his chin. Suddenly his eyes had all the warmth of shotgun muzzles.

"Hmm . . . well, in that case, you'll be dismissed instanter. And you'll never work for an employer more caring of his men than me. That is, if you can find another situation in these hard times."

Abe Patterson saw Buttons's crestfallen look and his face softened a little. "Here, have a drink." He opened a desk drawer and produced a bottle of Old Crow and three glasses. He poured the whiskey and said, "I know how you men feel, and I don't have a heart of stone. Your maidenly fears have not gone unheeded, and that's why I've chosen an easy run just for you . . . five theater performers to Houston, passengers as genteel and gracious as they come. Drink up, boys."

"I'll be driving the Gray . . ."

"Careful, Mr. Muldoon. I don't want to hear that name ever again, remember?"

"Driving ol' Number Seven," Buttons said, his face glum.

"Yes, and she's a beauty, ain't she?" Patterson said, beaming. "Red leather upholstery and curtains, special-order thoroughbraces so it feels like you're riding on a cloud. She's a work of art, by God, and once you get used to her ways, you lucky boys will love her."

Despite the warm caress of the whiskey, Buttons was still in a funk. "Three hundred and fifty miles of nothing but grass," he said, "on a route I've traveled only a couple of times afore, plus Apaches, the Griffin brothers, and road agents takes a heap of loving."

"And that's exactly why I kept the Houston run for you and Mr. Ryan," Patterson said. "The Apaches and the Griffin boys are raising hell to the west of us so you'll be well away from those savages. And Luke Powell need not concern us. The Ranger said he stays close to towns, especially Fort Smith and New Orleans, where there's whiskey and whores and pilgrims to be fleeced. I can't see him crossing an empty prairie, even to get his revenge on Miss Erica Hall." Abe spread his hands. "I'll tell you about her later. Now, Mr. Muldoon, don't complain. It will be an easy run. The way is smooth and the weather is fair. It will be like taking a bunch of flowers to your favorite maiden aunt for her birthday." He smiled. "And you boys can see paddle steamers in the Houston canal. Now, that's worth the trip, don't you think?"

"If we get there alive," Buttons said. "If ol' Number Seven doesn't decide to do for us like it did to them others."

"Well"—Abe's smile was as sincere as the grin on a Louisiana alligator—"it's come down to this . . . You boys have a choice to make and I can only hope it's the right one."

"And that is?" Buttons said.

"Get on the stage or get fired. Think it over."

"We've thought it over," Red Ryan said.

"And?" Patterson said.

"We'll ride the stage," Red said.

Buttons looked at him aghast. "Are you out of your mind?" he said.

"Study on it," Red said. "Summer's almost over and winter will come down fast. We got a cozy enough berth here in San Angelo and don't need to be spending December with empty bellies riding the grub line."

"And here's a kicker, a real humdinger as they say up Montana way. A twenty-dollar bonus for each of you after you deliver your passengers safely to the Diamond music hall in Houston, where they expect to be hired in a heartbeat, and I reckon they will," Abe said. "So there it is, gentlemen, an extra double eagle each for a nice, easy drive in the late summer sun. Even if you were my own sons, my own flesh and blood, I couldn't say any fairer than that."

"We'll take it," Red said. "When do we start?"

Abe glared at Buttons. "You don't look too sure, Mr. Muldoon."

"All right, I'll drive the gray stage," Buttons said. "I'm not a one to believe in ghosts and ha'ants an' stuff, but the first time it comes up with something spooky, I'll mount the passengers on the backs of the team and leave Number Seven right where it's at."

"It won't come to that pass," Abe said. "Trust me, you'll have a safe journey, I guarantee it. Now, let me read you the passenger list I got from Long John Abbot. Remember, these are all theater performers, what they call vaudeville artistes, so needless to say there will be no cussing, tobacco spitting, or crude jokes when you're around those nice people. Do I make myself clear?"

Red nodded, and Abe took that as a yes from both of the men. He balanced a pair of pince-nez spectacles at the end of his nose and read from a scrap of paper.

"As I said, all this is from Long John," Abe said. "He said the artistes came from Fort Worth to San Angelo on two different C. Bain and Company stages, and that Erica Hall is the main attraction. She's a fan dancer from England and by all accounts is a lovely lass."

"What's a fan dancer?" Buttons said. He was surly. He guessed fan dancing was another of those fancy, big-city notions that were steadily eating away at the already shaky foundations of the Western Frontier.

"According to Long John, Miss Hall dances naked around the stage with two Chinese fans, but she uses the fans to cleverly cover up her lady bits so nobody ever gets a glimpse," Abe said. He saw the puzzled expressions on Buttons's and Red's faces, shrugged, and said, "That's what Long John told me. I've more to say about her, but I'll leave that till later. The other woman is a singer, goes by the name of Rosie Lee. Then there's the Great Stefano, a knife thrower, Paul Bone, a song and dance man, and Dean Rice, a juggler." Abe took off his spectacles and laid them on his desk. "All in all, an interesting group of people."

"Boss, you said there's more to tell about the dancer gal," Buttons said. "Does she ever drop them fans?"

"I don't know," Abe said. "Maybe at the end of her turn."

"I'd sure like to see that," Buttons said. "I reckon I've never seen the like before."

"Maybe she'll dance for you on the trail," Abe said. "Stranger things have happened."

"Hee-haw! Now, wouldn't that be something," Buttons said.

"Boss, what else were you aiming to tell us about her?" Red said. Something deep inside of him feared that this was news he really didn't want to hear. And he was right.

Abe Patterson thought for a while and then said, "All right, you boys are boogered enough and I figured I wouldn't tell you, but now I've studied on the right and wrong of the thing, my conscience won't allow it. One thing about Abe Patterson, he's always fair."

"Now you got me worried, boss," Red said. "Wring it out.

Tell it slow and easy so we understand. Me and Buttons don't want any head scratching."

"Well, see, this is how it is, plain and simple," Abe said. "You know I told you that Luke Powell left Fort Worth with just one eye."

"Yeah, we know," Red said. "He's got a patch over it."

"Well, it seems that Miss Erica Hall made him that way," Abe said.

"What way?" Buttons said.

"The one-eyed way," Abe said. "Rosie Lee told Long John Abbot that Miss Hall took out one of Luke's eyes in Fort Smith with a hot curling iron. It was a quarrel over Luke cheating her out of some money and it turned violent. Rosie said it was Luke's shooting eye that got poked and he ran out of the hotel screaming in search of a doctor. Well, sir, Miss Hall packed a bag and wisely skedaddled on a C. Bain and Company stage that was just pulling out of town headed for San Angelo. Later Powell came back looking for her with a knife in his hand and only one eye in his head only to find that the bird had flown. Four days afterward, the other artistes talked with a driver who remembered the beautiful lady who boarded his stage at the last minute and the next day they fled in another C. Bain stage to San Angelo with all the luggage, most of it Miss Hall's."

"Luggage? Seems to me all she needed to pack was two fans," Buttons said. "Me and Red ain't boogered none by that story. It don't scare Red and me any."

"You ain't boogered because that ain't the scary part," Abe said. "The scary part is that chances are Luke Powell also talked to the same stage driver and by now he could know where Miss Hall is at. He's left Fort Worth, and

Rosie Lee says he vowed to take both Miss Hall's eyes and kill all he finds with her."

"All he finds with her . . . You mean, like me and Buttons?" Red said.

"That's what he means, all right," Buttons said. "And kill all he finds with her . . . It ain't a friendly thing to say."

"I told you, and now I'll tell you again," Abe Patterson said, "Powell will stay close to settlements. You won't see hide nor hair of him between here and Houston, trust me on that. And besides, Houston has an excellent police force. I'm told twenty-two stalwart officers stand ready to uphold the law and protect the innocent." Abe sighed and rose to his feet. "See, you boys got nothing to worry about. Now, if you will excuse me, I got to talk to the bank about a business loan." He shook his head. "Hard times coming down, boys, hard times."

CHAPTER THREE

"'Hard times coming down,' Abe says," Buttons Muldoon said. "Yeah, for us, not for him."

"You got that right," Red said. He seemed glum.

"It occurs to me Long John Abbot could've washed the blood off the seat before he had this monstrosity pushed over to the Patterson depot," Buttons said. He was up in the box under a high and hot sun, a scrubbing brush in his hand. He tossed an empty galvanized bucket to Red and said, "Fill that again."

"How much blood is up there?" Red said.

"A lot," Buttons said. "Look." He held up the brush and a cloth he'd been using. Both were stained pink. "That's how much blood. Long John said his boys were shot to pieces."

Red refilled the galvanized bucket at the pump and handed it back.

"Now I see it up close, I got to say that it's a fine-looking stagecoach," Red said. "The paintwork is first-rate. Best I've ever seen. It looks like a china egg on wheels."

Buttons paused in his work. "You know why it looks that way, don't you?"

"Because it was a special order, I guess," Red said. "Special orders get special treatment, paint and upholstery an' sich."

"No, that's not the real reason. It's because it's the devil's coach," Buttons said. "That's what the *D* on the door stands for . . . D-e-v-i-l . . . Devil."

"That ain't so," Red said. "It was made for a foreign gent and them foreigners have all kinds of fancy names that start with a *D*."

Buttons paused in his scrubbing. "Like what?" he said.

"Well, for one, do you mind Russian Bill? For a short spell he ran the Cow Horn Creek station down Medina County way," Red said. "Nice feller, but melancholy in drink. I mean crying-into-his-whiskey melancholy."

"No, I don't recollect no Russian Bill," Buttons said.

"Sure you do. He had a red beard down to his belt buckle and a Mexican wife that kept poorly. She had long black hair down to her butt and it shined in the sun."

Buttons suddenly saw the light. "Oh yeah, now I remember them. Nice enough couple, good with horses. And I recollect that they had a simple son. I think his name was Brenda."

"Brennan," Red said. "Well, Russian Bill's real name was Dimitri. That's a foreign name and it starts with a *D*."

Buttons was not convinced. "It wasn't a Russian who ordered this coach, it was the devil himself. I can feel its bad luck coming at me like steam off an overheated horse."

"Buttons, we're taking this thing all the way to Houston and back again," Red said. "So we got to look on the bright side. It's a brand-new coach. It will fog it real good between here and Houston."

"There is no bright side," Buttons said. "It's a bad luck

stage and that's the end of it." He glared at his dripping brush as though it were to blame for all his troubles and then went back to his scrubbing.

"All right, then, here's another bright side," Red said. "Now, quit that scrubbing for a minute and listen up. Here it is . . . the bright side is that bad luck chases away worse luck. See what I mean? It's real simple to understand. Think about it . . . A man can't have bad luck and worse luck at the same time. It just ain't nature's way."

Buttons stopped what he was doing, his face thoughtful, and then he said, "You know, Red, you may be onto something there. I mean, studying on it, bad luck ain't really bad, but worse luck can pretty quick lay a man low." He rubbed his chin with the back of the hand that held the scrubbing brush. "I never thought of it that way."

"I did. I've been thinking about it all morning, since we first saw the gray stage. And what I said is a natural fact," Red said.

"Yeah, a natural fact, and truer words was never spoke," Buttons said. "We can't have worse luck on the Houston run because we already got bad luck to chase it away."

"Now you're talking sense," Red said. "Finally you got your saddle on the right hoss. We'll hold on to our bad luck and we won't let it go until we're back here in San Angelo, all safe and sound."

"I like the sound of that," Buttons said. "There are times when bad luck can be a good thing."

"Now you're talking," Red said.

Red Ryan didn't know it then, but luck was waiting for him and Buttons just around the corner . . . and it was worse, much worse, than bad.

CHAPTER FOUR

As a general rule, rancher, lawman, and gambler Texas John Slaughter was not one to sulfurize a man's reputation, but he made an exception for a ranny by the name of Ben Lloyd. In a 1913 *Arizona Daily Orb* interview he called the sometime cowboy, outlaw, and gunman, "a vile, loathsome creature, sly, cowardly, and lowdown and a back-shooting varmint."

Slaughter summed him up nicely. Ben Lloyd was all of those things, and more.

Early that summer, he'd ridden into San Angelo carrying with him vague notoriety as a lethal gunman who'd notched the walnut handle of his Colt seven times. He soon took up residence in Paddy O'Hara's saloon, where he quickly revealed himself to be a bully, a braggart, and a mean drunk. He also played pimp and claimed pretty young saloon girl Charlotte Gentry as his woman. The trouble was that Red Ryan and Charlotte were friends, not sharing-a-bed friends, but friends nonetheless since they both had a liking for calico cats and the works of Edgar Allan Poe.

Ben Lloyd was a tall man, muscular with the narrow

hips of a horseman. He was handsome, a flashy dresser, blond with unblinking, pale blue eyes, and he sported long hair that fell over his shoulders in ringlets and his top lip bore the great dragoon mustache that was then in fashion. He affected the dark frock coat, snowy white linen, and string tie of the professional card shark and on the little finger of his left hand he wore a silver ring, the mark of the gambler.

To set the record straight, most experts agree that Ben Lloyd killed a man, a Mexican drover, on a cattle drive to Kansas in 1878. Five years he later outdrew and gunned a teamster named Waters or Walters in a Dallas saloon. His third and most notorious killing happened a year before he rode into San Angelo. Lloyd and Deputy Sheriff Ira Knox, another mean drunk, were arguing in a saloon in the Reservation, Waco's red-light district. It's unknown what the argument was about, but it could've been over the favors of a black whore named Callie Crawford. The bartenders, fearing the quarrel would escalate into gunplay, disarmed both men and told then to go sleep it off. But, according to several witnesses, before he left the saloon Knox told Lloyd that when he saw him in the street, he'd "shoot him down like a mangy cur." The next day Lloyd was told that Knox was eating crackers and cheese at the counter of the Emporium mercantile and was still voicing threats about killing "that damned lowlife Lloyd."

After hearing this intelligence, the always careful Lloyd armed himself with a ten-gauge Greener, crept into the store by the rear entrance, and let Knox have both barrels in the back. The deputy was carried to the Regency Hotel, where he lingered for three hours and died cursing Lloyd.

At Ben Lloyd's trial for murder, the jury, since Ira Knox

had made threats, called the killing a clear case of self-defense and Lloyd was acquitted. But after thinking it over, coupled with an overload of caution, Ben decided he'd worn out his welcome in Waco and left town in a hurry.

None of this was known to Red Ryan when he and Buttons stepped into Paddy O'Hara's saloon in search of a beer and the Irishman's free roast-beef-and-pickle sandwiches that he kept under a glass dome on the bar.

Apart from the bar's huge French mirror, the saloon's walls were covered in paintings of Irish landscapes, but pride of place went to a portrait, draped in black crepe, of Robert Emmet, Erin's great patriot and martyr. Paddy O'Hara loved to tell the curious the story of Robert Emmet, a man condemned before his trial and hanged by the British in 1803 for rebellion against the Crown. Buttons Muldoon never tired of the tale and shed many a salty Irish tear when O'Hara told it.

As it happened that day, the sandwiches were all gone and Red and Buttons sipped on their beers while O'Hara, an affable gent, retired to his kitchen to cut some more.

The saloon was busy with the lunchtime crowd, mostly businessmen, clerks, off-duty army officers, and a few cowboys in from the range and Red didn't right away see the trouble coming. But after a few minutes he watched it build and then rise to the surface like a gas bubble in a swamp.

Ben Lloyd, his pants shoved into tooled black boots with two-inch heels, was losing heavily at the chuck-a-luck table and he took out his frustration on Charlotte Gentry, who stood next to him, her hand on his shoulder. She'd earlier returned from shopping at the mercantile and hadn't yet changed out of her plain cotton day dress into the gaudy corset and short skirt worn by O'Hara's saloon girls.

Lloyd grabbed her by the arm and pushed her roughly away from him. "Beat it!" he yelled. "You're bad luck."

The push was forceful enough that the girl staggered across the floor and crashed into a table, upsetting drinks, scattering cards and money. The four men playing poker saved Charlotte from falling and set her on her feet again.

And if the incident had ended there, Red Ryan would not have gotten involved.

But it didn't end . . . and all kinds of hell broke loose.

Charlotte, no blushing violet, called Lloyd a no-good son of a gun and swung her purse at his head. The purse was small, silk, embroidered with flowers, very feminine, but it was weighted with a Colt single-shot derringer, heavy enough that it bounced off the left side of Lloyd's head and split the thin skin of his cheekbone. Blood streaming from a crescent-shaped wound, the man roared a vile curse and jumped to his feet. He grabbed the woman by the arm again and snarling like a wild animal, slapped her back and forth across her face so hard the blows sounded like gunshots.

There are some who say that if Lloyd had slapped the woman only once, say, hard enough to render her unconscious, Red Ryan might not have intervened. Others claim that, like everyone else in the saloon that day, Red was cowed by Lloyd's gun rep. But that notion was palpably false. Red knew nothing of the man. It was only when Buttons Muldoon said to him, "Do we put a stop to this?" that Red, already moving, acted. "Damn right we'll put a stop to it," he said.

Red crossed the floor, grabbed Lloyd by the shoulder, and as the man turned, he planted a hard straight right to his chin. Red was over six foot tall that summer, weighed 180 pounds, and his punch had some authority behind it.

Lloyd's legs went out from under him and he staggered back, his arms cartwheeling, before he did what Charlotte Gentry had done earlier . . . crashed into a table. But this time there were no card players to break his fall. The table splintered under his weight and spilled him, sprawling, onto the floor.

As soon as his eyes focused again, Lloyd looked up and saw with terrible clarity a red-haired man dressed in a worn buckskin shirt, pants held up by wide army suspenders, scuffed boots, a gray plug hat on his head, and a gun on his hip. The man stood relaxed and confident, legs wide, fists up, and an alarm bell clamored in Lloyd's brain with one insistent warning . . . *Leave this man the hell alone*. Lloyd's kills had come easy, none against a skilled opponent, but Red Ryan looked as though he'd been there a few times before. All at once sick to his stomach, Lloyd knew if he didn't react, he could never again hold his head high in the company of men. A coward at heart, now forced to it, he worked up the courage to do the unthinkable . . .

He sat upright and went for his gun.

Red Ryan was surprised. His opponent was on the floor, his Colt unhandy, yet he tried for the draw, his face a furious, vindictive mask. In later years, Buttons Muldoon would recall that Lloyd fired the first shot, too hurried and too high.

"But Red didn't give him a second chance," Buttons said.

In one smooth, practiced motion, Red pulled his Colt

and thumbed off a shot that hit Lloyd high in the chest. It was a killing wound. Ben Lloyd knew it, Red knew it, and everyone in the saloon knew it.

"Don't shoot me again," Lloyd said, a yelp of fear, blood frothing on his lips. He tossed his gun aside. "I'm out of it." He tried to get to his feet, fell forward, and died with his face in the sawdust, his blue eyes open, seeing nothing.

A moment later the saloon doors slammed open and big-bellied Sheriff John Coffin stomped into the room. Now sliding into comfortable middle age, he'd been a whaler out of Nantucket, fought in the War Between the States, tried his hand at the bank-robbing profession, and finally decided to stay on the right side of the law. Coffin knew and liked Red Ryan, but he spoke first to Paddy O'Hara, who stood wringing his hands dry on his white apron. He stared impassively at the dead man, a sight he'd seen many times in the past.

"Call it, Paddy," Coffin said.

O'Hara said, "His name is Ben . . ."

"I know what his name is," Coffin said. "Call it."

"Lloyd went for his gun first, got off the first shot, missed, and Ryan drew and killed him," O'Hara said. "There, John, I've called it."

"Then it's a clear case of self-defense," Coffin said. He seemed relieved.

O'Hara nodded. "Seems like."

"What happened, Red?" Coffin said.

"He was abusing the young lady and I stepped in," Red said.

"And you socked him, he fell on the floor and went for his gun," Coffin said. "I guess that's how I read it." He turned to Charlotte Gentry and said, "I've heard you called a number of things, Charlotte, but 'young lady' ain't one of them."

"That's because you don't mix with the right kind of people, Sheriff," the girl said. Her bottom lip was puffed and a violet and yellow shadow around her left eye suggested that it would very soon turn black. "Yeah, Ben grabbed me and he slapped me around." She extended a slender arm. "Look at the bruises and here on my face."

"You saw Lloyd go for his gun?" Coffin said.

"He drew down on Red and Red shot him," Charlotte said. "It's simple. That's what happened, Sheriff. There isn't any more."

"Lloyd fired first?" Coffin said.

Charlotte sighed. "Yeah, he did, and missed. Red didn't miss."

"Seems like you're off the hook, Ryan," Coffin said.

"Sheriff, he was never on the hook," Buttons said, irritated. "What are you talking about?"

"Talking about doing my job," Coffin said.

"Lloyd threw down on Red. You got three eyewitnesses telling you what happened."

Coffin nodded. "Maybe so. Ben Lloyd was a low person and something of a bully, there's no doubt about that."

"He shouldn't have drawn down on me," Red said. Then, a question to himself and everyone else: "His gun was unhandy, so why did he do that?"

"He got off the first shot," Coffin said. "I reckon his gun wasn't that unhandy."

"Why go for his gun at all?" Red said. "We could've settled it with fists."

Coffin said, "Not after you punched Lloyd and dropped

him like an anvil fell on his head. Right there and then you lowered him in men's eyes, or so he thought. The only way to regain his standing as a hard case was to kill you. I've seen it happen too many times in my life, a young fellow dies because of foolish pride."

He turned as Silas Woods, the undertaker, a man with a coyote's nose for carrion, tapped him on the shoulder and said, "Sheriff, where is the dear departed?"

"You're standing on him, Silas," Coffin said.

Alarmed, Woods did a little crow hop to the side and looked down. "Ah," he said, "a gunshot to the sternum. Good. Sheriff Coffin, I'm sure you understand by now that in my profession one prefers a gunshot to a cutting." He sighed. "The blade can be messy. Yes, indeed."

"See if Lloyd has enough money on him for a burying, otherwise send your bill to the city," Coffin said.

"This is my third one today," Woods said. "You heard about Phineas Doyle and Dewey Wilcox? What a tragedy."

"Of course I know about them," Coffin said. "How many does that make? Six?"

Buttons Muldoon said, "Yeah, six." He sounded like a mourner at a funeral.

"I hear Long John Abbot sold up," Coffin said. "He's out of the stagecoach business for good."

"You heard right," Buttons said. "He only had one coach and he sold it at a big loss to Abe Patterson."

"It's gray, that stage," Coffin said. "Unusual color around these parts. I've never seen one like it."

"It's called the Gray Ghost and it's cursed," Buttons said. "And the curse has struck again." He watched the undertaker and his assistant carry out Lloyd's body and said, "That feller is its seventh victim."

"How do you figure?" Coffin said. "Lloyd had nothing to do with the stage."

"Yeah, he did," Buttons said. "Listen up, Sheriff, before me and Red walked into the saloon, we washed Phineas Doyle's lifeblood from the Gray Ghost's box. If we'd finished just a minute later than we did Ben Lloyd would still be alive." He saw the doubt on Coffin's face and said, "A minute later and me and Red would've walked into the saloon when it was all over. A whore got roughed up by her pimp and she was already in her room crying her eyes out. No harsh words. No punch from Red. No gunfight. No dead man. It could've been simple, but the Gray Ghost didn't plan it that way."

"It's thin, Buttons," Coffin said. "Mighty damn thin. A stage that thinks for itself is a hard pill to swallow." He looked at Red. "What do you think, shotgun man?"

"Me and Buttons have different opinions on the stage," Red said.

"Do you think it's cursed?" Coffin said.

"Like wearing a dead man's boots, it can bring bad luck maybe, but it's not cursed," Red said. "It's just a stage like any other. Fancier for sure, but a stage nonetheless."

A swamper arrived with a mop and bucket and Coffin said, "Red, I'm closing the range on this killing. It was self-defense and there's no argument about that."

"I'm obliged," Red said. His face was shuttered, his normally bright eyes bleak.

"And thankee kindly, Sheriff," Buttons said. "You did the right thing."

Coffin stepped around the swamper and left, to be replaced by Paddy O'Hara.

"I've cut some beef sandwiches for you boys, if you're still interested," he said.

Red shook his head. The pink water in the bucket looked like it had come from the Gray Ghost. "No thanks, Paddy," he said. "I guess I've lost my appetite."

CHAPTER FIVE

Whitey Quinn left O'Hara's saloon after witnessing the gunfight. He was unimpressed. The dead man was a wannabe and it showed. The youngster wearing the plug hat had been pretty quick on the draw and shoot, but his play was nothing to boast of. Whitey knew he could take him any day of the week, any hour of the day. That was good to know.

A compact, smallish man in his mid twenties with pale yellow hair showing under his hat, Whitey walked along the boardwalk toward the false-fronted Addie hotel, where a dust devil spun and then collapsed, spent, into the street. The sky was blue, the sun hot, and the air smelled of dry timbers and of an outhouse situated too close to the board-walk.

Dressed in a frayed, black ditto suit, collarless shirt, and flat-brimmed hat, Whitey looked like a penniless preacher in search of a congregation. But looks were deceiving. On closer inspection, Whitey's boots were of the highest quality as were his cartridge belt and holster. He carried a Colt .44-40 revolver. Special order. A three-inch barrel with no ejector rod, no front sight, a hair trigger, and a custom staghorn handle. He was good with the piece and since he turned twenty-one had put eight men in the ground with it, including Elijah Riggs, the feared Yuma drawfighter. So Whitey's reputation grew and more and more his name was mentioned where men gathered to talk about guns and gunmen. A wanted man on the scout, no one recognized Whitey Quinn in San Angelo and if Sheriff John Coffin had, he'd have looked the other way.

The gunman stepped into the Addie and as was his habit he stood for a moment adjusting his eyes to the gloom of the lobby before he stepped to the desk. The hotel smelled of paint and recently sawn timber and the relentless Texas dust covered everything. The clerk was young, bespectacled, and his thin brown hair was parted in the middle and pomaded flat. His name was Archibald and he insisted that no one call him Archie. His brown eyes met Whitey's green ones and they gave him a shiver. It was like looking into the eyes of a cobra.

"Can I help you, sir?" Archibald said. Nervous. His voice broke on the question.

"Yes, you can," Whitey said. "Is Miss Erica Hall in residence?"

"She is," the clerk said. "But Miss Hall regrets she's unable to meet any gentlemen callers today."

The gunman pretended disappointment. "I'm sorry to hear that. I saw her dance in Fort Worth and when I heard that Miss Hall might be right here in little ol' San Angelo, why, I immediately set out to find her. I'd admire to compliment her on her artistry, you understand."

"Yes, I understand," Archibald said. He relaxed a little. "Can I have your name? I'll tell her you called."

"She won't know me, but my name is John Smith," Whitey said. Then, "Perhaps I can call again tomorrow?"

"I'm afraid that is impossible," Archibald said. "Miss Hall is leaving on the morning stage for Houston, where she hopes to be engaged as a dancer at a newly built theater in that fair city."

"What's it called, this theater?"

"I don't know . . . wait . . . I think it's called the Diamond."

Whitey now knew all he needed to know.

"Then perhaps I'll see her again in Houston," he said.

"I'm sure you will, sir," the clerk said.

It was a relief to see John Smith leave. The man scared him.

Whitey's next stop was the telegraph office, where he sent an urgent wire to New Orleans that included Erica Hall's destination. He then crossed the street to Ma's Kitchen and ate steak and eggs and peach pie before riding out of town.

"Yeah, she's there all right, boss," Whitey Quinn said, grinning. "We could go drag her out of the hotel tonight, have some fun with high-and-mighty Miss Hall, and then you can take your eye for an eye."

"Did you send the wire to New Orleans?" Luke Powell asked. "That's important."

"Sure did, boss," Whitey said. "I mentioned Houston, but the rest is worded just like you laid it out to me."

"That's where she's headed?"

"Yeah, Houston," Whitey said. "A big railroad town."

"It's more than that—streetcars, gas lamps, a lot of people. It's a big city."

"She could lose herself in a big city."

"We'll find her. I have to recover the merchandise she stole or we're all dead men," Luke Powell said.

A man used to fine tailoring and expensive fabrics, he felt uncomfortable in range clothes and it showed. "And no, Whitey, we're not doing anything tonight, so close to Fort Concho," he said, irritated. "I don't want to raise the alarm and have the army come after us." Then, frowning, "Why Houston of all places? Why not El Paso or Dallas?"

The gunman lifted the coffeepot from the fire and then paused. "The hotel clerk told me that there's a new music hall in Houston and she plans to try her luck there."

Powell touched the brown canvas patch over his right eye. "Her luck ran out when she did this to me," he said. "The music hall in Houston isn't going to sign on a blind woman."

Whitey Quinn laughed, as did the four other men gathered around the fire. "Ain't that the truth," one of them said, a beetle-browed gun and knife fighter out of New Orleans named Bill Cline, real name Loris Barca. He was big, bearded, dangerous, and almighty sudden. He'd killed three men with the gun and four with the blade, and Luke Powell set store by him.

"Houston has a big police department," Powell said. "So we'll catch up with Erica somewhere on the open prairie between here and the city. Out there in the long-grass country she'll have nowhere to run, nowhere to hide." Then, as the thought came to him, "Whitey, who's the stage messenger? Anybody we know?"

"I saw a feller by the name of Red Ryan outdraw and

shoot a man in Paddy O'Hara's saloon," Whitey said. "From what I could gather from the talk around him he's a messenger."

Powell, tall, with jet-black hair, and still handsome despite the eye patch, looked serious. "A gun-handy man like that could be a problem."

Whitey smiled and shook his head. "Boss, I saw him on the draw and shoot. He was fast, but I can take him."

"I know you can outdraw most anybody, Whitey," Powell said. "But just to make sure we'll target the messenger first, use rifles, and blow him clean out of the damned box."

Whitey said, "Sounds like a good plan, boss, but even if it is Ryan, he ain't much."

Powell nodded. If a gun like Whitey Quinn said the man called Ryan was third-rate, then he was. There was no questioning his judgment.

Luke Powell, real name Luciano Tiodoro, looked across the low flames of the campfire and studied the five men gathered around him. Like himself, a couple were members of the New Orleans Mafia's Matranga crime family. They'd camped in a grove of mesquite and wild oak three miles east of San Angelo under a waxing moon, hard cases inured to every hardship, all named gunmen because Powell would have no other, outlaws lacking in empathy for man, woman, child, or animal, whoring, whiskey-swilling killers each and every one. Men without mercy. Men without pity. Foul rattlesnakes in human form, the scum of the frontier. The baddest of the bad. Dangerous beyond measure. Beside fighting men like these, even the Apaches paled by comparison.

Even with just one eye, Powell liked what he saw. Short of a cavalry regiment, his boys could handle anything thrown at them. "When we catch up with the stage"—he waved a hand to the west—"out there in the wilderness, here's how we'll come down hard on Erica Hall."

"We're listening, boss," a young Texas drawfighter called Wesley Fuller said, coffee cup poised at his mouth.

"It's dead easy," Powell said. "We'll kill everybody on the stage, driver, messenger, the other performers that travel with the witch, but we keep her alive. You get my drift? I don't want her harmed."

"Sure do, boss," Fuller said. He wiped coffee off his mustache with the back of his hand. "And then what?"

Powell grinned. "And then you boys make her regret that she was ever born."

This raised a cheer and when the voices died away, Whitey Quinn said, "And when we're done with her?"

Powell's handsome face was wide, hard-boned, and his black, remaining eye glittered in the firelight. "Then I burn out her eyes and we leave her alone and naked and blind on the prairie. Let the wolves and coyotes finish her."

He looked around at his men. "*Giuro su Dio* . . . I swear to God, Erica Hall will rue the day she took the eye of Luciano Tiodoro."

CHAPTER SIX

"She wallows like a sow in a mudhole," Buttons Muldoon said. "Can't you feel it?"

Red Ryan shook his head and said, "Nope. She rides just fine to me."

Buttons turned his head and glared at Red. "That's because you ain't a driver. What does a shotgun messenger know about how a stage rides?"

"Nothing, nada," Red said. "I leave all that kind of professional stuff to you."

Somewhat mollified, Buttons said, "I should think so. When I say she's a sow in slop, then she's . . ."

"A sow in slop," Red said. "The hotel is coming up, looks like our passengers are already waiting for us." He smiled. "Beside a mountain of luggage."

Five people stood outside the door of the Addie hotel under an amber sky that cast a strange light on San Angelo, and beyond the town limits the vast expanse of grass rippled like a shoaling green sea. As the stage rattled to a halt a wind rose and slapped at the dresses of the two women on the boardwalk and the three men with them held on to their hats. The wooden HOTEL sign hanging above the door danced on its chains and the wind was now strong enough to sigh around the building and sail triangles of mustard-colored dust from the street.

Buttons handed Red the passenger list, glanced at the sky, and like a man whispering in a sepulchre said, "This wind ain't right. It ain't natural, I tell you, coming up all of a sudden like that."

Red climbed down from the box, looked up at Buttons, and shouted over the gusting roar, "Big winds happen all the time on the prairie. You know that better than I do."

But Buttons was spooked and he shook his head. "No, it ain't natural," he said. "And it's a hot wind, so it's blowing from hell."

"Can we board now, or do we stand here in this tempest all day getting stung by sand?"

That from an elegant and extremely beautiful young woman. She wore an emerald green traveling dress with a tight-fitting, cuirass bodice that flattened her belly and flattered her breasts and featured the smaller bustle dictated by French fashion. Her auburn, ringleted hair was piled high, held in place with gold pins, surmounted by a veiled miniature derby hat. She had a wide, expressive mouth, high, well-bred cheekbones, and her eyes were hazel and lustrous under perfectly arched brows.

Red thought the woman the loveliest female creature he'd ever seen in his life and he tried to speak but the words jammed in his throat and he remained silent.

"Well?" the woman said. She had to raise her voice above the blustering wind and seemed annoyed that to do so was most unladylike. "Do we ever get to board the stage or do you just leave passengers here?"

Red found his own voice and said, "Your name, ma'am?"

"Erica Hall." A pause then, "Of the Charleston Halls."

Red made a show of consulting the passenger list and then with a flourish opened the door. "Please board now, Miss Hall."

"It's about time," the young lady said.

Red gave Erica his hand as she entered the stage. She smelled like wildflowers and of the Pears soap so loved by the famous actress Lillie Langtry.

"Me next." A petite brunette girl stood at his elbow. Like Erica she wore a traveling dress, but in demure brown cotton with no tight bodice and her hat was a straw boater with an artificial white flower on the brim. She was not pretty but attractive, nonetheless. She held on to her hat by pressing on the crown with the fingers of her left hand.

"Name, ma'am?" Red said.

"Rosie Lee. I'm a singer."

"Then I'd admire to hear you sometime," Red said. He opened the door. "Please board."

"Thank you," Rosie said. "You are very gallant. You must be the driver."

"No, I'm the messenger," Red said. "I ride with a shotgun so no harm will come to you."

"Then it's good to know I'm in safe hands, Mr. Shotgun Man."

Rosie Lee was followed by three men, Paul Bone, Dean Rice, and a heroically mustached man who called himself "the Great Stefano." He would not part with a slim black case that he declared was both wife and child to him, and carried it inside.

Red took his seat beside Buttons and said, "We're ready to go."

"Got the Greener?" Buttons said.

Red took the shotgun from beside him and settled it over his knees.

Despite the early hour and the relentless wind a few onlookers had gathered to watch the stage leave. It was always expected that the driver would grandstand and drive out of town in true showboating style.

"Look at those people expecting a show and my heart ain't in it," Buttons said.

Red smiled. "Then do the best you can, old fellow."

"Well, here goes nothing," Buttons said.

He took hold of the reins and slapped the six-horse team into a gallop. The Patterson stage left San Angelo with a sound of rolling thunder, and Buttons, looking like an old pagan god, stood in the box and cracked his whip to supply the lightning. A scattering of voices raised in cheers as the stage hurtled across the city limits, dust clouds in its wake, and then rocked headlong into the wilderness.

Inside the stage, Erica Hall held on to the Great Stefano's muscular arm and said, "Oh my."

The Abe Patterson and Son stage was an hour out of San Angelo when Red Ryan spotted the Apache. Without turning his head Buttons Muldoon said, "Yeah, I see him."

One with the wild, untamed land, the Indian emerged from the prairie like an apparition. Where there was once only grass, he was suddenly visible, keeping pace with the stage out of rifle range, reining his paint pony to a canter. The Apache wore a white breechcloth, knee-high moccasins, a blue headband, and no shirt, but a rectangular white beaded breastplate hung on his wiry brown chest. He carried a Winchester rifle and a holstered revolver.

"Red, what do you reckon?" Buttons said, his eyes now on the Indian.

"He's a scout, sizing us up," Red said.

"Sizing us up for what?" Buttons said.

"Do I really need to answer that?" Red said.

"No, I guess not," Buttons said. "Keep an eye on him. There's no one on God's earth as notional as an Apache. He might take it into his head to attack us or he might not." He looked around at the endless prairie. "No sign of the Griffin breeds, but they could be close."

Red checked the loads in his Greener and laid it across his thighs. "He's drifting nearer," he said. "He wants to know who we got in the stage. Six Texas Rangers on a hunting trip could sure spoil his day."

"Red, tell the passengers to roll down the curtains," Buttons said. "Keep that buck guessing."

Red leaned out of the box and was about to yell down Buttons's orders when tragedy struck. A panicked man's voice from inside the stage yelled, "Stop the stage! Rosie is gonna be sick!"

CHAPTER SEVEN

Buttons Muldoon was horrified. He reined in the team and yelled, "Get that woman out of there!" Then to Red, "Go see if you can help."

"If she's aiming to puke there ain't much I can do," Red said, feeling a little panicked himself.

"Then let her puke in your hat or something," Buttons said. He was badly on edge. "Keep her away from the red leather."

Red climbed out of the box. The wind had dropped and he looked at the Apache who was still a ways off but now sitting his pony, watching with keen interest all that was happening. "Keep an eye on that damned Indian, Buttons," he said.

"Yeah, yeah, yeah," Buttons said. "Now, git the sick woman out of my stage. Abe Patterson is mighty proud of his red leather."

But Rosie Lee had already been assisted from the stage and now she was bent over, loudly throwing up, while Erica Hall stood by and made soothing, cooing noises.

"How is she?" Red said, knowing how limp that question was. It was pretty damn obvious how Rosie Lee felt.

"She's seasick," Erica said.

Buttons called down from the box, "What ails her?"

"She's seasick," Red said.

"She's whaaat?" Buttons said.

"Seasick," Red said. "She's seasick. What you get on a boat."

Buttons shook his head. "Now I've heard everything. Folks don't get seasick in the middle of the prairie."

"Well, Miss Lee sure did," Red said. "I've never seen the like."

"She'll be better in just a few minutes," Erica said. "It's the coach, you know. It's like being in a boat. Constant motion, mile after mile."

"It does rock some," Red said. "But I've never had a passenger get seasick before."

Erica smiled, looking gorgeous, Red thought. "There's a first time for everything, isn't there, shotgun man?"

"Seems like," Red said. "Miss Lee has just proved that."

Then from the box, "Red!"

Red stepped away from the stage and looked up at Buttons. "What?" he said.

"The Apache's gone," Buttons said.

"Thank God for that," Dean Rice, the juggler, said.

That's when Red Ryan noticed two things that troubled him . . . Rice, small and slender, dressed in a pale blue ditto suit, stood very close to Erica Hall, too close, kissing-kinfolk close, and his hands wandered over her waist and hips as though helping her to keep upright. The woman didn't seem to mind, but the Great Stefano scowled at Rice and there was thunder in his eyes.

Trouble brewing, Red decided. It was a situation to watch.

Finally Rosie Lee stopped retching and straightened. Erica dabbed at the girl's mouth with a small handkerchief and asked if she was feeling better.

"I . . . I . . . guess so," Rosie said. "I've got nothing left in my belly to throw up."

Erica winced a little at that last. Unless she could cover her mouth with a fan and whisper, a lady of good breeding never mentioned her body parts, especially in the presence of men.

"The coach does rock," Erica said, echoing Red Ryan.

"And we're crossing an ocean of grass," Rosie said. "That's why I got seasick."

"Are you feeling well enough to travel, Miss Lee?" Red said. "The health and welfare of our passengers is of major concern to the Abe Patterson and Son Stage and Express Company."

"Red!" Buttons yelled from the box. "Ain't that gal puked enough yet? We got a schedule to keep, you know."

"She's fine now," Red answered.

"Then get her inside and let's get rolling," Buttons said. He shook his head. "Seasick." The word snapped from his lips like the crack of a whip.

The Patterson stage was still an hour out from the Victor Potts station when two events happened that spooked Red Ryan and Buttons Muldoon and that a later historian described as "unholy harbingers of things to come."

The first of these was the thunderstorm that swept in

from the north with the savage ferocity of a wounded cata-mount. The second, and perhaps more serious, was that song and dance man Paul Bone, half-drunk, took a slug from his whiskey flask, swallowed, said, "I feel like danc-ing," and then promptly keeled over and died of apoplexy.

Lightning flashed, thunder crashed, and Rosie Lee screamed as Bone toppled forward and fell on top of her. The shriek was so loud that Buttons heard it up in the box.

"Now what?" he said, but his words were smothered by a massive thunder burst.

"Huh?" Red said.

"I said, 'Now what?'" Buttons said. "Didn't you hear the scream?"

"No, I didn't."

"Well, it was loud enough. One of them gals screamed about something."

"Maybe it was a spider," Red said.

Buttons brought the team to a stop and stomped on the foot brake. The smell of ozone and rain was in the air, then came tiny pattering drops . . . lightning scrawled across the sky like a signature of a demented god . . . thunder banged . . . and the heavens opened and the downpour began.

"Get out our slickers, Red," Buttons said. "Hurry."

The slickers were under the seat, covering the mail sacks, but Red left those to the tender mercies of the rain and grabbed both garments. Despite the downpour and still fairly dry, he and Buttons quickly struggled into the slickers then climbed down from the box.

The menacing, lightning-torn sky was black and dark-ness shaded the day into a convincing semblance of night. The huge gray stage glistened with rain and glimmered in the gloom, trembling on its thoroughbraces like a thing alive.

Buttons grabbed the handle, swung the door wide, and a dead man tumbled out of the stage and fell like a rag doll onto the grass at his feet.

Buttons hopped a step back, looked in horror at the dead man, and said, "What the hell do we have here?"

Rosie Lee had gone from sickness to hysterics. "He fell forward and died right on top of me," she yelled. "I couldn't get him off me no matter how hard I pushed. What killed him? Oh my God, he might have the cholera or something catching."

Red Ryan had examined Bone's body and now he stood in the downpour, his slicker gleaming, and said, "It's nothing catching. I think his heart just give out."

"He was a dancer," Rosie said. "That never happened to him before."

"No, I guess he never died before," Red said.

Rain and thunder made the horses restive and their harnesses jangled as they acted up in the traces, jolting the stage.

"We're about an hour from Vic Potts's station," Buttons said, rainwater dripping from the brim of his hat. "Vic's got a graveyard behind the corral, mostly dead passengers and road agents and the like, and he keeps it cleaned up real nice. We'll plant him there."

"Driver, I don't want to share a seat with a dead man," Erica Hall said. "You can't put him in here."

"No, you can't," Rosie said. "I didn't like Paul Bone when he was alive and I like him a lot less now he's dead. Somebody close his eyes. I swear he's looking at me, getting ready to fall on top of me again."

Lightning sizzled across the turbulent sky and rain drummed on Buttons's hat as he said, "Mr. Bone is a fare-paying passenger of the Abe Patterson and Son Stage and Express Company and as such he's entitled to ride in the stage, dead or alive. That's written in the rule book somewhere." He turned to Red, "Help me get him inside."

It was then that Buttons and Red discovered that their fabulously feminine fan dancer had fangs.

They found themselves looking into the black eyes of a Remington derringer, .41 caliber, lethal enough close up, and Erica Hall was close up. "I'll tell you again," she said. "You're not putting the stiff in here under any circumstances."

Buttons was enraged. He looked like he was about to explode, but Red headed off his wrath. "He's one of yours, lady," he said. He waited until a roll of thunder passed and then added, "Where do you suggest we put him?"

The torrential rain slanted around the coach, hissing like a baby dragon in a clock box and lightning tore the sky apart.

"I don't care where you put him," Erica said. The derringer didn't waver. "And he's not one of mine. Paul Bone was a morphine addict and a drunk who couldn't dance any longer. Back in Fort Smith I took pity on him, that was all."

As rain did a drumroll on his hat and shoulders, Buttons said, "Madam, threatening an employee of the Abe Patterson and Son Stage and Express Company with a gun is a very grave offense. When we reach Houston you will have to face the law and explain your actions."

"And you will explain yours, driving man," Erica said.

She batted her long, dark eyelashes. "Who is poor Erica? She's just a dancer lady who was undone and terrified for her life when the driver and messenger of the Patterson stage, singularly rough and violent men both, tried to lock her up with a dead body that might have been contagious." She fluttered her eyelashes again like two small fans, and Red thought she was very good at it. "So, much afraid, it was a matter of the greatest moment that she pick up a firearm to defend herself."

Erica smiled. "Who will the law believe? You two ruffians or little ol' me?"

Buttons sensed defeat, but battered by rain and the woman's words, he tried to salvage the situation. "Now, see here, young lady," he said, "I can throw you out of my stage and leave you at Potts's station. I don't think you'd like that very much. Now, make room in there for the deceased."

"Abandon me in the wilderness? Do that cruel deed and my lawyer will sue you and the Patterson stage company for every penny you've got," Erica said. "Isaac Spearman is a tough, uncompromising attorney and he has a particular dislike for men in positions of authority who abuse helpless women. Go ahead, ditch me if you dare."

Red Ryan said, "Lady, you don't look so helpless with that stinger in your hand."

"And I'll use it if I have to," Erica said. A question mark of dark hair fell over her forehead. "Leave Bone there and pick him up on your way back to San Angelo, why don't you?"

"That suggestion ain't ladylike," Buttons said.

"Mister, I've always been ladylike, but I stopped being

a lady a long time ago," Erica said. "It didn't get me any-where."

"For God's sake we have to do something," the Great Stefano said. He had a huge head crowned with a shock of black hair and his mustache was waxed into points that curled over his cheeks. "We can't sit out in the middle of the prairie in a thunderstorm all day. I'll help you put Bone's body on the roof. He isn't heavy."

Buttons would've argued further, but Red settled the matter. "Right, on the roof with him. We don't have far to go."

Buttons glared at Erica. "You haven't heard the last of this."

The woman smiled and returned the derringer to her purse. She didn't seem in the least concerned.

Red Ryan sat beside Buttons Muldoon in the rainswept box, a dead man's feet thumping into their backs.

"The Gray Ghost killed him," Buttons said. "The curse struck again. He was hale and hearty one minute, dead the next."

"He was an old man with a bad ticker who took mor-phine and drank too much," Red said. "It was bound to happen sometime."

"It didn't happen until he stepped foot in this stage," Buttons said. "Damn it, Red, don't you see that the Gray Ghost murdered him? It was a warning, telling me I'm next in line."

"Whiskey done for him," Red said. He turned his head and said, "Hey, Mr. Bone, what killed you, booze or the

Gray Ghost?" Red waited for a few moments and then said, "No answer, Buttons. I guess he doesn't know."

"That ain't funny, Red," Buttons said. "Just wait, something else will happen, something really bad."

Five minutes later they heard the sound of gunfire.

It came from Potts's station.

CHAPTER EIGHT

The thunderstorm lingered and Victor Potts's station, a long timber cabin with two doors in front and three shuttered windows, was under siege.

From his vantage point in the box, Buttons Muldoon watched from a distance as Apaches, using every scrap of cover, kept up a steady fire on the cabin, splintering its thin boards. He couldn't see the Griffin brothers but he was certain they'd be there somewhere.

"They got the place surrounded," Buttons said.

"Seems like," Red said.

"They haven't seen us yet," Buttons said.

"Not yet, but they will."

"I need time to think."

"About what?"

"Stay or go? We could head for the next station."

The Patterson stage was hidden behind a gray veil that the torrential rain had thrown over the landscape. But Buttons and Red knew they would not be invisible for long.

"Well, what do we do?" Red said.

"Vic Potts has two grown sons," Buttons said. "That means three rifles and Mrs. Potts reloading."

"You mean they're well-handed and we leave them to their fate?" Red said.

"I didn't say that," Buttons said. "I got a tired team that needs changed."

"Hey, driver, what's happening?" Dean Rice yelled above the relentless racket of the rain.

"The station's under attack from Apaches," Buttons said.

"In the rain?" Rice said.

"Apaches don't care about the rain," Buttons said. "They'll kill folks in any kind of weather."

"Then drive on to another station," Rice hollered, an edge of panic in his voice.

Buttons was silent for a long moment and finally he said, "I can't do that." And then to Red, "Are you ready?"

"I ain't sitting on my gun hand," Red said.

"Then let's go," Buttons said.

He whipped the already thunder-spooked team into a gallop and from somewhere in the stage Dean Rice yelled, "Nooooo . . ."

A hurtling gray coach charging out of the gloom took the Apaches by surprise, especially half a dozen warriors who'd left the cover of a brush-covered rise to converge on the cabin. Brown faces registering shock and surprise turned to the stagecoach and six galloping horses that bore down on them, a madman standing in the box, whip in hand, yelling like a demented banshee.

Caught in the open, with little time to react, the Apaches tried to turn and run, but the team hit them with devastating impact. A few warriors were thrown aside, others trampled as the now wild-eyed, panicked horses sped past the cabin. In a single, flashing instant as the scene rushed by, Red saw a white man back away, levering a Winchester. Holding the Greener like a pistol in his left hand, Red triggered a shot. He did it only to make an aggressive noise, knowing a hit was impossible. The shotgun kicked like a mule and when Red looked back, he discovered that any action is only impossible until it's done. He caught a fleeting glimpse of the white man. He still stood, but he was already dead, his entire face shattered into blood and bone, like a cherry pie dropped on a bakehouse floor.

Red didn't see the man fall. Buttons drove the stage past the station toward the corral, where he reined in the team. Immediately one of the big, 1,250-pound wheelers next to the coach went down, dead in the traces. Buttons later discovered that the horse had suffered five bullet wounds but had gamely stayed alive until it reached the corral.

Red reloaded the Greener and jumped down from the box. Next to him, Erica Hall leaned out the stage window, extended her arm, and triggered both shots from her derringer. Red reckoned that she didn't hit anything, but he admired her spunk. As it was, the two rounds from the woman's Remington were among the last fired at what was to be remembered by western men as the Relief of Potts Station because of the timely arrival of the Patterson stage. Messenger Red Ryan got special mention. According to one newspaper account, "He drew his deadly revolvers and charged into the midst of the blood-lusting savages, killing an even dozen ere the rest broke and ran." Red would later write a scathing letter to the editor about this falsehood but never received a reply. As a result, the legend stands to this day.

Shaken by Buttons Muldoon's charge, their four dead warriors, and renewed fusillades from the cabin, the Apaches withdrew, melting into the teeming rain and murk like phantoms. Among the slain was Uriah Griffin, a death that would call for a reckoning and put Red's life in danger like never before.

Buttons and his passengers walked from the corral to the cabin and Victor Potts met them outside. Potts, tall, lanky, with lively brown eyes and a trimmed, spade-shaped beard, grinned, shoved out his hand, and said, "Dang it, Buttons, you saved our lives."

"Happy to oblige," Buttons said, shaking the man's hand. "I've got a horse down, Vic, and a dead white man lashed to the top of the stage."

Potts's expression asked a question and Buttons answered it. "He died about an hour ago. He was a song and dance man who drank too much."

"Sorry to hear that," Potts said. I'll see to the horse and you'll want the man buried, I guess," Potts said.

"Yeah, I do," Buttons said. He glanced at the dead men, puddles of bloody rainwater formed beside them. "You've more to bury."

"I'll drag the Apaches out into the prairie, let the coyotes deal with them," Potts said. "I'll bury the white man."

"Half-white," Buttons said. "He's a breed, one of the Griffin brothers."

"Half-white?" Potts said. "Then I'll bury him shallow."

Buttons looked past Potts, his eyes searching, "Where are your sons?"

"They're inside," the man said. "Martha is tending to

their wounds. They were both grazed by bullets." He smiled. "Lucky they have hard heads."

"Oh my God," Rosie Lee shrieked. She shrank away from the sprawled bodies. "They're dead, like Paul Bone, they're all dead . . . and . . . and . . . bloody."

"Sure are, little lady, dead as hell in a parson's parlor," Potts said. He glanced over the bodies and waved a hand. "Seems that them two were killed by the stage and the one with the red headband looks like his neck is broke. T'other is shot through and through, and Buttons, I'll take your word on it that the ranny over there is a half-white man. It's hard to tell."

"Look at his hands and the brown hair under his hat," Buttons said. "He's a breed, all right, one of the four Griffin brothers and they're all poison."

Potts looked up at a silver streak in the sky where black clouds parted and then said, "How come they're riding with Apaches?"

Red Ryan said, "The story goes that their mother was a Chiricahua Apache, their pa an Irishman who was done in by drink. The mother raised her sons as Apaches but also taught them the white man's tongue and his ways. After she died, they ended up in the San Carlos reservation up in the Arizona Territory, where they made a lot of shady friends. With some other renegades, they broke out of there a couple of years ago and ever since they've played hob in Texas and the Indian Territory, murdering, raping, and robbing. They know how to kill a man slow, like an Apache, using fire on him over two or three days until his screaming wears him out and he eventually dies. Like Buttons says, they're poison."

Buttons directed his surprise at Red. "How come you know all that stuff?" he said.

"Because I read the *San Angelo Standard*," Red said. "It's a good newspaper, keeps me informed about stuff that's happening."

"I'll have to start reading that," Buttons said.

"Good idea. It will improve your mind," Red said.

He turned away from Buttons and walked to the dead Griffin brother. Red rolled the corpse over on its front, straightened up, and said to a puzzled Vic Potts, "I don't need to remind myself what buckshot from a ten-gauge shotgun does to a man's face."

Potts nodded. "It ain't pretty."

Erica Hall stepped beside Rosie Lee and looked at the dead men with no change of expression. Her hands were steady as she fed two stubby .41 rounds into her derringer, closed the gun, and shoved it back in her purse. To Potts she said, "Do you have brandy inside?"

The man shook his head. "No, but I got whiskey."

"I suppose that will have to do," Erica said. Then to Red, frowning, "No more talk of Apaches and the Griffin brothers around Miss Lee, if you please. She's of a nervous disposition."

Rosie Lee's eyes were as round as coins as Erica put her arm around her shoulders, ushered the trembling girl to the cabin, and stepped inside.

CHAPTER NINE

Two gangly young men and a plump, matronly woman in a blue, flowered dress were in the cabin when Erica Hall and Rosie Lee stepped inside. The woman tied off a bandage around the younger man's head and said, "You're with the Patterson stage. God bless you, you arrived just in the nick of time to rescue us."

Erica smiled. "I didn't do much, fired two shots from my derringer and missed both times. Apart from that I was terrified."

"Me, too," Rosie Lee said, shuddering. "It was too terrible for words."

Shiny brass cartridge cases littered the cabin's wood floor and the wall opposite the two windows was pockmarked by bullets, as were the shelves that held a variety of pots and pans, canisters, and plain white cups and plates, a few of them shattered. A fire still burned in the stove, where a sooty coffeepot and a large bean pot simmered, an indication of how sudden the Apache attack had been. A timber mantel held some oval tintypes of plain-featured kinfolk along with a few china knickknacks and in the middle, obviously a prized possession, a walnut mantel clock. Frayed easy chairs that looked like they'd once belonged to somebody's great-grandma stood one on each side of the stove and four rickety wooden chairs surrounding a round table that held a large Bible and an oil lamp completed the furnishings. Two narrow and uncomfortable-looking mattresses lay on the floor, shoved against the far wall, and a poorly executed portrait of a Confederate private with a memorable chin beard hung above an ajar door that led to a windowless bedroom where a brass bedstead covered with a patchwork quilt was just visible.

The cabin smelled of horses, sweat, and gun smoke, displayed little comfort, and spoke of a hard, joyless life on the frontier's raw edge.

"I'm Martha Potts," the woman said to Erica. "These are my sons, Joshua and Ephraim. As you can see, they're both wounded, but only slightly, thank God."

"After I got hit, I slept on the floor through most of the fight," Joshua said.

"It was a close thing," Martha said. "Joshua is our best rifleman."

Ephraim, a sparse covering of hair on his top lip stating his claim to manhood, said nothing, his wide, unbelieving eyes fixed on Erica. He had seen female passengers before, a few of the pretty wives of army officers, but none that compared to this woman's spectacular beauty. She was a vision apart, a lovely, exotic creature who lived in an elegant world of men and women and manners he could only guess at and could never aspire to enter.

For her part, Erica recognized the naked worship in the youth's eyes and was mildly amused. The rube was besotted and she expected that at any moment he'd drool at the mouth.

With a mother's instinct Martha Potts saw what was happening and abruptly ordered her sons to go help their father and Buttons Muldoon with the new team. The two youths left, neither of them handsome, nor smart, nor rich, nor cultured, attributes that Erica Hall looked for in a man. But she thought them amusing.

Martha closed the bullet-riddled door behind her sons. She crossed to the stove, lifted the pot lid, sniffed, and said, "Thank the good Lord my vittles didn't burn. It's salt pork and beans if you'd care to make a trial of it, ladies."

Outside the rain had stopped and men's voices were raised as the dead Apaches and the Griffin brother were dragged away.

"I'd like a cup of coffee with whiskey in it," Rosie Lee said. "A lot of whiskey in it."

Erica said, "I'll have the same."

Martha smiled. "Coffee and whiskey is the very thing. It will settle our nerves and do us all good."

Erica Hall and Rosie Lee sat at the table with Martha Potts when Red Ryan and Buttons Muldoon walked into the cabin with the Great Stefano and Dean Rice in tow. "Drink up, ladies," Buttons said. "We got a schedule to keep." Then to Martha, "What's in the pot?"

"Salt pork and beans," the woman said.

"Ladle some of that for me and the passengers," Buttons said. "What about you, Red?"

"I'll pass," Red said.

Buttons shook his head. "I swear, Red, a bird eats more than you do."

A few moments later the door opened and Victor Potts

walked inside. "The dead man's off your roof, Buttons," he said. "And I seen something strange."

"How strange?" Buttons said.

"He had a couple of bullet holes in him and so did the horse you lost," Potts said. "But there's none in the stage. Peculiar, that."

"It's not so strange," Red said. "There's no bullet holes in me or Buttons. Or the passengers. We took the Apaches by surprise and they didn't get a chance to shoot up the stage."

Buttons held a plate under his chin, forked some beans into his mouth, then spoke as he chewed. "They had their chance, all right," he said. "It's because the stage is a ghost. You can't put bullet holes in a ghost."

"It looks solid enough to me," Potts said. "I've never seen a fancier or better-built Concord, and I've seen a few."

"It's a killer," Buttons said. "When I get the thrice-damned thing back to San Angelo, I'll burn it."

Red was shocked by Buttons's features as he said that. His normally pleasant, round Irish face with its ruddy cheeks and twinkling blue eyes looked drawn and haggard and closed down, as though all the worries of the world sat on his shoulders. From his Irish mother he'd inherited the gift, some said the curse, of second sight, the ability to see the future through a misty window, and it showed on him.

A few minutes later as Buttons herded his passengers out the door to the waiting stage, Red took him aside and said, "What the hell's troubling you? You look like your biscuits are burning."

"Everything's troubling me," Buttons said. "Every damn thing . . . past, present, and future."

CHAPTER TEN

Holding the wire he'd received from Luciano Tiodoro in his stubby fingers, Antonio Matranga looked through his second-story office window and smiled as he watched children play among the trees or ride the carousel in the park opposite his opulent, Garden District villa. Matranga always thought that New Orleans looked its best in late August, the magnolia and live oaks washed clean by the summer rains. A streetcar drawn by a gray horse trundled past, two ragged street urchins running behind it, jeering at a fat kid in a sailor suit who sat beside his fond mama and tried his best to ignore them. A couple of fashionable belles strolled under his window, one in a dress of blue silk, the other in yellow ruffles. The young women's parasols were open against the afternoon sun and the one in blue carried a small dog that barked incessantly. At dusk, the electric streetlamps would come on and bathe the park in a soft opalescent light, but by then the children would be gone, leaving the night to lovers.

Matranga, the city's Mafia capo dei capi, boss of bosses,

sighed as he again studied the wire he already knew by heart.

ERICA HALL EN ROUTE TO HOUSTON WITH
STOLEN HEROIC MERCHANDISE STOP I AM
IN PURSUIT OF HER STAGE STOP LUCIANO

Matranga shook his head. This was bad. He'd trusted Erica Hall and Luciano Tiodoro with what the German scientists who made the new drug were now calling heroin. And at first, they'd done well in Fort Smith's seething swamp of depravity, Hell's Half Acre, pushing a kilo a week of the powder as a cheaper substitute for morphine and opium. But it was just as addictive and the profit margin was huge, as much as five to ten thousand dollars a kilo. Cut with dried milk it could be smoked or snorted, unlike the crude, black tar heroin that was now coming up from Mexico in small doses and could only be dissolved and injected into a vein. Antonio Matranga was already heavily involved in racketeering, extortion, prostitution, armed robbery, contract killing, money laundering, counterfeiting, and kidnapping, but he was anxious to expand his sales of morphine and opium and was now testing the waters with the new heroin. The theft of ten kilos of the as yet hard-to-come-by merchandise was a setback . . . a setback that needed to be corrected.

Matranga palmed his desk bell and the door to his office almost immediately opened and his secretary entered. Sophie Boudreaux was a tall, slender, middle-aged Creole who was angular and not pretty, a ring with a huge, red glass stone on her wedding finger. The ring had nothing to do with marriage, but everything to do with voodoo. She was efficient, clever, and fiercely loyal to the Matranga family as she was to the memory of Marie Laveau, the voodoo queen who'd adopted her as a child.

"Miss Boudreaux, send a boy to bring in Leoluca Vitale," Matranga said.

"Right away," the woman said.

She didn't know why Leoluca Vitale was summoned nor did she need to know, and Vitale himself would answer the call without question.

"Before you go," Matranga said. "Look out the window. Do you see that ragged bum on the park bench?"

"I see him."

"Be nice to him. Smile. Set him at ease. Give him two silver dollars and tell him they came from Antonio Matranga."

"Right away," the woman said. Again, she asked no questions.

After a while Matranga looked out the window and saw Sophie Boudreaux say something to the tramp—he wore a battered coachman's hat and some kind of old army greatcoat—and then she gave him the coins. The man rose to his feet, kissed the dollars, and hurried off to spend his money, probably on whiskey. It didn't matter. It was good business to spread around a little charity.

CHAPTER ELEVEN

"You got here in good time, Leoluca," Antonio Matranga said.

The young man smiled. "I took two fast streetcars."

He was of medium height, slender with black hair and eyes, and he used short, quick motion when he walked. He was alert, intelligent, and best of all in Matranga's eyes, a dependable, efficient killer.

"Leoluca, are you still living with that little Cajun girl . . . what's her name?"

"Babette Romero."

"Is she a good Catholic? Says the rosary and attends Holy Mass on Sunday?"

"Yes, she does those things and takes Communion. She's a good girl, capo."

Matranga nodded. "That is the sweetest music to my ears." He waved his beringed hands. "It is good that my *soldati* have such women. Leoluca, you must talk to her often, or there can be no relationship. Respect her. Where there is no respect there is no love. And trust her as she trusts you. Without trust there is no reason to continue together."

"As always, capo, you have great wisdom," Vitale said.

"You have met my wife?" Matranga said.

"I have not had that pleasure," Vitale said. He had killed, by his own count, seven people.

"I keep her out of the family business," Matranga said. "Like your Babette, she is a good woman and she prays novenas for me."

Vitale quickly crossed himself and said, "God bless her."

"'A good woman is hard to find and worth far more than diamonds.' That is from the Book of Proverbs," Matranga said. "And it is a woman who has brought you here."

"A good woman?" Vitale said.

"That remains to be seen," Matranga said. "If she's played me false, I may ask you to put an end to her."

Vitale didn't flinch. "Capo, I will do your bidding. Just give me the order."

Matranga picked up Powell's wire and handed it to Vitale. "Read that."

Vitale scanned the wire and said, "I stand ready."

Both men wore expensively tailored ditto suits in the latest fashion, short, tightly fitted jackets with slim sleeves, the lapels extremely narrow and small, buttoned so high the necktie was barely visible. Vitale's coat was cut a little looser in the chest to accommodate a .32 Long Colt Model of 1877, a double-action revolver in a shoulder holster, an assassin's weapon. Both men wore gold watch chains, a visible sign that they were prospering, and a silver Miraculous Medal hung from Matranga's chain.

The capo said, "This woman, Erica Hall, is a performer. She dances with a couple of Chinese fans to cover her nakedness, and she's very skilled."

"Alluring, I imagine," Vitale said.

"Yes, that, too," Matranga said. "A year ago I saw her perform at the St. Charles Theatre here in New Orleans and after the show I met her backstage. A man has his needs, you understand, and my only interest was to get Erica Hall in bed. But then, as we talked over a bottle of champagne, I had a different, and shall we say, a better idea. And that reminds me . . ." Matranga rang his desk bell and his secretary entered. "Wine, Miss Boudreaux, if you please."

When the woman returned, she poured wine for the men and left.

"Now, where was I?" Matranga said.

"I think you decided to put business before bed, capo," Vitale said.

"Ah yes, and so I did," Matranga said. He smiled. "'Business before bed.' That was very good, Leoluca. And let me tell you, it wasn't easy. She's a very beautiful woman."

Vitale picked up his glass, the wine as red as blood, and prompted, "And your idea, capo?"

"Miss Hall travels with a troupe of other acts and they constantly move from city to city to perform in the music halls," Matranga said. "She told me she follows the money, and the western towns pay more than most. That's when I thought, *Then why not sell my merchandise when you're at it?*"

Vitale, a loyal *soldato* who was being groomed for bigger things in the Matranga organization, said, "I hear that there's too much competition for business in the big eastern cities like New York and Chicago, too many gangs, too much war, but the West is wide open and there's a lot of money to be made."

"Exactly!" Matranga said. He sipped wine and then took time to light a cigar before he said, "To make a long story short, Erica Hall agreed to push the heroin for a ten percent cut and five percent of the opium and morphine sales. I sent her to Fort Smith to join Luciano Tiodoro, who was already there. And, of course, I suggested to the owner of the Variety music hall that he hire her as a dancer. That way she'd meet all the right people, you understand, actors and artists and the like willing to try something new, a new drug to make them feel good and happy enough to spread the word."

"Luciano Tiodoro changed his name, didn't he?" Vitale said. "I heard that."

"Yes, he calls himself Luke Powell now and he was a notorious bandito before I took him on as a favor to his father, a man I respect," Matranga said. "His papa was worried about young Luciano and hired Pinkertons to find him. Then three years ago he brought him here to New Orleans, where he was born and raised, for me to talk sense into him." He shook his head. "Luciano stood right there in front of my desk, big hat, boots, looked like a damned cattle drover, and he spoke Italian like a peasant."

"You took him under your wing, capo?" Vitale asked.

"No, not that," Matranga said. "Not under my wing. But I put him to the test. I told him to take care of a man who was making trouble for me, a Cajun pimp in St. John the Baptist Parish by the name of Henri Fontenot. The man was confused, he wasn't thinking straight, and he demanded a bigger cut from prostitution and opium. So now I tell you how the Fontenot affair went. 'Be courteous to Henri Fontenot, Luciano,' I said. 'Lean on him lightly, buy him jambalaya, meet his family, bring candy canes for his kids. Then talk to him. Tell him how much more generous I'll be when business picks up. In the meantime, I'll take good care of him like I was his patron saint. Tell him that. But if all words fail and he's deaf to my promises and still determined to be obstinate, you know what to do. That is when you go to the *pistola*.'"

"And did he go to the gun?" Vitale said. "Or was Luciano patient with Fontenot?"

Matranga was a man who sighed a great deal and he sighed now. "Too far, Leoluca. Luciano went way too far. Henri Fontenot refused to cooperate and threatened to go to the police, confess his sins as a pimp and opium dealer, and then blow the entire organization sky-high. He threatened to break the code of omertà and sing loud and long about my business and the black businesses on South Rampart Street, the whole kit and caboodle. Sing like a canary. Now, maybe a *pistola* muzzle to the man's head and a kind word might have changed his mind, I don't know. But Luciano claims he tried that and when Fontenot still refused, he pulled the trigger and blew his brains out. But he didn't stop there. He also triggered the man's wife and kids and their pet Pomeranian." Matranga slowly shook his head. "My, my, my, it was an ill-done undertaking, but nevertheless I saw in Luciano Tiodoro a man I could use. I needed his ruthlessness in Fort Smith, where my business was falling off a cliff, and he deleted a few people and quickly turned things around. Indeed, he was doing well until this Erica Hall affair came up."

Leoluca Vitale drained his wineglass and said, "You need me in Houston, capo."

"Yes, I do," Matranga said. "A train leaves tomorrow morning at seven for Houston. Be on it, Leoluca. On your way out talk to Miss Boudreaux and she'll provide you with hotel and other expenses." Matranga opened a desk drawer and produced a photograph in a cream-colored paper folder. "This is a carte de visite of Erica Hall and it's a good likeness. Take it with you and study it."

Vitale studied the portrait and said, "She's a beautiful woman."

Matranga nodded. "Yes, she is. It would be a great pity to"—he waved a hand—"put a bullet through her fan. But you must do what you think is best." He looked at Vitale intently. "Wire me when everything is done."

Vitale got to his feet. One of the most dangerous professional assassins in the nation, he looked like a well-dressed warehouse clerk who cooked the books and skimmed off a few dollars here and there. But his appearance was deceiving. Leoluca Vitale was a stone-cold killer who cared nothing for the men he murdered and they didn't disturb his sleep at night. After a few days he couldn't even remember their faces. So far, he hadn't killed a woman, but there was a first time for everything and he wouldn't hesitate to destroy Erica Hall. Vitale had a quirk. After every killing he put a flower in his lapel. In Erica Hall's case he'd find a rose, preferably red.

"I'd like receipts for your hotel and meals, Mr. Vitale," Sophie Boudreaux said. "Can you do that for me? Mr. Matranga likes to keep track of expenses."

"Sure thing," Vitale said. He turned his head as the

office door opened and Matranga stood big and bulky, framed in the entrance.

"Leoluca, when you meet up with Miss Hall, be kind, be understanding, respect her as a woman," the capo said. "Talk to her, show her the error of her ways. I never did find out if she's a Catholic, but if she is, maybe you could talk her into saying the rosary with you, get on her good side. Then, if she returns the heroin, kiss her on the cheek and let bygones be bygones. Do you understand?"

"And if she doesn't cooperate?" Vitale said.

"Then you must make her talk. You know what to do."

"I'll interview her," Vitale said. "I'll find out where she has the merchandise. And if she doesn't talk, well . . ."

Matranga sighed. "No, don't tell me. Violence disturbs me so, and I leave that part of the business to you, Leoluca. Do what you have to do, I don't care, just bring back my merchandise. Oh, and there is one more thing to do in Houston."

"I'm listening," Vitale said.

"Take a downtown electric streetcar to Quality Hill, that's a residential area in the Houston business district. Look for number 85, a big house on Chenevert Street with six Greek pillars in front. The man who owns that house is a Sicilian by the name of Vincenzu Grotte. He owns a music hall, a couple of restaurants, and a high-class brothel called the Silver Garter and he owes me favors, a lot of favors, *capiche?*"

Vicente nodded. "Sure, capo, I understand."

"Good. Now, listen. Talk to Grotte, mention my name, and tell him why you're in Houston," Matranga said. "He likes to think of himself as an honest businessman, but he dabbles in extortion and contract killings and he has associates all over the city. He'll help you track down Erica Hall. If she's in Houston, Grotte will find her for you."

"I'll talk to him, capo," Vincente said.

"Good. *Buona fortuna*, Leoluca."

The door to Antonio Matranga's office closed.

CHAPTER TWELVE

An owl, a bird of ill omen, flew silently over the heads of the Apaches as they rode away from the Potts's station fight and they talked among themselves and agreed that their medicine was bad. Apaches have no word for good-bye, so they simply left to mourn their dead, leaving the three Griffin brothers alone on the prairie. The grassland was splashed in moonlight, the only pools of shadows a few, and very rare, circular depressions, wallows made years ago when buffalo still wandered the plains. The three Griffins had made camp in a thin stand of mesquite and post oak and two of them roasted chunks of jackrabbit meat on the end of sticks. At a distance, near the tethered horses, a white woman sat with her head on her knees, her dress a ripped and torn wreck of what it had been just a week before when she was a rancher's wife. Her hair was unbound, tangled, and fell over her shoulders and face. She'd been beaten and raped many times by all four brothers and could no longer talk.

"Uriah's soul cries out for vengeance," Cyrus Griffin said. He was the youngest brother, just twenty-one. He was vicious, mentally disturbed, a wild animal barely human. Like the others he wore shabby, stained range clothes he'd stolen from dead men, but the Colt he carried and the Winchester that lay beside him were oiled and well cared for. He had his Irish father's blue eyes and red hair and there was nothing of the Apache about him, though he spoke the Athabaskan tongue fluently.

"We will eat and then follow the tracks of the stage," Ira Griffin, at thirty the oldest brother and their leader. He was black-eyed, black-haired, and looked more Apache than the others. "Fear not, Cyrus, our brother will be avenged."

Jeremiah Griffin, a year younger than Ira, said, grinning, "Their deaths must be long and painful. I want to kill them a small piece at a time and hear them scream."

"For days," Cyrus said. "Many days."

"I saw women in the stage," Jeremiah said. He jerked his chin in the direction of the quiet, sitting woman. "Prettier women than the hag we've got."

"I knew a woman down in Chihuahua in old Mexico who ran a brothel," Ira said. "Her name was Estelle and she served up the prettiest whores you ever did see. They were Chinese, and none of them was taller than five feet. Of course they didn't last very long so you had to git while the gittin' was good." Ira smiled and nodded. "I'll always remember them whores."

"We was talking about Uriah," Cyrus said, scowling.

Ira grabbed a chunk of half-raw rabbit and chewed on it before he said, "Eat, and then we will follow the tracks of the stagecoach. We will catch up sometime after first light and destroy them."

"Save the women," Cyrus said. Then he motioned to their captive. "What about her?"

Ira shrugged. "Leave her here. I'm finished with her."

The other two nodded in agreement, but Cyrus spat into the fire and stood. He walked to the woman, who still sat with her head on her knees, shoved the muzzle of his gun into the back of her neck, and pulled the trigger. He returned to the fire, grabbed a chunk of rabbit, shoved it into his mouth, and said around it, spraying meat, "Look at her. She's dead and hasn't moved."

Jeremiah, black hair falling to his shoulders under his high-crowned, flat-brimmed hat, glanced at the woman and then looked away. "A whore is better."

"Sometimes," Ira said. He looked at the woman. "But she was too much trouble."

"Think about it," Cyrus said, shaking his head. "We're still sitting here eating jackrabbit and she's already met her Maker."

"You think she's told him about us?" Ira said.

"Sure," Cyrus said. "And all of it bad."

"Who cares? We'll all end up in hell anyway," Ira said, his face red in the firelight. "Now, saddle up. And we got to find coffee someplace. I'm craving a cup."

"Maybe they'll have some on the stage," Cyrus said. "Or there will be a station close by."

"I've had my fill of stage stations," Ira said, getting to his feet.

"The Potts place sure done for Uriah," Cyrus said. "Ira, we should head back that way again and even the score with Victor Potts and his sons and his wife."

"We will, depend on it," Ira said. "But only after we've done for people on the stage."

Forgotten already, without a second glance at the dead

woman, the Griffin brothers mounted up and picked up the stage tracks heading south.

After riding for an hour, Ira called a halt, swung out of the saddle, and examined some horse droppings. He rubbed a sphere of manure between his thumb and forefinger. It was soft and still held some warmth.

"We're close," he said.

"How close?" Cyrus said.

"We'll catch up soon, that's how close," Ira said.

"How soon?" Cyrus said.

"The stage will be in sight just after sunup," Ira said. "We'll take it by surprise and shoot the driver and the shotgun guard."

"I saw men in the stage, but I can't say how many," Jeremiah said.

"No matter how many. The men we kill, the women we keep for ourselves," Ira said. Then a rare smile. "Cold nights coming soon."

His wide, high-cheekboned face was deeply scored from his right ear to the point of his chin from a knife fight, the scars livid white against his bronze skin. His features were hard, his glittering black eyes merciless, and in his time he'd tortured, or gleefully helped torture, a dozen men to death, nine of them white, the other three black buffalo soldiers. Like his brothers he was emotionless, scarcely human, and General George Crook, a soldier who knew Apaches, once called him "a ravening wolf in a human's hide." Like all Apaches, in war Ira played by no rules. His philosophy was simple, right to the point: *If you are my enemy, I will destroy you.* That was his belief in its entirety. There was nothing else and talk of mercy would have made him laugh.

Ira Griffin stepped into the saddle, glanced at the luminous night sky, and then said, "The stage has left us an easy trail to follow." He spat and then kneed his horse forward. "Pah, we chase after children."

"The messenger killed Uriah with a shotgun," Cyrus said. "He is dangerous."

Ira nodded. "We will respect his shotgun," he said. "As soon as the light starts to change, we'll attack the stage from his side. He'll be the first to die."

Jeremiah raised his rifle above his head and shrieked the Apache war scream, "AAAAAARRR!"

Ira turned his head, smiled, and said, "You are ready, my brother?"

"Yes, ready. I think of the booty that will be ours," the young man said. "Scalps, six horses, and women. The Mescaleros who left us will regret their desertion."

"That is so," Ira said. "The Mescaleros will envy us and look the other way when we ride past."

But to the others their brother spoke in a distracted manner because his full attention was on the distance where a red point of light looked like a cinder fallen from a shooting star.

Then Cyrus and Jeremiah saw what Ira saw.

"It's a campfire," Cyrus said. "Large, a white man's fire."

Ira drew rein and the other followed suit.

"Rangers?" Ira said. "Or soldiers?"

"Unlikely to be Rangers out so far on the grassland," Cyrus said.

"Soldiers, then," Ira said.

"Only one fire," Cyrus said. "If it is soldiers, they are few in number."

As always, Jeremiah looked to his older brother for leadership. "Ira, what do we do?" he said.

Cyrus said, "We can circle around them, whoever they are."

"Or catch them asleep," Ira said. "Where there are soldiers there are guns and horses." He touched his tongue to his top lip. "And coffee."

"In the past White Painted Woman"—Cyrus called the goddess Esdzanadehe, her Apache name—"has given us her protection and the gift of long lives. Perhaps she has led us here to this fire."

"Then where was she when Uriah met his death?" Jeremiah said.

"Uriah never asked the goddess for her protection," Ira said. "He did not believe in her and therefore she was deaf to him."

"What do we do?" Jeremiah said.

After a moment's thought, Ira Griffin said, "It's many hours until sunup. We ride to the fire where we may be made welcome."

"What if it's soldiers?" Cyrus said.

"They won't see us as Apaches, but as white men," Ira said. "If we are welcomed, then all will be well. But if we're chased away as filthy savages, we will kill them all."

"But if there are too many?" Cyrus said.

"Around one campfire, their number will be few and they will be easy to kill," Ira said.

Jeremiah, more fearful than his brothers, stared at the distant fire, sensing danger, and said, "I hope that will be what White Painted Woman has planned."

CHAPTER THIRTEEN

"Do my eyes deceive me or do I see riders coming in?" Whitey Quinn said. He stood at the edge of the firelight, looking into moonlit darkness. Mesquite crackled in the flames, that night perhaps the only sound in all the vast plains.

Luke Powell rose to his feet and stood beside the little drawfighter. Despite his rough clothing, he wore a gold watch and chain and rings on his fingers. "It's riders, all right," he said. He summoned Wesley Fuller, the Texas gun handler, and the knife fighter Bill Cline to his side. His two other men, Gus Finley and Ross Glenn, were of little account. Finley, gray-haired and approaching middle age, was stove up from his cowboying days and walked with a limp. He was a stocky man, going to belly, and his unshaven face was ruddy from the heat of the campfire and the greater heat of forty-rod whiskey. He was rumored to have killed a deputy town marshal in Abilene and a stock detective somewhere in the New Mexico Territory. A man of little ambition, Finley was a hanger-on and he clung to Powell's coattails. He'd served well as an enforcer in Fort Smith and Powell tolerated him. Ross Glenn was younger, stocky, with an oddly shaped head as though the top of his skull had been flattened by a falling rock, and his mustache was full, black, and thick. He was emotionless, unfeeling, and joyless. To him the spring rain never fell, the warm sun never shined, and a woman in his bed was as enjoyable as a cold drink of water. As far as is known, Glenn never killed a man though some historians credit him with the murder of a teller during a bank robbery in Missouri when Jesse and Frank James were present. But that has never been proved. Suffice it to say that Ross Glenn was a soulless, dead-eyed man with no past, no present, and little chance of a future.

"Three men coming in," Whitey said. "White men, by the look of them."

"Yeah, even with one eye I can see them," Powell said. "Whitey, you and Wes get ready for the draw and shoot. They may be Rangers."

Wes Fuller, a baby-faced, twenty-one-year-old killer whose burning ambition was to be another Billy the Kid, adjusted the hang of his gun and said, "Just give the word, boss." Like Whitey and Bill Cline, his gun had been of great value in Fort Smith and Powell held him in high esteem.

Luke Powell watched the riders come closer and then, well within rifle range, revealing that they came in peace, the Griffin brothers drew rein and Ira called out, "Hello, the camp!"

Whitey smiled. "At least they're polite. Rangers would've charged right in."

"Come half the distance closer and state your intentions," Powell said.

The Griffins rode to within twenty yards of the camp,

drew rein again, and Ira said in a normal tone of voice, "We'd like to share your fire for a spell and I could sure use a cup of coffee."

Powell whispered, "Keep a weather eye on them, boys." Then louder, "Come on in smiling and your hands away from your guns like you were calling on kinfolk."

"Suits us," Ira said. "We're coming in, riding easy."

Powell watched the riders closely. One of them had long black hair and the look of a breed. Like him, the other two were shabbily dressed, but all three rode good horses and carried belt guns and Winchesters. *It takes one to know one,* the old saying goes, and Powell pegged them as outlaws of some kind who didn't seem to be prospering of late.

The three men dismounted, ground-tied their horses, and stepped into the circle of the firelight. Ira splayed his hands to the heat and said, "Feels good." He looked directly at Powell and said, "Name's Ira Griffin. These are my brothers Cyrus and Jeremiah. The one with the long hair is Jeremiah. Coffee smells good."

"Pot's on the fire. Help yourself," Powell said.

"I put out my name, what's yours?" Ira said.

"Name's Luke Powell. You don't need to know the others."

"No offense," Ira said.

"None taken," Powell said.

Ira got down on one knee beside the fire and Ross Glenn tossed him a tin cup. The breed poured himself coffee and blew across the cup a few times and then tasted. He nodded. "Good coffee," he said.

"Arbuckle," Glenn said.

"The best kind," Ira said. He got to his feet and drank

again and then said to Powell, "Where are you boys headed?"

"Why do you need to know that?" Whitey said.

"No reason. Just being sociable," Ira said.

He had already assessed the situation and ruled out a gunfight. Three against six were not good odds, especially at close range, and all of Powell's boys looked like they'd be gun handy.

"We're headed for Houston," Powell said.

"Business trip?" Ira said. "Or are you going to see the sights?"

"You could say business trip," Powell said. "But we might do some sightseeing."

"Big city, Houston," Ira said. "A lot of people."

"You been there?" Powell said.

"Only once. Me and my brothers, there were four of us then, rode in to see what a big city was all about."

"What did you see?" Powell said.

"Tall brick buildings, electric streetcars, crowds of people everywhere, and the city all lit up at night," Ira said. "It was a sight to see."

"How were the women?" Whitey said, hostile but interested.

"Right pretty," Ira said. "Me and my brothers visited Happy Hollow, that's what they call Louisiana Avenue where the brothels and the whores are."

"And how was it?" Whitey said, eager.

"We wasn't made welcome," Cyrus said, scowling.

"How come?" Whitey said.

"Were you broke?" Wes Fuller said.

"No, we had money but nowhere to spend it," Cyrus said. "It got out that we were breeds and the police and a bunch of the citizenry ran us out of town. At one point the citizens were going to hang us, but the lawmen stopped them."

"What kind of breeds?" Whitey said. "My guess is you had an Indian ma."

"Our mother was Mescalero Apache and our father that we never got to know because he never stayed in place for long, was an Irishman."

"Too bad," Whitey said.

"What's too bad?" Ira said. "That we're breeds?"

"No, that you was thrown out of the brothels," Whitey said. "That can make a man feel low-down."

Ira shrugged. "It was no matter. We ended up in Galveston, where the whores weren't so picky."

Whitey slapped Ira's back and grinned. "Well, good for you, half-breed!"

Ira's smile was thin and unamused. He stared hard at Whitey, burning the man's face into his memory . . . a white man to kill one day.

Powell saw that glance, didn't like it, and to ease the tension said, "Where are you boys headed?"

"South," Ira said.

"You visiting kin?" Powell said.

"No."

"Then what?"

"We're following a stage."

Whitey said, "Hey, so are—"

"Why?" Powell said, stopping Whitey dead in midsentence.

"It's a story," Ira said. "I could use some more coffee."

"He'p yourself, breed," Whitey said.

"Whitey, the gent's name is Ira," Powell said. "Call him by his name."

"I don't care what he calls me," Ira said.

He took a knee, poured coffee, and stood again.

"Don't your brothers want coffee?" Powell said.

"They don't have cups."

"Whitey, give them cups."

"What am I? A waiter?" Whitey said. But he rounded up a couple of tin cups and gave them to Cyrus and Jeremiah. "Drink up, boys," he said.

"We have corn cakes," Ira said.

"Huh?" Powell said.

"In our saddlebags, we have corn cakes," Ira said. "We have enough to share."

"Sure, bring them on," Powell said.

Ira walked back to his horse and returned to the fire with a bulging flour sack.

Whitey took a flat corn cake and said, "Hey, pretty good." He chewed and smiled, "They ain't bear sign, but they're right tasty. Hey, breed, I mean Ira, is that honey I taste?"

"Yes, Apache women gather it from hives in agave and yucca plants," Ira said.

"I bet them squaws get stung a lot," Wes Fuller said.

"They get stung, but not a lot," Ira said.

Powell said, hearing distant alarm bells in his head, "Why are you following a stage?"

"There is no need for you to know," Ira said.

"There is. I also have an interest in that stage."

"You wish to rob it?"

"Maybe."

"Then it's yours. We will ride on and leave it to you. Thank you for the coffee."

Powell gave Whitey Quinn and Wes Fuller a sidelong glance, then said, "Wait up. Tell me why you were following the stage."

Ira Griffin thought about that, then said, "The messenger killed my brother."

"Where did this happen?"

"At Potts's station, a few miles from here."

"Why were you there?"

"Grub," Ira said. He hesitated over the white man's word, as though he didn't say it often. "It is said that Victor Potts always has beef and beans and good coffee."

"Why did the messenger kill your brother?" Powell said.

Whitey and Fuller were listening intently to this exchange, sensing trouble.

The night was still, the prairie wind hushed, the moon big and bright spreading a mother-of-pearl light over the long grass. One of the horses stamped and snorted, suddenly restless as a hunting pair of coyotes called to each other close to the camp. A burning mesquite log dropped into the fire and showered a brief cascade of sparks into the darkness. Time suddenly dragged, slow as molasses in winter. Edgy men heard their own breathing.

"Why did the messenger kill your brother?" Powell asked the question again.

"I don't know," Ira Griffin said. "He just did."

"You planned to shoot the messenger and the other men and take the women and the horse team."

"No. Just the messenger."

"His is the only scalp you planned to take?"

Ira's eyes moved across the men facing him, summing them up in his mind. There were too many. Six men, all gunmen. He looked at his death.

"Yes, only the messenger."

Powell said, "What about the women? There are two white women on that stage. Savages lust for white women. They use and abuse them and then kill them. Isn't that right, half-Apache?"

"We want the messenger, no one else," Ira said.

"One of those women on the stage is very important to me," Powell said. "I don't want her harmed."

"We don't want your woman, only the messenger. He is a murderer."

Whitey smiled. "And you ain't?"

"We will go now," Ira said. "The coffee was good."

Cyrus and Jeremiah moved their hands closer to their holstered Colts.

"Yes, we will go," Cyrus said. "We have no quarrel with you."

"You're going nowhere, you damned, lying animals," Powell said. And then, a yell, "WHITEY!"

Twenty years after these events, the former puncher Gus Finley, then in his late seventies, wrote a letter to his younger sister in Philadelphia and gave her a full account of the gunfight that followed Powell's call to action . . .

After Luke Powell called out Whitey Quinn's name, the gunfighter (sic) drew his holstered revolver with lightning speed and shot Ira Griffin in the heart, killing him instantly. The youngster Wesley Fuller also drew and fired at Cyrus Griffin but hurried his shot and missed. Griffin returned fire and Wes went down, shot in the belly. After that guns roared and flared and the firing became general. I shot at Cyrus but to this day I do not know if my ball did any execution. Beside me, Ross Glenn fired. Dear Bessie,

I told you about him and his association with Jesse and Frank James. As far as I could tell in the gloom, Glenn scored a hit because I heard his exultant yell. I'm sure Luke Powell did not shoot because of his reduced vision, having earlier lost his right eye and half his sight and as far as I could tell, Bill Cline, a knife fighter, did not fire. But no matter, Whitey Quinn, a deadly shootist, was more than a match for the surviving Griffin brothers. Both, if I remember their names correctly, Cyrus and Jeremiah, went down to his gun. Whitey put two bullets into Cyrus's forehead, so close Luke later covered the wounds with a silver dollar, and Jeremiah suffered a shot so deadly that several of the stone beads he wore around his throat were driven out the back of his neck. Sweet Jesu! The poor savage lay on his back and dug his bootheels into the Texas earth, choking to death on his own blood. How long did all this shooting last? I'd say in a space of time it takes a man to blink three times. Dear Bessie, I'm sorry to be so sanguinary about this matter, but I wanted you to know that this was just one of the many melancholy trials and tribulations your brother endured during his time on the Western Frontier. Now my eyes grow weary and my hand cramps from the pen therefore the later tragic events that befell me in Houston I will relate to you in a future correspondence.

Clouds of gun smoke drifted across the camp and, illuminated by the moonlight, glided into the grassland like a file of gray phantoms. A strange, echoing silence hung in the air and gathered around the still bodies of three dead men. But young Wesley Fuller, gut-shot, was far from still. In dreadful pain, he clutched at his belly with bloodstained hands, groaned, screamed, groaned again . . . a loud and seemingly endless nocturne of a lingering death.

Luke Powell helped the others to drag the Griffin bodies away from the camp into the darkness where they would not be seen, but Fuller's constant shrill shrieks shredded his nerves.

"*Mio Dio*, will he never stop?" he said, the heels of his hands jammed against his head.

The four others reacted to the dying man in different ways. Gus Finley's face was ashen, strained, but Ross Glenn and Bill Cline seemed indifferent. Only the draw-fighter Whitey Quinn's face showed any real emotion, the suffering of Wes Fuller, one of his own kind, affecting him.

"Can't you do something to help him?" Finley said.

"He's gut-shot," Quinn said. "He's beyond help."

Bill Cline looked down at the suffering man. "I can cut his throat," he said. "Make it quick."

"Bill, try that and I'll kill you," Whitey said.

"He's joshing," Ross Glenn said. "Ain't you just joshing, Bill?"

"Yeah, just joshing," Cline said. "Let him scream his lungs out, I don't much care."

"He'll die soon," Finley said, more in hope than certainty.

"Sometimes a gut-shot man will scream for a whole day and night," Cline said. "Seen it happen more than once." He shook his head. "Look at him. I bet he wishes he was dead."

"Let him die in his own time," Whitey said.

"Maybe we should say a prayer," Finley said.

"I don't know any prayers, Gus," Whitey said. "Do you?"

Cline said, "Dear God, help this gut-shot man. There, I said a prayer."

His gaze burning across the night with green fire, Whitey said, "Bill, someday I'm gonna put a bullet in you."

"Anytime you feel like it, Whitey, just shuck the iron and have at it," Cline said, grinning.

"Shut the hell up, both of you," Powell said. Then, his face strained, "I never watched a man die this hard before."

"Me, neither," Finley said. "And I hope to God I never see another."

The dark, dreary night ground on . . . an hour passed . . . then another . . . Wes Fuller continued to suffer. He was pale, the skin cold and covered in sweat, and between shrieks he gasped for breath. The youngster was dying in agony and Powell, his own terrible wound fresh in his memory, couldn't take it any longer.

He took a knee beside Fuller and said, "Die, damn you, die. Get it over with."

The young man arched his back against a pain spasm and tried to talk, but could mutter only a long, drawn-out groan that pierced Powell to the heart. He stood and drew his revolver. Without looking at anyone, he said, "Enough is enough, I'll put him out of his misery."

"No, you won't."

Powell turned his head. Whitey Quinn had his own gun drawn.

"Damn it, Whitey, he's holding us up," Powell said.

"At this rate we'll never catch the stage before it reaches Houston."

Whitey's Colt was steady. "Let Wes meet his Maker at his own pace," he said.

"It could be hours," Powell said.

"Then let it be hours," Whitey said.

"All right, then, you stay with him," Powell said. "Boys, let's saddle up and follow the stage like we intended." No one moved and he said, calling Bill Cline by his given Italian name, "Loris, are you with me?"

Cline replied in similar fashion, shaking his head. *"Luciano, non possiamo farlo da soli."*

"We won't have to go it alone," Powell said. "Finley, Glenn, you'll ride with us, won't you?"

Finley, more fearful than the others, said, "I won't hold up the stage without Whitey's fast gun."

Irritated, Powell said, "Glenn?"

"Hell, I don't care," Ross Glenn said. "I'll ride."

"Then saddle up," Powell said.

"I'll take the bay one of them Griffin brothers rode," Glenn said. "It's a better hoss than my own."

"Nobody's going anywhere until Wes dies," Whitey Quinn said. "We're in this together and I want him to pass on with his friends around him."

"Whitey, I ain't his friend," Cline said. "I wasn't his friend back in Fort Smith when he took Lily Lawson out of my bed, and he ain't my friend now."

"Lily was a whore," Whitey said.

"Yeah, she was, but she was my whore," Cline said.

"And you lost her," Whitey said. "Because you're so

damned ugly and you should've taken a bath now and then."

Cline's hand dropped an inch toward his holstered gun.

"Go ahead, Bill, try it," Whitey said. He smiled like a malevolent cobra. "I can shade you anytime of the day or night."

"Stop it right there," Powell said. "We have a job to do and there will be no gunfighting among ourselves."

"Until the job is over," Cline said. He looked big and dark and menacing.

"Sure thing, Bill," Whitey said. "Call on me."

The big man nodded. "Depend on it."

Then Fuller managed a gasping, pain-strangled cry: "Boys, don't leave me to die out here alone. I don't want to die in the dark."

Powell snapped, "Damn it! All right, we'll wait until you're coyote bait." He glared at the young man. "Die soon, you hear me? Die soon."

CHAPTER FOURTEEN

"Buttons, what's eating you?" Red Ryan said. "I swear you're as fidgety as a kid in church."

"I got a bad feeling," Buttons said.

"About what?"

"I don't know about what. It's just a bad feeling."

"The stage is running well, and so are the horses."

"And that's the problem. Everything is going so good something bad is bound to happen. Maybe we're lost."

"Buttons, you never got lost before," Red said. "Keep the North Star at your back and we'll be heading due south like we're supposed to."

"You still got the army compass you won in a poker game that time in El Paso?"

"Sure. It's in my pocket."

"Good. Because we may need it. I just remembered that I took this route afore, but it was years ago," Buttons said. "Dusty Dixon was my messenger then. Do you recollect him?"

"Can't say as I do," Red said.

"Well, here's a story." Buttons's sensitive fingers moved on the ribbons, making an adjustment. "That off swing ain't pulling his weight. He's a shirker. Knowed that the minute I laid eyes on him."

"You got a story to tell," Red said.

"Oh yeah, the story. Well, how it came up, back in the winter of '74 me and Dusty got snowed up in the Montana Territory in the Bridger Mountains country. I was driving for Wells Fargo back then, carrying a strongbox full of bank drafts that were worth more than gold at the time. Thank God we found a line cabin with a sheltered corral out back and a good supply of firewood and grub, coffee, flour, beans, and salt pork and the like. I later discovered that the cabin belonged to a rancher named Driscoll and Wells Fargo paid him for what we ate and what the team ate and it was a considerable amount."

Buttons glanced over his shoulder at the night sky and said, "We're heading south, right enough. Houston is a ways off, but it's straight ahead."

Red waited a few moments and then said, "And that was the story? How you got snowed up and ate twice your wages in groceries?"

"Hell, no. That's only half the story."

"Tell it. I can't see anything around me but blackness, so I got nothing else to do but listen."

Buttons nodded. "Well, sir, there were two books in that line cabin, a Bible and one other."

"Which was?" Red prompted.

"I still remember that book plain as day," Buttons said. "It said on the cover, *An Illustrated History of the Black Death* by Professor Marmaduke Tweng."

"Who?"

"That was the professor's name, Marmaduke Tweng."

"A ten-dollar handle, for sure."

"Beats Red Ryan any day, don't it?"

"And Patrick Muldoon."

"I wouldn't go that far," Buttons said.

"So what happened?"

"We was snowed up for the best part of two weeks and in that time Dusty read the book from cover to cover. Every time I looked at him his nose was buried in the pages and I swear what little hair he had left on his head was standing on end."

"It scared him, huh?" Red said.

"Yeah, it did. There were pictures in there that no Christian man should ever see. Dead bodies being thrown into pits and maybe some of them only half-dead, and the like. And there was a picture of His Holiness Pope Clement who never did get the plague even though his cardinals were dropping around him like flies."

"How come?"

"Well, his doctors told him to sit between two roaring bonfires, even in the heat of summer, and Sir Marmaduke says that's what saved Pope Clement's life. After he read that, Dusty sat in front of the stove for days on end and he never did catch the Black Death."

"So he figured he'd never get it, huh?"

"You could say that, but it wouldn't be true. After seeing all those pictures in the book he was never the same man again, went from a fair to middlin' sociable ranny to a mean ol' sourpuss. And, believe me, worse was to follow." Buttons shook his head. "That off swing is tiring. He's slowing us down."

"How did Dusty become worse than mean?"

"He became a cat man, that's how."

"I'm not catching your drift."

"Dusty took to carrying cats around with him, usually just one, but sometimes two or three. He kept them in a cage and they were the most evil, vicious cats you'd never want to meet."

Intrigued despite himself, Red said, "How come he did that?"

"Did what?"

"Carried cats with him."

"Because of rats. He was terrified of rats."

"How come?"

"Well, Professor Marmaduke Tweng said that rats caused the Black Death, and Dusty had read in the book what a terrible misery the plague was, killing hundreds and hundreds of folks in a single day. He showed me a picture in the book of a rat biting a healthy man as he slept. In the next picture, a day later, that same man was all swollen up and dead as hell in a parson's parlor."

"So Dixon didn't want to catch the Black Death so he carried cats with him to kill the rats," Red said. "That makes sense."

"You got that right," Buttons said. "Dusty was so terrified of the plague he wouldn't walk into any room or stable or anywhere else until his cats went in first and told him it was all safe to enter."

"His cats spoke to him?"

"So he said. Of course it ruined ol' Dusty's career as a messenger. Wells Fargo fired him. You can't have a cage of mewling cats up in the box upsetting the passengers and annoying the driver."

Red grinned. "Whatever happened to Dusty? Did the plague get him in the end?"

"Hell, no. He tripped over one of his cats, fell off the

second-story balcony of a Denver brothel, and broke his fool neck. Some say a whore who had sneezing fits around cats pushed him, but that could never be proved."

"Buttons, have you just told me a big windy?" Red said.

"Nope, everything I told you is a natural fact," Buttons said. "Would I lie about His Holiness the Pope? Ah, there's a light ahead. It must be the station at last."

CHAPTER FIFTEEN

The stage station was a decaying sod building with a wood shingle roof and an iron chimney pipe that trailed gray smoke. There was a corral, an outhouse, and a small smokehouse. To the right of the sagging timber door a wood trestle held a water basin, a stained towel, and a bar of yellow lye soap. A communal toothbrush hung on a string. Nearby, a huge sow and half a dozen piglets wallowed in mud at the base of a rusty, screaking windmill. The whole ramshackle place looked as though it was held together with baling wire and twine and the smell of dung and the odors from the outhouse spoke of dirt and squalor.

The station master was a stocky, bearded, and shaggy-eyebrowed man that Buttons did not know and he in turn addressed Buttons as "jehu," a name then used for stage-coach drivers after the Old Testament king of Israel who was known for driving his chariot at breakneck speed.

And the man's greeting was hardly welcoming. "Drive on, jehu," he said. He held a lantern high, splashing amber light on his face and his eyes were wild. "For pity's sake, drive on!"

Buttons was suddenly angry. "Get ahold of yourself, man," he yelled. "I got a tired team here."

The station master's head swiveled to the opening door of the stage and he wailed, "Oh my God, it's too late."

Two events happened quickly . . .

Rosie Lee stumbled out of the stage and immediately doubled over and began retching horribly. Seasick again. Then the cabin door slammed open and two large men stepped from the yellow lamplit interior into the darkness. They stood in a rectangle of light, grins on their bearded faces, big men wearing bearskin coats and fur hats with untied earflaps, the rawhide strings hanging loose.

Red Ryan's hands tightened on the Greener and his belly tightened at the same time. In the gloom the men looked as big as grizzly bears and he knew this might shape up to be trouble.

Unaware that he was about to dance with the devil, Buttons made things worse. To the station master he said, "I want this team changed and I want it changed now. What do they call you, mister?"

"My name is Jenks, Art Jenks," the man said. "Been called that man and boy." He cast a fearful glance at the grizzly bears and said, "You picked a wrong time to get here, jehu."

"The horses pick the time, not me," Buttons said. "Now, let's get the spare team out." He stood up in the box. "And, mister, I'm driving a bad luck stage and on top of that I don't need any sass or backtalk."

"Your bad luck ain't started yet," Jenks said.

Heat lightning flashed on the horizon, thrumming inside distant clouds, filling them with a fleeting violet glow. The lightning lent an eerie cast to the night and made the gray stage stand out in stark contrast to the flickering gloom. One of the bearskin men opened his coat, revealing a huge Walker Colt in a cross-draw holster. His eyes were on Buttons.

Erica Hall stepped out of the stage and walked to Rosie Lee's side. She placed a hand on the girl's back and said, "Are you all right?"

"Fine, I'll be fine," Rosie said, gasping, but she didn't straighten up.

Both fur-coated men stepped closer to the women, looking them over, liking what they saw.

"Hey, you," the man with the Walker said.

It took a while before Buttons said, "You talking to me?"

"Yeah, I'm talking to you. Are you in charge here?" the man said.

"Who wants to know?" Buttons said.

Red casually pointed the Greener at the man. He figured Buttons could handle him, but it was better to be safe than sorry.

"Name's Ben Wilson." He waved a hand. "This here is my partner Milt Hensley."

Hensley grinned at Buttons but didn't say anything. "Me and Milt are wolfers and bear hunters and out here in this wilderness it can be a lonely profession. Do you catch my drift?"

"No, I don't catch your drift," Buttons said.

"Then I'll say it plain," Wilson said. "Fifty dollars in gold for the women."

"Go to hell," Buttons said. "Now, clear the way there, I've got horses coming out."

"Sixty," Wilson said.

"The two ladies are paying passengers of the Abe

Patterson and Son Stage and Express Company and are under my protection until we reach Houston," Buttons said. "So back off. And go somewhere else. I'm downwind of you and, mister, you could use a bath."

"Heard that before," Wilson said. "I killed the last man who said it." His hand moved to his gun. "Well, the hell with you, maybe I'll just take them."

"Try that and maybe I'll drop you right where you stand," Buttons said.

"I want no trouble here," Art Jenks said. "Jehu, I know these men and they're not to be trifled with. Sell them the women and make yourself a nice little profit on this trip. That's what Phineas Doyle would've done."

"And maybe that's why he's dead," Buttons said.

Jenks was shocked. "Phineas is dead?"

"Yeah, him and Dewey Wilcox. Gunned down by road agents while they were driving this stage."

"Sorry to hear that," Jenks said. "But I still say you should sell the women."

"Mister, you're even lower down than them wolfers," Buttons said. He looked at Rosie and Erica. "You ladies get back in the stage instanter. You'll be safer, and Jenks has nothing inside you'd want to eat anyway."

But Erica Hall was not a woman to be stampeded.

"Jenks, how much for the wolfers?" she said. "I'll give you two bits for the pair."

Wilson growled, "Is that supposed to be funny?"

"No, it's not funny," Erica said. "And Mr. Muldoon is right, I can smell you from here, like a gut pile in an alley behind a butcher's shop."

Wilson was enraged. "Now I'm gonna hurt you,

woman," he said. "I'm gonna drag you into the cabin and hurt you real . . . real . . . bad."

"Don't even try," Red said. "From up here I can put two barrels of buck in your belly."

But Ben Wilson wasn't listening.

As the silent lightning flashed above him, arrogant and just twenty-five years old, he took a single step that instantly turned into a giant leap into eternity.

"Ahhrgh . . . ahhrgh . . ." Wilson clutched at his throat and did a strange little jig, his lips stretched wide into a grimace of mortal agony, blood splashing over the front of his bearskin coat. A broad-bladed knife had buried itself to the hilt just under his Adam's apple, a slaughtering, horrendous, killing wound.

The Great Stefano, whose expert knife throwing had many times entertained the crowned heads of Europe, leaned out of the open stage door and yelled, "Take that!"

Wilson collapsed to the ground, gurgling blood, and for a long moment time seemed to stand still . . . a frozen tableau of stunned people lit only by Jenks's lantern and the flickering lightning.

Milt Hensley was the first to recover.

"Damn you!" he yelled. He hardly acknowledged the Great Stefano's presence, his whole attention fixed on Erica Hall, the cause of Wilson's death. He took a step back, opening his coat to get at his gun, and died right where he stood.

BLAM! BLAM!

Two shots. Fired from a Remington derringer. Even in the uncertain light, Erica aimed, her right arm fully extended. At a distance of ten feet she put both bullets into Hensley's chest, by any measure revealing considerable shooting skill with a stingy gun. Later there were some who said that either Red Ryan or Buttons Muldoon must also have fired because two rounds of .41 Short could not have dropped Hensley, a man said to be six foot, three inches tall, weighing in excess of 250 pounds. But the then widely read magazine, *Frank Leslie's Popular Monthly*, later tested the normal 130-grain .41 bullet and put the lie to that assertion. At ten feet the bullet passed through a three-quarter-inch pine board, more than adequate killing power if the shooter did his or her part.

And that night Erica Hall did her part.

As she'd done before, after she fired on the Apaches at Potts's station, Erica immediately reloaded the derringer and put it back in her purse. Such was the habit of experienced shootists and it occurred to Red Ryan that the woman had been taught well and had just proved herself to be an apt pupil.

Art Jenks was a man in shock. He looked at the two dead men and turned his ashen face to Buttons, who'd come down from the box. "Was it murder?" he said.

"The lady was threatened by both those men," Buttons said. "As a representative of the Abe Patterson and Son Stage and Express Company, I declare it a clear-cut case of self-defense. Red, what do you think?"

"I don't think she or the knife thrower had any other option," Red said. "Those two were looking for trouble and they found it."

"They never gave me any trouble in the past," Jenks said. "Drank their whiskey quiet and paid their score."

"You got a woman inside?" Buttons said.

"Hell, no, what woman would want to live out here? And what woman in her right mind would want me?"

"There's your answer," Buttons said. "They saw our female passengers and it drove them crazy."

Jenks opened his mouth to speak, seemed to think better of it, and clammed up again.

"Out with it, Jenks," Buttons said. "Say what you want to say."

"A six-month ago, Ben Wilson and Milt Hensley killed a man here and took his woman and his poke," Jenks said. "He was a parson who'd run off with somebody's wife and the contents of the poor box." He looked at Erica. "Maybe you need to know that, lady."

"Why would I need to know that?" Erica said. The only emotion on her face was anger. "I shot a wild animal and my conscience is clear."

"What happened to the parson's woman?" Buttons said.

"I don't know. They showed up here yesterday without her. Probably sold her off to somebody or she died."

Buttons shook his head. "Jenks, you run a mighty fine establishment, and that's a guaranteed natural fact."

Jenks's smile was slight. "Would you want this job, jehu?"

Buttons shook his head. "No, I would not," he said. "It was this accursed stage that brung you this bad fortune and it will leave once we're gone. Now, let's get this team changed."

"This kind of stuff always happens to me," Jenks said. "Now I got two men to bury."

"Search their pockets," Buttons said. "If they was here eating your grub and drinking whiskey, they probably have enough money to make it worth your while. And talking about grub, what you got to eat in there?"

"Boiled salt pork and mustard. But the pork is kinda fatty and it's got green spots."

"I'll take a pass on that," Buttons said.

"Then feel free to help yourself to the mustard," Jenks said.

Despite Jenks's rundown place, the new team was well cared for and rested and Buttons Muldoon grudgingly admitted that Jenks might be a good man with horses after all.

He and Red were up in the box, side lamps lit, the dark prairie ahead of them. But to the east a band of blue light showed above the horizon, heralding the coming of morning.

After a long silence, Buttons said, "That Stefano ranny is good with a knife."

"Seems like," Red said. "And Miss Hall is handy with a derringer."

"It didn't trouble her none," Buttons said.

"What do you mean?"

"I mean killing a man. It didn't faze her. Did you see Rosie Lee? She eyeballed the two dead men and threw up again."

"That little gal pukes all the time," Red said. "But you're right, it looked like Erica Hall had been up that road before."

"Maybe a few times," Buttons said. "Damn, this coach rolls like a brig in a typhoon."

"Buttons, it rides just fine, smooth as silk," Red said.

Buttons turned his head and stared at Red. "It's a bad

luck stage and if we don't get shed of it soon, it's gonna be the death of us." Then, a shriek. "Now what?" Buttons said.

"Sounds like Rosie Lee wants to puke again," Red said.

Buttons cussed enough to turn the air blue and then reined the team to a halt. He leaned over in his seat and yelled, "What's happening in there?"

The juggler Dean Rice answered: "Rosie Lee saw the Great Stefano clean blood from his throwing knife and went a little hysterical. I'm holding her hand and she's fine now."

Buttons shook his head and said, "Red, we're doomed, I tell you." He spelled the word, "D-o-o-m-e-d. Doomed."

Red smiled. "Seems like," he said.

CHAPTER SIXTEEN

"You telling me the woman killed both of those men?" Luke Powell said.

"Only one of them," Art Jenks said. "A knife thrower done for the other one."

"Stefano," Powell said. "He calls himself the Great Stefano."

"I don't know what he calls himself," Jenks said. "But he can sure throw a knife. How's the fried salt pork?"

Whitey Quinn answered as he threw his fork onto his tin plate. "It would gag a maggot. It ain't fit for nothing but a slop bucket."

"You should be shot for serving up that kind of grub," Bill Cline said. His hand dropped to his gun. "Maybe I should do it right now."

"Bill, let it go," Powell said. "Wes Fuller is lying out there in the prairie and he ain't cold yet. We've had enough shooting for a while."

Jenks refused to be intimidated, or perhaps Powell's words gave him backbone. "Still gonna cost you two bits a man," he said. "The mustard is free."

"Mister, don't push your luck," Powell said. "He sipped

from his cup, made a face, and said, "Your coffee is no better than your grub."

Whitey Quinn said, "Boss, seems like we ain't gonna catch them up before they reach Houston."

"Jenks, where's the stage depot in Houston?" Powell asked.

"According to the driver, it was a Patterson stage, but I guess he'll use Long John Abbot's depot on San Jacinto Street. Thanks to the railroads, I reckon it's the only stage depot left in Houston."

"Then we'll start from there," Powell said. He addressed a question to Jenks. "Are there hotels around there?"

"A few," the station master said. "But if I was looking for somebody, a runaway woman maybe, I'd stash my horses at the depot livery stable and take a streetcar to the downtown area where all the big hotels are."

"Where are the music halls?" Powell said.

"I don't know, but probably downtown."

"You ever heard of the Diamond Theater?" Whitey Quinn said.

"No. But that doesn't mean it ain't there," Jenks said. "Houston is a big city."

Whitey walked to the cabin window and looked outside, where morning light was stealing across the grasslands. "Sun's up, boss," he said.

Powell nodded. "Yeah, if we leave now, we can be in Houston before dark."

"Then what?" Whitey said.

Powell adjusted the canvas patch over his empty eye socket and said, "It ain't difficult to figure out. We find Erica Hall, take back the heroin she stole, and then I deal with her."

"You got to deal with her somewhere quiet," Whitey said. "Like the man said, Houston's a big city."

Powell grinned. "I'll find a way."

"You always do," Bill Cline said. "If the knife man is somewhere close, let me take care of him."

"Sure thing, Bill, he's all yours," Powell said.

Then Art Jenks, displaying incredible stupidity, came real close to getting his fool head cut off.

"I seen that man toss a knife," he said. Then speaking directly to Cline, "Mister, I don't think you're a match for him."

Cline sat on a bench drawn up to Jenks's scarred and incredibly dirty and greasy rough pine table and his hands cradled a tin cup of boiling hot coffee. Jenks stood a little to his right, a stained dishrag in his hands. The instant the last word fled the man's lips, Cline moved, displaying incredible speed and coordination for such a big man. He leaped to his feet, threw the coffee in Jenks's face, and then grabbed him by the front of his shirt and pulled him close into the blade he held in his right hand, the point pricking Jenks's belly. His mouth just an inch from the other man's ear, Cline whispered, "Now I'm gonna gut you like a hog."

Most historians believe that Art Jenks lacked sense but possessed a certain amount of sand, but all agree that he shrieked in terror that dawning morning as Cline, the definition of a psychopathic killer, threatened him with a terrible death.

"Loris! No!" Powell yelled. "Let that man be."

Powell was raised in the Mafia doctrine that associates show a certain amount of gallantry toward ordinary people who should only indirectly be harmed by their crimes. He could not countenance, for no real reason, the cold-blooded killing of a nonentity like a stage station master.

Cline lowered his knife, placed his left hand on Jenks's face, and shoved hard. The man's arms and legs cartwheeled as he staggered across the dirt floor and slammed into the cabin's far wall. Jenks slid slowly to the ground, his glazed eyes rolling in his head.

Powell glanced at Jenks and said, "Loris, from now on you'll use the knife only when I tell you to use it. *Capiche?*

"Yes, I understand, but I was only kidding, capo," Cline said, his head bent as he slid the New Orleans–made stiletto back in the sheath.

"And I'll tell you when to joke," Powell said.

Whitey Quinn said, "I was never tempted to use a knife on a man."

Gus Finley said, "Me, neither," and Ross Glenn shook his head.

"Because no one taught you gents to use the blade," Cline said. "I was trained by my pa in the *scherma di stiletto siciliano*, the Sicilian school of knife fighting. You make the kill by shoving the knife deep into your opponent's body and then twist the blade sharply in various directions before you withdraw it. The stiletto's sharp point does dreadful damage to a man's guts and kills quickly. I know, because I've done for four men in that fashion." Cline smiled. "Stuck them like pigs and in the end they all squealed like pigs."

Powell said, "Bill is telling the truth. I remember one of those men. Frank Grant was his name."

"Yeah, boss, that's right, you were in on that killing," Cline said. "He was good at dealing morphine and opium, was Frank, but he got greedy and skimmed too much off the top."

"He was damned treacherous and low-down," Powell said. "He took advantage of my good nature."

"Well, after that night in the Fort Worth Fun House brothel I cut his purse strings for good," Cline said.

"Remember how the whore who was with him hollered blue murder?" Powell said. He smiled. "That was funny."

"Yeah, I remember. Frank's blood was all over her cot. She even had it in her hair."

"It took twenty dollars to calm her down," Powell said. "So even in death, Frank Grant cost me money."

He rose to his feet and laid a couple of silver dollars on the table. To the now fully conscious Jenks, he said, "Thanks for your hospitality. Now we have to ride."

"And thank Mr. Powell that you're still alive," Whitey Quinn said.

Art Jenks stood outside the cabin door and watched the four riders leave. A surge of anger spiked at him and he threw the two silver dollars after them. "Take back your money and be damned to ye,'" he said, low enough that they couldn't hear.

But an hour later he picked up the coins again and put them in his cashbox.

CHAPTER SEVENTEEN

Buttons Muldoon and Red Ryan had never seen the like.

Houston was a city of streetcars, tall brick buildings, lamplit boulevards, and throngs of people walking with purpose, as though everybody was headed somewhere important. Somewhere in the distance a riverboat steam whistle wailed into the evening half-light and closer a locomotive's bell clamored as it neared the new Grand Central Station on Main Street.

"Busy place," Buttons said, his hands tight on the reins.

"Seems like," Red allowed. "I've never in my life seen so many people in one place at one time."

In fact, as the railroads increasingly shoved aside stage lines, a stagecoach like the Gray Ghost was no longer a common sight in the city, nor were its flamboyant, brass-buttoned driver and shotgun-armed messenger.

Giggling Texas belles, colorful as meadow flowers in the latest French fashions, strolled the gaslit promenades, trailing an admiring coterie of beaux dressed like mail order catalogs on the hoof as they sang snippets from

Messrs. Gilbert and Sullivan's *The Mikado*, then hugely popular among the younger set.

What had been Long John Abbot's depot on San Jacinto Street consisted of a small timber cabin and corral, added as an afterthought to the large T. D. Scriver livery stable and boardinghouse that catered to the streetcar horse trade and offered carriage rentals, "Wedding Conveyances a Specialty."

Buttons drew rein outside the cabin and immediately a tall young man dressed in canvas pants, ankle boots, and a collarless shirt stepped out of the stable and walked to the stage.

"And you must be T. D. Scriver," Buttons said.

"Wrong first time, jehu," the man said, impertinence in his face. "I'm Tom Scriver, T. D.'s son and heir." He held open the stage door and, visibly impressed, assisted Erica Hall outside, a little less impressed when he did the same for the pale Rosie Lee. The Great Stefano and Dean Rice he allowed to fend for themselves.

Buttons and Red climbed down from the box and Scriver said, "There are bunks in the cabin for you two and I can accommodate your passengers overnight."

"I'd rather find a hotel," Erica said. "Can you recommend one, preferably close to the Diamond Theater."

"That music hall is downtown," Scriver said. "Plenty of hotels within walking distance." He looked over the bulging luggage boot. "Those bags might be too much for a streetcar." He smiled. "Push it right off of its tracks."

"I need all of mine, including the steamer trunk," Erica said. "Carrying my luggage is out of the question."

Red Ryan looked at the woman. Three days on a stagecoach and Erica Hall was still beautiful and as fresh as mint, hardly a wrinkle in her travel dress. By comparison, Rosie Lee's pretty face was pale, exhausted, and she looked like she'd spent the night sleeping in a haystack. The Great Stefano and Dean the juggler, who never juggled, both seemed tired and in need of a shave.

"Buttons, maybe we could drive Miss Hall to her hotel," Red said.

"I'm sure it's agin the rules," Buttons said. "You can bet that ol' Abe Patterson has it wrote down somewhere in black and white."

"He'll never know," Red said. "How could he know? I'm not going to tell him."

"Abe is like God, he knows everything," Buttons said.

"Never fear, pretty lady," Scriver said, "I have an Italian fellow who can take you downtown. His name is Rocco and I hire him now and again. He's respectable enough."

"And my luggage?"

"Rocco has a carryall cart, ma'am. There are seats for all of you and plenty of room for luggage. I can have him here in twenty minutes. In the meantime, may I invite you and your friends into the boardinghouse for coffee?"

"Have you anything stronger?" Erica said.

Scriver smiled. "I'm sure we have a bottle of bourbon somewhere."

"Then lead on, Mr. Scriver," Erica said.

"Ahem," Buttons said. "What about unharnessing my team?"

"I'll be right back once I send a boy for Rocco and get Miss Hall settled," Scriver said. "May I make bold enough to ask for your first name?"

"It's Erica."

"A lovely name for a lovely woman," Scriver said.

Red Ryan could've cheerfully shot him.

"A corncob mattress," Buttons Muldoon said, standing by his iron cot. "Seems like Long John was just as much a miser as Abe Patterson."

"At least the sheets are clean," Red said.

"I hate sleeping on corncobs," Buttons said. "I've got delicate skin."

Red laughed. "You've got a hide like an ornery old longhorn steer."

Buttons let the corner of the mattress he held fall back on the cot and then gave Red his full attention. "Tell me what you think of that furriner."

"What furriner?"

"The ranny with the flat cart."

"I don't think anything. He loaded up the passengers' luggage just fine, including the big steamer trunk without any complaint."

"I figured he looked shifty."

"You think most folks look shifty."

"And most folks of our acquaintance do."

Red shook his head. "You need some grub. You willing to try the restaurant down the street that Scriver told us about?"

"He told us about it because it's cheap," Buttons said, refusing to shift from his cranky mood. "He looked us over and said, 'It's cheap.'"

"He hung his saddle on the right hoss, didn't he?" Red said.

"I still say that furriner looked shifty. I don't trust furriners."

"Steak and eggs," Red said. "How does that set with you?"

"It's a cheap restaurant. The steak will be tough and the eggs tougher."

In that, Buttons Muldoon barked up the wrong tree. The steak was tender, the eggs fresh . . . and that night he slept on the corncobs like a dead calf.

Buttons Muldoon rose at dawn in a better frame of mind. In fact, he told Red Ryan that a breakfast of bacon and eggs at the cheap restaurant would set him up for the rest of the day.

"After we eat, we'll hitch up the team and head for San Angelo," Buttons said. "And then we'll get rid of the Gray Ghost and its bad luck for good."

Red shook his head. "That's not how Abe Patterson will see it. I reckon we're stuck with the gray stage for good. Maybe you could convince him to repaint it Patterson brown and change its luck. But I doubt Abe will go along with that."

"Well, he don't have to go along with it," Buttons said. "Because I'm gonna set the damned thing on fire . . . burn it right down to the wheel rims."

Red smiled as he built a cigarette. "Buttons, I never took you for an arsonist."

"I never was until I met the Gray Ghost. Step outside. I

want to show you something. It's a strange thing I noticed last night."

Red walked outside with Buttons and said, "So show me."

"Lookee over there where the Gray Ghost is parked. What do you notice?"

"Nothing. Except a stagecoach and a couple of barn cats."

"Damn it, Red, study on the thing. Look closer."

"All right, now I see a stagecoach and one barn cat."

"It's crouching," Buttons said.

"What's crouching? The cat?"

"No, the stage. Look at it. It's ready to pounce."

"Pounce on what?"

"On a new streak of bad luck. It's piling up dead men."

Red was spared having to comment when Tom Scriver walked toward them with an army sergeant in tow. "Good news, Muldoon," he said. "I have a couple of passengers for your return trip."

The sergeant was a beautiful cavalry soldier, erect, broad-chested, sporting a magnificent dragoon mustache, but the hair under his kepi was clipped short. He wore a canvas gun belt around his waist, a Colt butt-forward in a glossy black leather holster, and stood resplendent in a blue coat, shiny brass buttons, and golden chevrons.

"I'm told you men are from Fort Concho and plan to return there," the sergeant said. He didn't have a normal voice, more of a hound dog woof.

"We're returning to San Angelo," Buttons said.

The sergeant nodded. "Good, good, then I have a couple of passengers, soldiers' women, that need transportation.

They're currently residing in a boardinghouse near my recruiting office."

"A hundred dollars each, five dollars for meals, and no army scrip," Buttons said. He instinctively didn't like the sergeant and his good mood of the dawn had completely evaporated.

"The women have money for their fares," the sergeant said. "They've been bouncing around here and there for several weeks trying to procure suitable transportation. Finally they came to the army for help." The man managed a tight smile. "I recruit soldiers, not women, so you're a sight for sore eyes."

"Officers' wives?" Buttons said.

The sergeant barked. "Didn't you hear me say, 'soldiers' women'? If they'd been officers' wives, I would've called them ladies." He took a folded piece of paper from his pocket, opened it with a flourish, and said, "The women are Mrs. Maggie Hannah and Mrs. Opal McDermott, wives of Corporals John Hannah and Henry McDermott, K Company, 19th Infantry. During the fort's deactivation process these wives will be employed as washerwomen . . ." The soldier closed the paper. "The rest doesn't concern you."

"I'd like to leave within the hour," Buttons said. "Will you bring the ladies, I mean women, here?"

"Impossible," the sergeant said. "It can't be done, not today."

"Well, we can leave early tomorrow," Buttons said. "Soldiers' wives must be used to getting up early."

"You can leave three or four days hence and at this time of the day. In the meantime the women will continue to be accommodated at the Rest and Be Thankful boardinghouse on Walker Avenue."

Buttons was flabbergasted. "What the hell . . . Why?"

"Paperwork," the soldier said. "Army rules and regulations. Literacy test for the wives, arrangements for remuneration of travel expenses, arrangements for suitable enlisted men's married accommodation at Fort Concho, medical examinations of both females here in Houston by a qualified doctor. And all this paperwork must be submitted for approval to the assistant officer of the assistant officer of the acting Fort Concho quartermaster."

Now Buttons was so incensed he spluttered. "Why not approve it yourself and let them women go?"

The sergeant was so taken aback his massive jaw dropped. "Out of the question, civilian. That would be gross insubordination. Soldiers have been shot for less."

"Then it's nothing to do with me," Buttons said. "I'm the driver of this stage and a trusted employee of the Abe Patterson and Son Stage and Express Company and I say we're leaving in an hour after I have breakfasted. Now, get your women here by that time or tuck your tail and light out, soldier boy."

The sergeant looked like he'd been gut-punched. Without taking his eyes off Buttons he said, "Mr. Scriver, order my detail to join me here on the double."

The man grinned. "Sure thing, General."

A few moments later six young cavalrymen, complete with sabers, lined up in front of their sergeant, who said to Buttons, "What is your name?"

"Patrick Muldoon. What's yours?"

"Sergeant Gunther Brandt and I'm impounding your stage until such time as you leave for Fort Concho. It will be guarded twenty-four hours a day until then."

"That's an outrage," Buttons said. "You can't do that. You can't keep us here."

Brandt said, "Oh yes, I can. I'm imposing martial law. Taylor, Davies, post yourselves by that gray stage, draw sabers, and let no one near it until you're relieved." The sergeant waited until his men had taken up positions on either side of the stage and cold steel glinted in the morning light and then said, "There, Mr. Muldoon, it looks like I've done it. When martial law is in effect, the military commander of an area, that's me, has unlimited authority to make and enforce laws and I'm making it a law that you can't move the stage without my permission."

Red Ryan spoke up for the first time. "Buttons, when the stage is just setting there it's not doing us any harm. I reckon our luck will change over the next four days."

"What do we do in this burg for four days?" Buttons said. "And us down to our last chip."

"Why, there's plenty to do," Sergeant Brandt said. "You can ride the streetcars, visit the bayous, and watch the steamboats. Take a walk downtown and talk pretties to the lovely ladies in the park. There's a lot a young buck like you can do in Houston if he has a mind to. And here's some advice. Don't carry those guns where they can be seen. The police don't like it and they'll knock you around."

"Sounds like a fun city," Buttons said.

"It is, if you behave yourself," the soldier said. "Now I must be about my duties. Different sentries will come and go, but I'll see you again in four days."

The sergeant talked briefly to the soldiers flanking the stage and then he and his four remaining cavalrymen left, kicking up a mix of dust, dung, and wisps of straw from their booted feet.

"I don't like that feller," Buttons said. "I don't like him one bit."

"I don't think he cottons to you much, either," Red said. "Let's have breakfast and then we'll take a streetcar downtown, sit on a park bench, and watch the pretty girls go by."

"Have I any choice?" Buttons said. "Hide your iron under your shirt, Red. We don't want to get knocked about by the law."

CHAPTER EIGHTEEN

Leoluca Vitale hopped off the streetcar as soon as it passed 85 Chenevert Street. Under a sky that looked like thin, whitewashed clouds on a blue canvas, he stood on the sidewalk outside the Greek-style house for a couple of minutes, studying the lie of the place. The mansion had six lofty Doric columns supporting a gable roof that made up the front facade. A flight of wide, stone steps led to a portico that framed the recessed doorway highlighted on either side by rectangular sidelights with stained glass windows in a geometric design, matched by the transom above the doorway. Seen from the sidewalk, the mansion and nearby carriage house looked larger than life, but clean and grand without being overwhelming.

It seemed that Vincenzu Grotte was a man of taste, or rich enough to hire a man of taste to design his house.

Vitale opened the iron gate and took a pathway between green, manicured lawns that led directly to the house. The air around the entire neighborhood seemed rarefied and smelled only of fresh-cut grass, flowering magnolias, and money.

Feeling that his every movement had been monitored by several pairs of eyes, Vitale lifted the ring knocker held in the mouth of a brass lion and let it fall three times, politely, but loud enough to be heard.

The door opened almost immediately and a magnificent creature appeared, a butler well over six feet tall, dressed in a black tailcoat with a satin collar and lapels, a white shirt and vest with a bow tie, narrow black pants, and highly polished shoes. He wore a trimmed mustache and his hair was parted in the middle and slicked down on both sides. But his square jaw looked like it had been hewn out of granite with a blunt chisel and he had the merciless gray eyes of a harpy eagle.

"Can I help you, sir?" he said.

Vitale noticed three things about the man . . . one was that he was not Sicilian, two that his beaky nose was held high as though he sniffed something bad, and the third was his coat, cut slightly roomy on its left side to accommodate a revolver.

"My name is Leoluca Vitale," the little gunman said. "I am here on behalf of my capo, Antonio Matranga, on a business matter of great importance."

The name Matranga was the open sesame that swung the door wide, but after he stepped into the foyer the butler stopped Vitale, patted him down, and removed his Colt from its shoulder holster. "I'll return this to you when you leave, sir." he said. He bowed. "I'll tell Mr. Grotte that you wish to see him."

Vitale paid little attention to the interior of the house. His impression was that it had wood floors, rugs, white walls and ceilings, and odd-looking furniture that looked like it was designed for reclining and not sitting.

It came as a relief that Grotte's office was a refuge of traditional American furniture, a vast mahogany desk, brass-studded leather chairs, and heavy walnut bookshelves and filing cabinets. The only picture on the walls was a medieval Russian icon of the Madonna and Child and the room smelled heavily of cigar smoke and bourbon.

Vincenzu Grotte had none of Antonio Matranga's intimidating size, rather he was a small, slight, and very neat man with the soulful features of a consumptive poet pining for a lost love. Coming from such a tiny frame, his voice came as a surprise, loud and powerful as a cannonade.

"Mr. Vitale, you have been sent by capo dei capi Matranga." he said. "What does my old friend want of me?"

Using as few words as possible, aware that Grotte was a very busy man, Vitale told him of the flight from Fort Smith of the trusted Erica Hall and her anticipated arrival in Houston with ten kilos of heroin.

Finally, Vitale finished by saying, "My capo wishes you to find the woman and I will get back the heroin."

"I'm not familiar with this heroin," Grotte said. "Inform me."

"Capo, it was derived from the opium poppy in England and Germany as a cheaper substitute for opium and morphine, but it's just as addictive."

"And how much is ten kilos of the stuff worth?"

"Depending on how it's cut, anywhere between fifty and a hundred thousand dollars."

"A considerable sum," Grotte said. He steepled his fingers. "A man could get rich selling the heroin drug."

Vitale was uncomfortable. Grotte had a habit of not looking at him directly but stared fixedly over his right shoulder. It made the man's eyes hard to read, and maybe that was the point.

"Indeed he could," Vitale said. "Capo dei capi Matranga is a mighty, flowing torrent to his people. He wishes us all to become rich."

"Then I will find this woman for you," Grotte said. "I return a favor, do I not?"

"Indeed you do, capo," Vitale said. "Capo dei capi Matranga will be most pleased."

"Where can I get in touch with you, Mr. Vitale?"

"I'm at the Monarch Hotel on . . ."

"I know where it is," Grotte said. He smiled. "You are interested in the device on my desk, are you not?"

"I'm puzzled as to what it is," Vitale said. "My guess is that it summons your butler."

"You've never seen one before?"

"No, I have not."

"Matranga does not have one?"

"No. But he has a bell on his desk to summon his secretary."

"I also have one of those, but this is called a telephone. With this device I can keep in touch with my business interests here in Houston and make a long-distance call as far away as Galveston."

Vitale was interested. "How does it work?"

"I pick up the receiver and an operator, sometimes a boy but usually a woman, asks for the party I'm calling," Grotte said. It's all very convenient and quick."

"I must tell capo Matranga about this," Vitale said.

"I don't know if there's a telephone line to New Orleans

yet, but if not there will be very soon, I'm sure." Grotte rose from his chair. He looked to be about five foot, four inches tall. "But I am remiss on my hospitality. He crossed the room to a small table that held several crystal decanters and said, "Sherry?"

Vitale said, "I've never tried it."

"You'll like it." Grotte's voice boomed, sounding more of an order than reassurance.

Vitale tried the sweet, heavily fortified wine and found it to his taste.

"This is excellent, capo," he said.

"I have a dozen bottles shipped from Portugal several times a year," Grotte said. He sipped from his glass and then said, "Are you married, Mr. Vitale?"

"Not yet. But it's in my plans for the future."

The little man nodded. "I have a wife, but I don't love her. She's from Campania and she let herself go and got very fat. Holy Mother Church does not countenance divorce, so I can't take that route to be rid of her." He smiled and for the first time met Vitale's cold eyes. "She's staying with her equally fat sister this week. Perhaps before you return to New Orleans you could do a favor for me?"

Leoluca Vitale nodded. "As a courtesy, yes."

"We will keep in touch," Grotte said. "The Monarch Hotel has a telephone."

On the way out of the Grotte mansion, Vitale asked the butler for his revolver.

"Double action, a fine piece," the man said. "But the caliber is small."

"It serves," Vitale said.

He spun the revolver, let the butt thud into his palm, and in one practiced motion smoothly slid the Colt into its holster. It was an experienced gun handler's marquee play and the lesson was not lost on Vincenzu Grotte's butler.

CHAPTER NINETEEN

Five heavily armed horsemen rode into what had been Long John Abbot's stage station, one with a patch over one eye that gave him a sinister look. The men drew rein outside the livery stable and studied the two young soldiers guarding a gray stage.

Finally Luke Powell, tired and dusty, swung out of the saddle and stepped to the troopers. "What goes here?" he said.

"Sir, this stage has been impounded by the United States Army for the next three or four days," one of the youngsters said.

"Why?" Powell said.

"The stage is to remain here until two soldiers' wives are ready to be transported to Fort Concho to join their husbands," one of the youngsters said.

"Where are the passengers who came in from San Angelo?" Powell said.

"Sir, that I do not know," the soldier said.

"Can I help you?"

Tom Scriver stepped out of the barn, dropped a pitchfork and bucket by the door, and then walked to Powell, who'd been joined by Whitey Quinn. Scriver was used to shady-looking characters visiting his livery, but the towhead who dressed like a parson but carried a gun in a low-slung holster put him on edge. He had the look of the killer about him.

"Where are the folks who came in on the stage?" Powell said. His face was hard, unfriendly. "One of them a fine-looking woman by the name of Erica Hall."

"There were two women with the stage when it arrived yesterday evening," Scriver said. "Along with the two gentlemen with them, they left to find a hotel."

"What's the name of the hotel?" Powell said.

"That, I don't know. All I can tell you is that they headed downtown."

"Where's the stage driver?"

"He and his messenger are having breakfast at a restaurant just down the street," Scriver said. "Ma Pettibone owns the place and she makes a right nice ham-and-cheese omelet."

"Will they come back here?" Powell said.

"They will eventually. The cabin is their sleeping quarters while they're in Houston."

Whitey said to Powell, "How do we play this, boss?"

"The driver might know where Erica Hall headed. We'll talk with him."

Scriver was about to say that Rocco Baldoni would know where Miss Hall was staying, but he decided against it. The four had the rough look of frontier gunmen, a dying breed in these modern times, but there were a few still around and those remained dangerous.

Scriver took a small, but perilous step. "You gentlemen can't wear your guns in Houston," he said. "The police will confiscate them." And then, echoing Sergeant Brandt, "And they might knock you around."

"Damn the police," Whitey said. "If they try to take my gun, I'll . . ."

"Whitey, shut the hell up," Powell said. Then to Scriver, "We'll leave our guns and horses with you. Make sure our mounts get oats. They've come a long way."

"Fine-looking animals," Scriver said.

"Yeah, they are," Powell said. "Make sure you treat them right."

"I will," Scriver said. "I'll brush them down good and be generous with the oats."

"Whitey, you and Bill Cline stay here and guard our guns and horses. Gus and Ross, you come with me."

"But, boss . . ." Whitey complained.

"This is not a time for hotheads," Powell said. "That will come later, but not now." He unbuckled his gun belt and handed it to Scriver. "You boys do the same."

Whitey grumbled but handed over his Colt as did the others. Cline kept hold of his stiletto, hidden under his coat.

Powell said something in Italian to Cline, and the big man nodded. *"Cosa certa,"* he said.

Whitey was suspicious. "Boss, what did you just say to him?"

"I told him to make sure you behave yourself and don't go off half-cocked if someone looks at you the wrong way," Powell said.

"And what did Cline say?"

"He said, 'Sure thing.'"

Whitey looked hard at the big, bearded man and smirked. "You reckon you could stop me, Bill?"

"Yeah, I could stop you," Cline said.

"Maybe one day you'd like to try," Whitey said.

"I don't like you, Whitey, so one day I'll kill you," Cline said.

Whitey was playing it tough, but he was taken aback by Cline's unemotional statement, as was Luke Powell.

"You two pull back on the reins," Powell said. "Our task here is to find Erica Hall and get back the heroin she stole. After that, you can have at it, I don't care. But until then, there will be no squabbling among ourselves. Do you understand me?" He waited until Whitey and Cline grunted agreement and then said to Scriver, "Those two obviously need coffee. Fix them up, huh?"

CHAPTER TWENTY

Ma Pettibone's restaurant was a long, narrow building jammed into a concrete canyon created by two towering office blocks, one with a wooden sign on its roof advertising DR. BRADLY'S BITTERS. Busy, steamy, smelling of coffee, frying bacon, and cigar smoke, the place was crowded, mostly low-paid clerks in ditto suits, several bosses in broadcloth, top hats at their feet, and a few young women, obviously secretaries, wearing off-the-peg, bell-shaped skirts gored to fit smoothly over their hips, shirts with huge, leg-of-mutton sleeves, and ribboned straw boaters. Amid that businesslike throng, a man in a brass-buttoned sailor's coat and beside him another wearing a beaded, buckskin shirt and a derby hat, his high-heeled boots visible under the table, stood out as rubes come to visit the big city . . . or a stagecoach driver and his messenger.

Luke Powell told Gus Finley and Ross Glenn to go back outside and stand guard. When they'd done that he made his way to Buttons and Red's table, earning the ire of a red-faced waiter who struggled past him holding a tray of filled plates over his head.

"Mind if I join you," Powell said. Without waiting for a yea or nay he dragged a chair closer to the table with the toe of his boot and sat. A waiter pounced on him like a hawk on a chicken and said, "What can I get you, sir?"

"Coffee and a ham-and-cheese omelet."

"Do you want toast with that?"

Powell was aware that the puzzled driver and his messenger were staring at him.

"Toast? Yeah, sure."

"We have sourdough, hearty white, or rye."

"Rye sounds good."

The waiter hurried away and, without any preamble, Powell said, "I'm looking for the man who drove a stage into Abbot's station early this morning."

"That would be me, and seeing as how you only got one side lamp, I'm guessing you're Luke Powell," Buttons said.

"You guessed right, mister," Powell said, his fingertips straying to his patch.

"We heard you'd been hung or got religion or something," Red said.

"And you heard wrong," Powell said. "I was in business in Fort Smith and prospering until Erica Hall stole some valuable merchandise from me." He looked at Red. "Since you came in on the stage, I want to talk to you. She was one of your passengers."

Red nodded at Buttons. "Speak to the jehu, not me."

"Where is Erica Hall?" Powell said. "Tell me the truth, now."

Buttons said, "Now, why the hell would a beautiful young woman give me her hotel and room number? Do I look like a great lover to you?"

Red grinned. "I thought you were a great lover, Buttons."

"I am. But only to certain kinds of women. Erica Hall wasn't one of them."

"I want to know where she is," Powell said, and clamped Buttons's wrist in his fist. "This isn't funny. I'm deadly serious."

"I know it isn't funny, Powell," Red said. "That's why under this table I've got a Colt pointed at a place that could ruin your own future prospects as a great lover for all time."

"You wouldn't shoot," Powell said.

"Try me," Red said.

Powell removed his hand as though Buttons's wrist were red-hot. "All right, let's keep this peaceful. A hundred dollars if you tell me where I can find Erica Hall."

"We don't know where she is," Red said. Despite the drone of conversation and the clashing clamor and clatter of the restaurant kitchen, the clicks were audible as he eased down the hammer of his gun.

"I'll up the ante," Powell said. "A hundred. Each. That's more money than you clowns make in a three-month."

"As Mr. Muldoon told you, we don't know where she is," Red said. "If she's a thief, why don't you go ask the police to find her?"

"Funny man. You're a very funny man."

"So people tell me."

The skin of Powell's face tightened against the bone. "If I was you boys, I wouldn't let the sun go down on me in Houston town. This burg is gonna become right unhealthy. You're due for bad cases of lead poisoning, you understand?"

"Powell, you're a low-life, tinhorn crook who made his

reputation killing women, half-grown boys, and old men," Red said. "You're scum, the lowest of the low, and I wouldn't piss on you if you were on fire. Now, get out of here before I forget myself and put a bullet into you."

"Tough talk. We'll see how tough you are when you go try to drive your stage out of here."

Powell rose to his feet and stomped out of the restaurant, pushing aside the waiter who was bringing his breakfast order. The man placed his tray on the table and wailed, "Ham-and-cheese omelet and rye. What do I do with it?"

"Leave it right here," Buttons said. Using his fork he pointed to the table in front of him. "Right here. I'll eat it."

CHAPTER TWENTY-ONE

The sun was high, the sky as pale blue as washed-out denim as Vincenzu Grotte sat at his desk and watched his gardener trim the lantana and paintbrush shrubs that formed the centerpiece of his lawn. It was about time, Grotte decided, they were starting to look a little overgrown. A child's nanny strolled past pushing a baby carriage and then stopped and talked angrily with a hurrying and grubby scullery maid for a few moments, shook a finger at her, and then walked on. Grotte smiled. It seemed the maid was late for work and the nanny was not too happy about it.

The phone bell on Grotte's desk dinged and he took the receiver and held it to his ear. A tinny woman's voice said, "Connecting to the Diamond Theater." A few seconds passed and then a man's voice, shouting as people did on the newfangled telephone, "Mr. Grotte?"

"Speaking."

"This is Dave Weathers."

A former actor, Weathers was now the Diamond Theater manager.

"Talk to me, Dave," Grotte said.

"Boss, I've got an act trying out here that I think you should see. In fact there's four acts, but this one's special."

"Tell me."

"She's a fan dancer."

"A what?"

"She dances naked but she covers herself with two Chinese fans."

"Did you see her naked?"

"No. She says she's reserving that for you."

"Is she pretty?"

"Boss, she's the most beautiful woman I've ever seen."

"Can she dance?"

"Well, she kinda glides and shimmies."

"To what music?"

"Hold on a second, boss," Weathers said. He called out to the piano player, "What's Miss Hall's music?" The woman answered and Weathers said, "Boss, it's the second movement of Charles-Marie Widor's Piano Quartet in A Minor. The music is to say the least . . . erotic."

"Who the hell is he?"

"I believe he's a Frenchman. Apparently, a few years ago Widor and the woman were lovers for a brief spell and he wrote the piece for her."

"And you say we have that music?"

"Yes, the dancer brought it with her."

"We already have dancers. Tell her I'll think about it and let her know. What's her name?"

"Erica Hall."

That silenced Grotte as his mind worked.

"Mr. Grotte?"

"Yeah, I'll be right over. Keep her there."

"You won't regret it, boss," Weathers said, a smile in his voice.

"Maybe, maybe not," Grotte said.

He hung up the phone receiver, palmed the desk bell, and got to his feet. When the butler appeared, he said, "Mr. Trapp, tell Niles Piper I need the carriage."

Trapp nodded and said, "Right away, sir."

"Oh, and tell him to arm himself."

"Of course, sir."

CHAPTER TWENTY-TWO

The Diamond Theater was located in midtown on Holman Avenue, an undistinguished granite building that from the outside looked like a grimy warehouse. But its interior told a different story. The theater sat six hundred people and had a rare wooden proscenium arch that gave the stage a picture-frame effect. Vincenzu Grotte boasted that his music hall had eight sets of painted scenery to be used as needed in his various productions, as they had in the big theaters back East. The Diamond had two tiers of boxes, a gallery and orchestra pit, and above everything hung a massive, gaslit chandelier, its crystals cut in the shape of diamonds that gave the theater its name. The dressing rooms were located under the stage as were a set of red-upholstered and brass suites with small bedrooms attached where some of the female actresses and performers entertained rich male clients who spent freely on sex and overpriced champagne.

When Grotte entered, Erica Hall sat on a front-row seat with Rosie Lee and Dave Weathers, a tall, slender man with dramatically blue eyes who had the look of the retired thespian about him. Dean Rice, a large, canvas carry bag balanced on his knees, and the Great Stefano and his ever-present black box sat in seats at the rear in semidarkness. Niles Piper, the groom, stood in the aisle close to them. The stage was illuminated and a middle-aged woman, her gray hair tied back in a severe bun, sat to one side at an upright piano and studied sheet music that Grotte figured must be What's-his-name's quartet.

Weathers rose to his feet and said, "Mr. Grotte, allow me to introduce Miss Erica Hall, the dancer I spoke to you about."

Grotte bowed over the woman's extended hand and said, "Charmed."

"Likewise," Erica said, her smiling scarlet mouth revealing white teeth. "Mr. Weathers has been very remiss. He failed to mention how handsome you are."

"You flatter me, madam," Grotte said. But he was obviously pleased. Like exploring hands, his eyes wandered over Erica's body, her loose robe of Chinese silk revealing little. "And you are stunningly beautiful."

Erica's laugh rang like a silver bell in the quiet of the empty theater. "Then we are a pretty pair, are we not?" she said.

An image of his fat, frumpy, and mustachioed wife sprang, unbidden, into Grotte's subconsciousness and he blinked, shutting out the picture, and said, "I'd like to see your dance, Miss Hall. I understand the music was written especially for you."

"Perhaps," Erica said. "The quartet was written by Charles-Marie Widor when I was very young and living in Paris with dreams of becoming a ballerina. He dedicated the piece to me on my twentieth birthday and I've used it in my act ever since."

"You never became a ballerina?" Grotte said.

"No, I grew too tall, but all was not lost. Ballet gave me strength, flexibility, discipline, and self-confidence and for all that I will be eternally grateful."

Grotte tested her. "Were you and the Frenchman lovers?"

"Yes, for three years, until I turned twenty-one and came back to the United States." Erica put her arms around Grotte's neck. He could feel her heart beating, her breath on his cheek. "I do so want you to like my dance," she whispered.

"Then let me see it," Grotte said. His voice was husky. He'd been around Erica Hall for only a couple of minutes but never before in his life did he want a woman so bad. She put even High Timber Zasha Travers, the flashiest whore in the Silver Garter, to shame, made her look like a cloistered nun by comparison.

In her scarlet robe Erica moved through the theater like a flame as she mounted side stairs that led to the stage and vanished into the wings. A few moments later, apparently on a signal from Erica, the pianist's fingers moved across the keyboard and the Widor music played.

Erica, naked, moved sinuously onto the stage and began her dance, every movement in harmony with the music. From where Grotte sat, he watched a beautiful ivory statue of a woman, two vivid, scarlet Chinese fans fluttering around her body like butterflies. As she danced, she seemed to reveal much, but showed nothing at all. Was that a glimpse of coral-tipped breast? Grotte leaned forward in his chair, mouth agape. No, it was just the magic of the fan. The swell of a hip? Perhaps . . . for a brief moment before it disappeared. He could not be sure. Then a graceful turn to the back, the fans dipping and gliding then a turn to the front, a plié on bent knees followed by a relevé that brought her upright again. The woman, the fleeting glimpses of velvet flesh, the sensual music, the hypnotic flittering of blood red fans had Vincenzu Grotte in thrall. Erica's sultry eyes stared right at him throughout the dance, teasing, tormenting, inviting, he was sure of that. Woman's wiles on display to the most erotic degree, designed to drive a man mad with desire. Then the climax to the bawdy ballet that almost made Grotte cry out in pain. The music ended and immediately Erica extended her arms like white wings, the fans in her hands. For the briefest of moments she stood stark naked in the middle of the stage, before she turned and performed an enchainment of elegant little side steps that took her offstage.

"Brava! Brava!" Grotte sprang to his feet, grinning, furiously clapping his hands. "Bravissimo!"

Erica stepped back onstage, wearing her robe. She dropped Grotte a little curtsy and then said, "Well, do I dance at the Diamond?"

As others have noted, Erica Hall was probably aware that on the side the theater was also a high-class brothel. It's likely that Dave Weathers told her that much. And it's reasonable to assume that even before she'd performed her Salome dance, she'd summed up Vincenzu Grotte as a crook, but a thug she could use.

"Of course you can dance here," Grotte said, beaming. "Two hundred a performance with three performances a week guaranteed and two percent of the box office."

"You're very generous, Mr. Grotte," Erica said.

"I can be even more generous. Do you want to talk about it?"

"Certainly. I'll listen to your proposition."

"I keep an office here. We'll chat over a bottle of champagne."

"Mr. Grotte, what about Rosie Lee, Mr. Stefano, and Mr. Rice?" Erica said.

"Who?"

Weathers said, "Mr. Stefano is a knife thrower and Mr. Rice is a juggler. Miss Lee is a songstress, and she's got a reasonably good voice."

The Great Stefano and Dean Rice stood and the knife thrower said, "I'll work for a hundred a performance."

"Me, too," Rice said.

"This is a theater, not a damned circus," Grotte said. "Good day, gentlemen."

Rice looked up at Erica, his arms extended in a pleading gesture, but the woman shook her head. "Sorry," she said, and walked offstage.

"What about me?" Rosie Lee said. She looked pretty in a pale blue day dress with a small bustle.

"Mr. Weathers says you have a good voice," Grotte said. "What do you sing?"

"Anything you want me to sing, Mr. Grotte."

"Can you sing, 'Always Take Mother's Advice' and 'I'm a Farmer's Daughter'?"

"Yes, I sing them often," Rosie said.

"Fifty dollars a performance," Grotte said. "Mr. Weathers will sign you on." He looked Rosie up and down and then added, "You're a plain little thing, so when you're onstage show more bubbies and ankle, get the menfolk involved."

Spent, Erica Hall and Vincenzu Grotte lay together, naked on the narrow bed in the room adjoining the man's office. Drowsily, Erica said, "When is my first performance?"

"Rehearsal at eleven tomorrow morning, your first performance tomorrow night," Grotte said. "Short notice, I know, but I want you onstage. You'll be a sensation."

"I'm so grateful that you hired me, Vincenzu."

"Your talents as a dancer made me hire you."

"Nothing else?"

"Yes, for your dance, and for what we just enjoyed."

"Three times," Erica said.

"I wasn't counting."

"Will you protect me, Vincenzu?"

"From what?"

"A man who wants to kill me. He attacked me and I put one of his eyes out with a curling iron. It happened in Fort Worth and he vowed to take both of my eyes and blind me."

"What's this man's name and where is he?"

"He's probably here in Houston. He goes by the name Luke Powell, but his real name is Luciano Tiodoro."

"Ah, *siciliano*."

"Yes. He has powerful friends in New Orleans."

"So do I. Don't worry your pretty little head, I'll take care of Mr. Tiodoro."

Grotte sat up, bunched a pillow behind him, and took a moment to light a cigar. He then put his arm around Erica's shoulders and yanked her closer to him, using more brute strength than was required.

"Now, tell me about the heroin," he said.

Despite the rough handling, Erica smiled. "I'm so glad you asked, Vincenzu."

CHAPTER TWENTY-THREE

At Buttons Muldoon's insistence he and Red Ryan left the restaurant and made their way back to the stage depot.

"There's always a chance the army sergeant changed his mind," Buttons said.

"I wouldn't count on it," Red said. "He seemed like a pretty determined feller to me."

"What about Luke Powell and them?" Buttons said.

"What about him?"

"He was mighty sore when he left the restaurant."

"Maybe because he knew you were going to eat his omelet."

"This is serious, Red. As far as I could tell, Powell's a finger looking for a trigger."

"How the hell would we know where Erica Hall was shacked up?" Red said. "He's barking up the wrong tree."

"Next time he'll go to the gun."

"Look around you, Buttons, what do you see? Buildings so tall geese crash into their upper stories. Streetcars, some electric. Fashionable folks strolling the sidewalks, not boardwalks. Constables in blue with helmets and truncheons in their hands, children playing in the streets, no wild saloons, but there are bars and restaurants and there are railroads, steamboats, and I heard men in the restaurant talking about steam-driven horseless carriages coming soon . . . you catch my drift?"

"No, I don't," Buttons said, genuinely confused.

"Houston is a civilized city," Red said. "Men like Powell won't go to the gun because they don't fit in here. This ain't Tombstone."

Buttons shook his head. "All that stuff won't stop a badman like Luke Powell. Red, we're headed for a gunfight. I feel it in my bones. And do you know what's to blame? I'll tell you what's to blame . . . a cursed stagecoach called the Gray Ghost."

"Buttons, there's nothing cursed about the stage," Red said. "It's just your imagination working overtime."

"It's not my imagination," Buttons said. "Mark my words, we're headed for trouble."

In that, as future, hell-firing events would prove, Buttons was right and Red Ryan wrong.

A couple of days later a blatantly inaccurate account of the first of those events appeared in the *Houston Age Semiweekly* newspaper, preceded by a cascade of headlines . . .

THE FESTIVE REVOLVER IS ONCE AGAIN HEARD IN OUR FAIR CITY

Two men hurled into eternity
in the space of a moment

A pair of desperadoes in custody

If guilty they'll hang,
vows City Marshal Alexander Erichson

Have the wild ways returned to Houston?

A couple of poorly executed ink drawings showed two scowling, tough-looking characters above a caption that read, "The accused pair are well known to Texas law enforcement. At left is Patrick Muldoon, an Irish teamster, his face revealing all the ignorance and brutality of his race. The other, known as Redheaded Ryan, is also an Irish teamster, a man with a fiery disposition said to be a deadly gunman. According to the *Age*'s sources Ryan and Muldoon are both heavy drinkers and quarrelsome under the influence of tornado juice."

Then came an abbreviated account of the "Gunfight at Abbot's Station."

As far as the Age *can piece it together, it seems that Muldoon and Ryan got into it with two others over the affections of a fallen woman, known to the participants as "the whore Ernestine Doll." According to one eyewitness, liveryman Tom Scriver, all four were drinking from jugs of busthead and the argument soon escalated into*

THREATS OF VIOLENCE

Scriver opines that one of the soon-to-be dead men, whose identity remains unknown as we go to press, called out to Ryan, "She's mine and you'll not

have her, so be damned to ye fer a scoundrel." And
proceeded to draw his

DEADLY REVOLVER

That man, whoever he was, and Ryan exchanged
shots and then Muldoon joined in the merry fray and
discharged a ball at the second man, identity also
unknown, and then the

FIRING BECAME GENERAL

The Age *is saddened to report that ere the smoke*
cleared two dead men, shot to pieces, lay stretched
out in the dirt

WELTERING IN THEIR BLOOD

It is reported by other witnesses who wish to
remain anonymous that Ryan and Muldoon laughed
at the dreadful execution they had wrought and
Ryan was heard to utter, "And so perish all who
would try to steal my woman."

The Age *is disgusted that this kind of gun*
violence still raises its Gorgon's head in our beloved
city and we urge the authorities to prosecute Ryan
and Muldoon to the fullest extent of the law and
after a fair trial frog-march them to the gallows.

The reality of the gunfight at the stage station was very
different from the *Houston Age Semiweekly*'s garbled and
invented version. The newspaper was interested in selling
copies, not truth.

* * *

It was not yet noon when Red Ryan and Buttons Muldoon returned to the stage station. The day was already hot and even as fall approached, Houston was covered by its seemingly endless summer sky. Away from the downtown traffic and bustling crowds, the air smelled of horses, but fresh and clean, holding a promise that all was well in the Bayou City.

Luke Powell was not there, but Whitey Quinn and Bill Cline sat on a bench in front of the station cabin. Both had retrieved their guns. Whitey had a pint of whiskey in hand that he corked when he saw Buttons and Red. He got to his feet, adjusted the hang of his revolver, and stepped in front of Red, an aggressive, tinhorn act, designed to intimidate.

"You're still alive," Whitey said. "I figgered Luke would've shot you by now."

"When you see him," Red said, "tell him he left the restaurant in such an all-fired hurry he forgot to eat his eggs."

Whitey didn't like that. He didn't like it one bit.

"If you're saying you put the crawl on Luke, you're a liar," Whitey said.

Red refused to be baited. "I said he didn't eat his omelet. Mr. Muldoon here ate it for him."

"You're a funny man, ain't you?"

Red smiled. "Powell called me that. Buttons, was that before or after I called him a tinhorn crook?"

"I can't quite recollect, but I'm sure it was after," Buttons said.

"Do you know who you're talking to, shotgun man?" Whitcy said.

"Can't say as I do."

"Name's Whitey Quinn. Does that name mean anything to you?"

"No, I can't say that it does."

"Where I come from when men hear my name, they walk wide around me and call me sir."

"Mighty small town, huh?" Red said.

Whitey slowly shook his head back and forth, like a metronome. His eyes were flat, dull as charcoal. "Ooh . . ." he said, "I'm sooo looking forward to putting a bullet in your brisket and listening to you howl." He turned and yelled to the young cavalry troopers at the gray stage. They looked like half-grown boys in dirty shirt blue. "You two, get over here."

The soldiers were tough farm boys with sand enough, but they'd heard of Texas drawfighters and had every reason to believe this aggressive little man with a gun on his hip could be one of them. They were also bored and ready for any distraction.

Whitey took a half-dollar coin from his pocket and handed it to one of the youngsters. "You and your pardner go buy some stick candy," he said. "Come back when the shooting stops."

The trooper was hesitant, but Red said, "Lose yourself for a while, soldier. We won't try to drive the stage away, I promise."

The kid thought that through for a while and looked from Red to Whitey and knew something bad was brewing, something he wanted no part of. "Well . . . I guess it will be all right," he said.

"It will be just fine," Buttons said. "Go. There's no point in you getting involved in gun business that ain't any of your making."

"Listen to the man. Now, git," Whitey said.

After the troopers walked from the depot into the street, Whitey grinned at Red and said, "Answer me one question, rube. It might save your life."

"Or yours," Red said.

"Funny man," Whitey said. "Always with the good jokes."

"What's your question?" Red said.

"Where is Erica Hall?"

"I have no idea."

"You're a damned liar."

"Maybe. But you called it and I answered your question. Now what?"

Whitey took a step back, his gun hand clawed over the butt of his Colt.

"Now you go fer the iron tucked into your pants and I kill you," Whitey said. "I seen you draw and kill a man in Paddy O'Hara's saloon in San Angelo, and mister, you weren't much. Now say something funny about that."

"You got a big mouth, Whitey," Red said. "All wind and piss."

Again, Whitey Quinn's unbelieving, slow shake of his head.

His hand dropped to his gun.

Whitey was mighty fast on the draw and shoot. A whole passel of hard-eyed men of experience had told him that. Hell, hadn't he killed Elijah Riggs, the feared Yuma drawfighter? But did Whitey's brother shootists know that

Riggs was lying in a stinking tent in Deadwood, fevered from smallpox, when the teenaged Whitey stepped inside and put five bullets into him for no other reason than to gain a reputation? Probably not.

By contrast, despite what later historians say, no one ever pegged Red Ryan as a fast gun. He was a messenger, a shotgun man, and was never considered a ranker among the frontier's gunfighting elite.

Imagine then, Whitey Quinn's surprise when a .45 bullet, with terrifying impact, crashed into his chest . . . and before the lights dimmed, his own gun hardly clear of the leather, he saw Red Ryan standing there staring at him, smoke trickling from the muzzle of his revolver. One shot. That's all it took. And Whitey carried that awful realization with him into eternity.

Bill Cline would go to the knife if he could. The moment Whitey fell, Cline had a split second of hesitation . . . use a knife or reach for his gun and throw down on Red Ryan? That moment of hesitation was the only edge Buttons Muldoon needed. He reached under his coat, grabbed the Remington from the waistband at the small of his back, and cut loose. Buttons hurried the shot, low and to the right. A hit. But not a killing shot. The bullet struck the top of Cline's femur and staggered him. Cline, fixated on Red, steadied, ignored Buttons, and triggered a shot. The bullet tugged at Red's sleeve as he returned fire. And in that moment Cline knew with terrible certainty that he'd signed his own death warrant in lead. That conviction was confirmed when two bullets slammed into his chest and the cartwheeling earth rushed up to meet him. Cline had time to shriek his wrath and fear before the silence of death took him and stifled his tongue forever.

Ere the gun smoke cleared, the police arrived. For a while that was the current belief in Houston after the gun-fight. But in fact fifteen minutes passed before the law arrived, four blue-clad constables and a new paddy wagon that had seen little use, summoned by both the young cavalry troopers and the distant hammering of gunfire.

CHAPTER TWENTY-FOUR

The police sergeant was a tall, well-built man in his early forties with a magnificent set of muttonchop whiskers and a stern expression. He had a Colt revolver in his right hand and a nightstick swung from a leather loop on his left wrist. His eyes moved from the dead men and to Red Ryan and Buttons Muldoon. He didn't seem very pleased to see them.

"Give me your names and then tell me what happened here," the copper said.

"I'm Patrick Muldoon. I'm a driver for the Abe Patterson and Son Stage and Express Company. The one in the plug hat is Red Ryan, my messenger. It's a clear-cut case of self-defense, Sergeant."

"Says you."

"They drew down on us and we defended ourselves."

"Says you."

"Of course says me. Who else would say it? Damn it, man, it was self-defense."

"Wise men in more exalted positions than mine will decide that," the policeman said. "Now, what happened?"

"I just told you what happened, you blockhead."

"Calling an officer of the law rude names will do nothing to help your case," the sergeant said.

Two of the lawmen disarmed Red and Buttons, and Buttons, his cheekbones flushed, said, "Is that strictly necessary?"

"If you murdered those two men, then yes, it's strictly necessary," the sergeant said. "Now, for the last time, what happened?"

Red described the fight, omitting any reference to Erica Hall, and then said, "The smaller one's name is Whitey Quinn. I don't know the other one, but they both ride with Luke Powell."

"Who's he?" the sergeant said.

"You've never heard of him?"

"No. That's why I'm asking you."

"I'm sure you've got wanted dodgers on Powell and his boys, including these two," Red said.

"I'm sure we don't," the sergeant said. "So, Mr. Ryan, you freely admit that you are the one who killed those two men."

"Yes, I admit it. To save my life and the life of Mr. Muldoon."

"Tell that to the judge and jury," the sergeant said. He nodded to the constables. "All right, boys, put the manacles on him."

"Where are you taking him?" Buttons protested, his angry face now brick red. "And may I remind you that, like me, Mr. Ryan is an employee of the Abe Patterson and Son Stage and Express Company and a gentleman of some standing in the San Angelo community. He's not to be handled in this way."

"I'm taking him to Caroline Street," the sergeant said.

"And what's on Caroline Street?"

"Police headquarters and some nice, comfortable cells."

"The shootings were in self-defense, Red told you that," Buttons said. "And I fired a shot, too, you know. Now, unhand him."

"That's not my decision to make," the sergeant said. "Don't worry, if he's found not guilty, he'll be freed."

"And if he's found guilty?"

"Then we'll hang him."

That was the straw that broke Buttons Muldoon's patience. "Then you're taking him nowhere and Abe Patterson will be informed of this. Take those manacles off him, instanter!"

"Buttons, let it go," Red said. "I'll get a good lawyer."

"Red, they're taking you nowhere," Buttons said. "This is not justice, you're being railroaded. It's an outrage."

It was then that Buttons made a big mistake. At a time when the Houston police were hired for their toughness, he rushed at the constables who held Red and managed to shove one of them to the ground . . . before a swinging nightstick made contact with his head and laid him out cold.

"How are you feeling, old fellow?" Red Ryan said.

Buttons Muldoon sat upright on the screeching iron cot and held his head in both hands and groaned, "What hit me?"

"A club. Made of oak, I believe, or it could've been mahogany."

"One of those blue lawmen did it."

"Yes, he sure did. Smack! Right on the noggin."

Buttons looked through his open fingers. "This is no good joke, Red. I was buffaloed."

"You were indeed. And to boot, you're being charged with assaulting a police officer and maybe conspiracy to murder."

Buttons dropped his hands and looked around him at a small concrete cell with a small rectangular window high on the wall opposite the iron bars and padlocked steel door. There was a bucket on the floor and the place stank of piss and ancient sweat overlaid with the ever-present boiled-cabbage smell that seemed to permeate just about every boardinghouse and public building in the West. Buttons opened his mouth to speak, but Red said, "The law calls this a holding cell. In our more permanent arrangement, we'll have our own bunk and bucket and three squares a day, or so I was told."

"What have they charged you with?" Buttons asked.

"We've been here for four hours and so far, nothing."

"I've been out for four hours?"

"You got a bad bump on the head, but I think you've been asleep for the last couple of hours."

"I put a bullet into that Cline feller, you know."

"Keep that to yourself," Red said. "There's no point in us both getting hung."

"Damn it all, it was self-defense."

"I know, but that doesn't seem to enter into the Houston lawmen's thinking."

"It's the curse. Lay an eye on it, Red, and it will look like a natural fact."

"The Gray Ghost strikes again."

"Now you're making sense. First chance I get, I'm gonna burn it."

"If the good citizens of Houston don't burn us first," Red said.

The door that led to the cells opened and two constables, one with a huge jangling bunch of keys hanging from his belt and a merry smile on his lips, stepped inside. "The city marshal wants to see you boys," the key man said. His smile slipped and he stared at Buttons in some distaste. "Do I have to shackle you, or will you behave yourself?"

"I'll corral that ornery hoss," Buttons said.

"See you do."

"Were you the one buffaloed me?"

"No," the lawman said. "I didn't have that pleasure."

CHAPTER TWENTY-FIVE

A cross town from the jailhouse, Vincenzu Grotte and Henry Trapp, his attentive butler, were in conference.

"She says she has ten kilos of the stuff," Grotte said to Trapp. "In American, that's about eleven pounds, and at ten thousand dollars a kilo . . ."

"A hundred thousand dollars on the barrelhead," Trapp said. He whistled through his teeth. "Boss, that's a pile of money."

"In any language," Grotte said.

"Where is the merchandise now?"

"At Erica Hall's hotel. In a steamer trunk."

"You want me to leave her dead on the floor and take it?"

"Hell, no. We'll take it, yes, but I don't want the woman dead, at least not yet. I still haven't explored all her possibilities, if you get my meaning."

Trapp smiled. "I sure do."

"But we have a problem."

"You pay me to take care of problems."

"No, two problems. One is a *siciliano* by the name of Luciano Tiodoro. He also goes by the name Luke Powell.

Before she stole the merchandise, Erica Hall took out one of his eyes and he badly wants to do the same to her."

"And the other?"

"Leoluca Vitale."

Trapp looked like he'd been slapped. "A made man, the one who visited you, carries a gun for . . ."

"Antonio Matranga," Grotte said.

"Boss, this already sounds bad. Why is he in town? Do I want to hear it?"

"Yeah, you want to hear it, that's why I pay you. The merchandise in question was stolen from Matranga by Erica Hall, and Vitale is here to get it back. And incidentally, so is Powell. As I said, he and Erica were working together in Fort Smith."

"Then we give it back to capo dei capi Matranga. We do him a big favor and we know he never forgets anyone who helps his business. It's a code he lives by."

"Too easy, and easy is not how I want to play it," Grotte said. "The bottom line is . . . I want the hundred thousand."

For a second time Trapp looked shocked. "But . . . but it's Matranga's money."

"I know, and I'm taking it from him," Grotte said.

"Have you thought this through, boss?"

"Sure I have. All I have to do is hold off Matranga for a while."

"Boss, heroin has never been tested in Houston. I mean, how long would it take to sell ten kilos of the stuff?"

"With Erica Hall's help, not long, just a few weeks, maybe. Every morphine and opium addict in town will want to try the new drug. I already have buyers lined up to buy the Diamond and the rest of my businesses. Then I get rid of my fat wife . . . and the world's my oyster.

Maybe I'll take Erica Hall with me." He shrugged. "Or maybe not."

"Boss, you're cutting it too close. Antonio Matranga makes a bad enemy and you'd be playing a dangerous game."

"I'm a gambler. I'll roll the dice because it's a game I'm willing to play."

Outside the streetlamps were being lit and as they lined up along the sidewalks mist drifting in from the bayou gave them pale blue halos likes rows of elongated El Greco saints. A brewer's dray drawn by a dappled Percheron rumbled past and crates of bottled beer rang like stacks of cheap tin trays.

"What about Vitale?" Trapp said. "I mean, he's right here in Houston and from all I heard he's a dangerous man."

"We set one problem against the other. I can have Tiodoro, or Powell, or whatever the hell he wants to call himself, take care of Vitale. Then you take care of Powell. Two problems solved and my hands are clean."

"Where is Leoluca Vitale?"

"He's at the Monarch Hotel. It's adequate accommodation for a soldier."

"And Powell?"

Grotte smiled. "Ah . . . where is Powell?"

Trapp said nothing.

"Powell is here. Right here in my home, probably drinking my bourbon," Grotte said. "He and two other men of no importance."

Trapp's baffled face betrayed his unasked question.

"He came here to talk with me not more than an hour ago. The maid let him in."

Another befuddled look and another answer.

"Although he's *siciliano*, Tiodoro told me he was never a made man, but worked as an associate for Antonio Matranga in New Orleans and then Fort Smith. Since I've been in business for a long while, he'd several times heard my name mentioned as an associate living in Houston and tracked me down."

Trapp was alarmed. "Boss, he tracked you down? I don't like the sound of that. It was way too easy."

"Apparently money changed hands, and one of my employees at the theater, a box office clerk, gave . . . let's just call him Powell for now . . . my address."

"Boss, I'll shut that damned traitor's mouth for good," Trapp said.

"It's already taken care of. He patted the telephone receiver. I gave the job to Niles Piper, and the clerk, apparently his name was Tompkins, is already squealing"— he crossed himself—"his guts out to Saint Peter."

"When do I meet this Luke Powell?" Trapp said.

"Not now," Grotte said. "Later, when I order you to erase him and you need to get close, it's better that he doesn't recognize you as someone who works for me."

"When the time comes, I'll take care of it," Trapp said.

"Of course you will. People live, people die, it's the way of the world. When all this is over, I still want you with me, Henry. You are not *siciliano* and therefore can never be a made man, but you will always be a trusted and valued associate."

"I am honored," Trapp said.

"I've never asked you this, but do you have a steady lady?"

"I have one such. Her name is Esther."

"Is she fat?"

"No, she is very slender and she has red hair."

"Then you must be happy with her."

"I am. Most of the time."

"Does she walk in the Catholic faith?"

"No, boss, she is a Jew."

Grotte nodded. "The son of our God was a Jew. It is well that we respect the Jewish people. Cherish her."

"I will," Trapp said.

He felt uncomfortable. His personal life and business life were two different entities, and he preferred to keep them apart. Esther believed, or at least she pretended to believe, that he was a butler for a rich man and it stopped right there. The men he'd assassinated for Vincenzu Grotte were not topics of conversation and would remain that way.

Grotte said, "Now, leave by the back door. Powell is with the other men in the parlor and I don't want him to see you. After he leaves, I'll light the doorway carriage lamps to let you know that it's safe to return." Grotte smiled. "Go, spend some time with your Jewess."

"So, what do I call you, Luke Powell or Luciano Tiodoro?" Vincenzu Grotte said.

"I used Powell during my adventures on the frontier because it was an easier name to remember when I sold my gun to rich men like yourself."

"You didn't answer my question . . . Powell or Tiodoro?"

"Luke Powell for now. When I return to New Orleans I'll become *siciliano* once again."

Grotte let that go and said, "Then just between us I'll call you Tiodoro. How is your eye?"

"Under this patch there is no eye, so that's how it is."

"Is it your shooting eye?"

"It was."

"It doesn't spoil your good looks, Tiodoro. The patch gives you . . . what's the word? Ah yes, a rakish air." Niles Piper stood at the office door, a short-barreled Army Colt carried openly in a shoulder holster. "What do you think, Mr. Piper? Doesn't he look rakish?"

Tall, lean, and hard-faced, Piper said. "Yeah, boss. Rakish."

Powell ignored that and said, "I really need your help."

"I know." Grotte's fingertips strayed to his own right eye. "You want to find the woman who gave you that?"

"Yes, an eye for an eye."

"Erica Hall is her name. An eye. That's all you want from her?"

Just a moment's hesitation, then Powell said, "Isn't that enough? I want to blind her. Let her go through the rest of her life sightless."

"You're a hard man, Tiodoro."

"And Vincenzu Grotte is not?"

A smile, then, "You have competition, Tiodoro."

"What do you mean?"

"There is another man who very much wants to meet up with Miss Hall."

Powell was surprised. "Who?"

"His name is Leoluca Vitale. Have you heard of him?"

Powell shook his head. "No, I have not."

"A made man. A soldier for capo dei capi Antonio Matranga."

That stifled Luke Powell for a few seconds before he finally said, "A jilted lover, perhaps."

"Perhaps. But Vitale told me that Miss Hall was working for Matranga in Fort Smith before she made off with ten kilos of a new drug called heroin." Grotte spread his hands. "We're talking about a hundred thousand dollars of merchandise here. But you know nothing about that, Tiodoro?"

Powell struggled to find an answer, but Grotte helped him out.

"It slipped your mind?"

"No, it did not, because I had no idea she'd stolen the heroin."

"But you knew it existed."

"Yes. Erica Hall and I started to sell the drug in Fort Smith for Antonio Matranga."

"How did it sell?"

"We could've moved the whole ten kilos in a couple of weeks, maybe less."

"That is excellent."

"It's easy to move the stuff. Opium and morphine addicts will pay any price for it."

"The trouble is, Matranga wants his heroin back and he sent Leoluca Vitale to fetch it. Whether or not Miss Hall lives or dies, is up to Vitale." Grotte looked at a point above Powell's head. The gas lamps on the walls spread an eerie, greenish light. He steepled his fingers and said, "Ah well, where do we go from here, Tiodoro?"

"Help me find Erica Hall, later tonight, tomorrow, the next day. I'll take care of her and then bring you the heroin," Powell said.

"I own the Diamond Theater," Grotte said. "She's a dancer, so she might come to me for work."

"Let me know right away if she does," Powell said.

"What about Leoluca Vitale?"

"I'll take care of him."

"You and the two you have waiting in the parlor?"

"No, not them. I have a couple of associates who can take the Leoluca Vitales of this world apart."

"Not with a gun. Gunfire will immediately attract the attention of the police."

"One of my associates is *siciliano* and an expert with the blade. He'll use the stiletto."

"Good. Excellent. Vitale is lodging in the Monarch Hotel. Dispose of him there and then report back to me. I suggest you book rooms close to his." Grotte waved a dismissive hand. "That is all. The night will fall soon and I grow weary."

Powell rose to his feet and stepped to the door that Piper opened for him. Grotte's voice stopped him.

"Oh, Tiodoro, you won't let the heroin slip your mind again, will you?" he said.

CHAPTER TWENTY-SIX

Red Ryan and Buttons Muldoon were pushed into the cramped, untidy office of acting city marshal Alexander Erichson, a tall, slender man who bore a remarkable resemblance to George Armstrong Custer.

Erichson sat behind a large oak desk that took up most of the room, a gun rack holding a dozen Winchester rifles behind his head. There were no wanted posters or any other bulletins on the windowless, faded yellow walls but a dark painting of an antlered, and apparently unhappy deer hung to the right of the desk with a brass plaque screwed to the frame that read, THE STAG AT BAY. Like the rest of the police station the office smelled strongly of boiled cabbage.

The marshal directed Red and Buttons into the chairs in front of his desk and looked them over in silence for a full minute. Finally he picked up a telegraph wire and said, "Whitey Quinn and Loris Barca, alias Bill Cline. Both men are wanted."

He read, "'Whitey Quinn and Loris Barca alias Bill Cline wanted dead or alive on charges of murder, rape, and robbery.'" Erichson stopped reading, laid down the wire, and said, "That came from the Texas Rangers a few minutes ago. It seems the great state of Texas owes you boys a favor and maybe a reward."

"Didn't I tell them damned knuckleheads of yours that those men were outlaws?" Buttons said. "And what did I get for it? I'll tell you what I got for it . . . a billy club bounced off my skull."

"I'm sorry, Mr. . . . You are?"

"Patrick Muldoon, of the Abe Patterson and Son Stage and Express Company."

"Mistakes happen, Mr. Muldoon. After all, you told my constables that Quinn and Cline were here in Houston with Luke Powell, an outlaw who's been dead for years."

Red Ryan said, "Powell isn't dead, Marshal, he's right here in Houston."

Erichson smiled. "Well, if you see him, please let us know."

"And suppose we have to shoot him in self-defense? What happens then?" Buttons said.

"Nothing, I guess. After all, you can't be hanged for killing a dead man, and as far as the law is concerned, Powell is dead." Erichson stood. "You can pick up your guns on the way out, and you, Mr. Muldoon, will pay a ten-dollar fine for assaulting a police constable. The clerk's office is to the right as you go out the door."

Buttons was indignant. "I didn't assault a constable," he said.

"You pushed Constable Dodson to the ground, did you not?"

"Just a little push and then he fell down."

"That was a felony assault. Pay your fine before you leave, Mr. Muldoon."

* * *

"Ten dollars for a push," Buttons Muldoon said. "What kind of town is this?"

"The kind that doesn't tolerate ruffians like you, old fellow." Red Ryan looked out the window of the streetcar at the passing parade of lamplit pedestrians, including some very pretty young women on the arms of their beaux. "I could get used to this," he said.

"I'm hungry," Buttons said. "All that gunfighting and police brutality has given me an appetite."

"The jehu up front says he comes close to the Scriver livery. We'll jump off then and head for the restaurant."

"A man guiding a mule that pulls a car riding on rails ain't a jehu," Buttons said. He was determined not to shake his bad mood.

"Well, driver, then."

"He ain't a driver, either."

"So, what is he?"

"How the hell should I know? Maybe they should call him a messenger."

"Testy, Patrick, testy," Red said, smiling. "You're still all riled up about the ten dollars."

"Robbers. Damned highway robbers, every single one of them."

"Who?"

"Them lawmen, constables, whatever you want to call them."

"Steak and eggs," Red said.

"Huh?"

"That's what you need, Buttons. Steak, eggs, and a wedge of pie."

And in that, Red was correct.

* * *

By the time he'd sopped up a blob of egg yolk with his last chunk of steak and then demolished a slice of apple pie and then sampled the peach, Buttons Muldoon, in a much better frame of mind, lingered over coffee.

When he and Red arrived at the livery, young Tom Scriver, who had a small room and office at the rear of the barn, was just about to turn in. It was full dark, with no moonlight, and he held a lantern high until he recognized their faces.

His face beaming with his newfound admiration for his gunslinging visitors, he said, "It was a hell of a morning, huh? I gave a reporter for the *Houston Age Semiweekly* a full account of what happened and he said it will make you boys famous. He said the story will be front-page news when it comes out in a couple of days." Suddenly Scriver looked confused. "How come you're out of jail? The reporter thought for sure you both were in line to get hung. He was going to write that in the paper."

"Never believe what you read in the newspapers," Red said. "All they print is corral dust."

"But . . . but the story," Scriver said. "I mean, you two getting hung is in the story."

"Sorry to disappoint you, but the men we killed were wanted dead or alive," Red said. "Turns out we're heroes, of a kind."

Scriver shook his head. "Well, if that don't beat all." He smiled. "Mr. Powell is gonna be sore upset."

"He was here?"

"Yeah, about an hour before you got here, him and two other men."

"You told him about Bill Cline and Whitey Quinn?"

"Didn't have to. Them two soldier boys over there did most of the talking."

"Except to reporters, like some I know," Red said, and Scriver had the good grace to hang his head.

Buttons said, "How did Powell take the bad news?"

"At first he was foaming at the mouth, but when he heard you two were likely to get hung, why, it cheered him up no end."

"I'm sure it did," Red said. "Where is Powell now?"

"I don't know," Scriver said. "Him and the other two picked up their guns and left."

"Horses?"

"No. Their mounts are in the barn."

"So Powell is still in town," Red said to Buttons.

"He won't leave until he evens the score with Erica Hall," Buttons said.

"He sure carries a grudge, don't he?"

"Wouldn't you?"

"I don't know."

"I would." Buttons peered into the gloom. "Those soldiers are still there."

"Leave them be," Red said. "We already got in enough trouble and we can wait a few days longer."

"We're gonna have big trouble with Powell sooner or later."

"Maybe we can stay out of his way."

"Not much chance of that. He'll come looking for us, depend on it."

Red nodded. "Yeah, you're right about that."

"Look at it, Red," Buttons said.

"Look at what?"

"You know what. The Gray Ghost. Look how it just sits

there, glowing, even though there's no light. It glares, that's what it docs, it glares like a wolf."

"Well, I'm gonna leave you and the stage to it," Red said. "It's me for my blankets."

"Damn stage, damn town, damn constables, damn Luke Powell . . . Why did I ever accept this run?"

"Because Abe Patterson would've fired you if you hadn't," Red said.

"Damn Abe Patterson," Buttons said.

"Amen," Red said.

CHAPTER TWENTY-SEVEN

As Red Ryan and Buttons Muldoon sought their bunks, Luke Powell had already booked into the Monarch Hotel, a shabby-genteel building constructed to look like a New Orleans manor house. It had wrought-iron balconies, tin ceilings, and boasted that there were "spring mattresses in every room."

Powell had no interest in any of that. His only concern was that Leoluca Vitale was in Room 21 and he was in Room 22, close enough for what had to be done.

Powell, Gus Finley, and Ross Glenn stood by the curtained window and shared a bottle of whiskey as they plotted their strategy.

"We decide here and now how we play this and when," Powell said. "It's got to be quiet. No guns. Seems like someone hears a shot and then the law and the whole city come running to find out who fired a gun."

Finley and Glenn exchanged glances and then Finley, older and wiser, spoke up. "Boss, are you talking about a blade?" he said. "I've never stuck a man."

"Me, neither," Glenn said. "But I'm willing to give it a try."

"I'll do it. You boys hold Vitale down and I'll skewer him," Powell said. "Hell, it ain't that difficult to shove a knife into a man."

"Unless that man has time to draw iron," Finley said.

"He's a soldier. He'll have a gun in his hand, depend on it," Powell said. "It's as though they never had a gunfight in Houston before—the whole damn town is talking about what happened to Whitey Quinn and Bill Cline. I wish they were with me tonight, instead of the dregs I'm left with."

"We've got to stop Vitale skinning his iron," Finley said. "That's what we're talking about, not dregs, because I ain't a dreg."

"I know you're not, Gus," Powell said, backing down. "I'm on edge, is all."

"How good is this Vitale, boss? Do you know?" Glenn said.

"He's a soldier. He'll be good."

"So we're not gonna have much time."

"A second or two, maybe less. Vitale will be mighty sudden."

Finley said, "He's got to come out of his room sometime. We can wait in the hallway and grab him as he walks out the door."

"A good way to get us all full of lead," Powell said. "Come on, think. I need better ideas. I want this done tonight."

"We have to get him to open his door," Finley said.

"How?" Powell said.

"A message!" Glenn exclaimed. Powell and Finley stared at him. "I knock on his door, but he won't open it until I tell him I've got an urgent message from Vincenzu

Grotte, and then he'll open wide. And I'll be right on top of him. How big is he?"

"I don't know," Powell said.

"It don't matter none, I can take him," Glenn said.

"He'll still be armed," Powell said. "He could get off a shot and ruin everything."

Finley smiled. "Ruin everything and put a bullet in you, Ross."

Powell thought for a while and then said, "A woman at his door could do it, put him off his guard."

"Luke, you're right, a woman!" Glenn said. "She says, *I'm a gift from Vincenzu Grotte.* Vitale opens the door and we're right behind her."

Powell looked at Finley. "What do you think, Gus?"

"It's thin. And where do we find a woman willing to do it?"

"A whore will do it, if we pay her enough," Glenn said. He smiled. "The desk clerk could probably get a woman here pretty quick if we drop him a few dollars."

"We'd need to be fast, very fast," Powell said. "Vitale will be fast. You can count on that . . . and it worries me."

Finley said, "The way I see it, if we don't use a woman, we're left with two options . . . kick Vitale's door down and gun him or get him in the street. He's got to go out to eat sometime."

"Both those options mean guns, and that's out of the question," Powell said. "To get to Erica Hall and the heroin, I've got to eliminate Vitale, and nobody ever said that he'll be an easy man to kill."

"Then we get the whore," Glenn said. "You ever read about the Sirens whose beautiful voices lured poor sailor-men to their doom on the rocks? No? Well, it doesn't matter, a whore will be our Siren."

Powell thought that through and then said, "Ross, go down to the front desk and tell the clerk we want a woman up here and ask him where we can find one." He reached into his pocket and pulled out a crumpled twenty-dollar bill. "Give him that. It's probably more than he makes in a month."

Glenn smiled. "Pretty or not?"

"What does it matter? We only need something that sounds female," Powell said.

Although Houston no longer considered itself a Wild West town, the Monarch was a typical frontier hotel. Its rooms were small, just six-foot-by-eight, and most of that space was taken up by the narrow bed. There were a couple of hooks on one wall to hang clothing, a wash-stand with a porcelain pitcher and basin, a place to hang a small towel, and an attached mirror. A small chair and a chamber pot under the bed completed the furnishings and the room was lit by a single gas lamp.

When he booked into Room 21 Luke Powell made a couple of big mistakes.

He did not take into consideration that the partition wall between his room and Room 22 was only six inches wide, constructed of plastered wooden slats with no insu-lation. At the American House Hotel in Abilene John Wesley Hardin once shot through such a wall and killed a man for snoring. But Leoluca Vitale, with the instincts of a predatory lobo wolf, was not snoring that night . . . he was listening.

The grandfather clock in the foyer had just chimed nine when Leoluca Vitale heard the drone of conversation in the room next to his. It sounded like three men, an unlikely crowd to share a bed. The Monarch's even-numbered rooms were a little larger, more expensive, and considered suites. One of the perquisites for the better-off guests was a carafe of water and a drinking glass beside the bed. Vitale held the rim of the glass against the wall, pressed his ear to its base, and listened.

Some of what he heard was garbled, but he caught the gist of it . . . Luciano Tiodoro, who called himself Luke Powell, was plotting to kill him and was talking about hiring a whore to lure him to his death.

Quickly, Vitale donned his shoulder holster and coat and then lowered the gas lamp to a dull glow. He quietly opened the door, closed it behind him, and on cat feet walked along the hall and into the foyer. As he expected, the young clerk dozed at his desk, his mouth open, a trickle of saliva on his pimply chin. Vitale walked out of the hotel, avoided the puddles of misty light provided by the streetlamps, and crossed the street. He stepped into the darkened doorway of a women's hat shop opposite the hotel and there, with a born hunter's patience, he watched and waited. A couple of minutes passed and then a man stepped out of the Monarch, looked around, and hurried away.

Leoluca Vitale settled in for a wait. There was no foot traffic, but an electric-powered streetcar carrying only one passenger rattled past and soon disappeared into the darkness. How long would it take to find a streetwalker in this low-rent part of the city? Five minutes, he suspected. Maybe less.

In fact, Ross Glenn, acting on the desk clerk's instructions, got lucky. He found a whore walking her gaslit beat within a couple of minutes. She said her name was Juliet and she wouldn't take less than two dollars, especially at this time of night when she was just about to turn in. Did the gentleman require other services? Those would be added to the basic price. Glenn told her that he needed her voice and that he'd give her five dollars. If the girl thought that strange, she didn't say. Not that it mattered, she'd very soon be dead.

Vitale watched the pair cross the street in the direction of the hotel.

Now! He moved. They had to be fast kills.

He stepped out of the shadows, walked quickly toward Glenn.

"You!" he said, talking to the man's back.

Glenn turned, saw the danger, and his face registered openmouthed panic. He tried to run but two bullets in the upper spine from Vitale's gun dropped him and he hit the cobbled street fast and hard. Vitale looked at the girl. "Prostitute?"

"Yes," she said, her lower lip trembling.

Vitale put a bullet between her breasts and she fell beside Glenn. In the distance somebody cried out and the triggerman melted into the misty darkness like a gray ghost. When the police arrived, Vitale was long gone.

Tomorrow he'd buy a flower for his buttonhole . . .

And tomorrow he'd ask Vincenzu Grotte why he sold him out to Luciano Tiodoro, the low-life piece of dirt who called himself Luke Powell, as though he was ashamed of his good Sicilian name. The concept of mercy and letting bygones be bygones had never taken hold in Leoluca Vitale. Grotte had wronged him and now he wanted the man's scalp.

CHAPTER TWENTY-EIGHT

The gunshots from outside drove Luke Powell and Gus Finley from the Monarch Hotel by the back door. They scampered across an area of bottle-strewn waste ground and ended up at the rear of a warehouse, where they stopped and listened into the darkness. The night remained quiet.

"Boss, I'm done," Finley said, breathing hard. "I'm riding out tonight, following the North Star out of this damned town."

"We don't know what happened," Powell said.

"Ross Glenn didn't have a gun," Finley said. "I've a pretty good idea of what happened. Three shots, two into Ross, the other into the whore he found."

"You saying Leoluca Vitale done for them?"

"Damn right he did."

"But how did he know?" Powell said.

"He listened at the keyhole. How the hell do I know what he did?"

"Yeah, he was listening! The wall. It was the damned wall."

"Huh?"

"Vitale was in the next room, but he wasn't asleep,"

Powell said. "The walls in a cheap hotel are thin. Damn him, he stood there listening and heard every word we said."

"Maybe that was the way of it," Finley said. "But one thing is certain, it was him who fired the shots. Ross Glenn is dead, you can bet the farm on that."

"I have the notion to agree with you," Powell said. "Men like Vitale do the job right."

A gibbous moon hung in the sky and away from the streetlamps the lee of the warehouse was as black as the inside of a coal house. A rising wind rustled like sandpaper among the clumps of bunchgrass that rimmed the open area but there was still no human sound from the direction of the Monarch.

Finley said, "Come with me, boss, and we'll shake the dust of this town off our feet. We could head back to Fort Smith and have ourselves a time."

Powell touched his eye patch. "What about this? What about Erica Hall and ten kilos of heroin? You want me to just walk away from it?"

"I will," Finley said. "And I won't look back."

"I have a score to settle, and I want that heroin."

"Hell, all you'll do is give it back to Antonio Matranga, make a rich man richer."

"Yes, that was my plan, but it isn't any longer."

"You mean you'd keep it for yourself?"

"Yeah, keep it all for me and move to some big city, New York maybe. Yeah. That's it. I could sell the merchandise to one of the Mick gangs, make a fast profit, and go into business on my own."

"Too dangerous for me," Finley said. "Fort Smith is about as big city as I care to go."

"You think small, Gus," Powell said. "That's always been your problem. But then, so have I. In the past I've thought small and now it galls me. Why should I give the merchandise back to Matranga? I've got as much right to it as he does."

"Maybe more, with the eye an' all," Finley said.

"Now you're starting to see the light with both eyes, Gus. Come with me to New York. I need your gun and I'll make you rich in no time."

"No, sir. I'll stay right here in Texas and settle down, maybe. Mary a widder woman with her own house and a little nest egg in the bank. That would be the ticket."

"That ain't you, Gus. You were meant to die of apoplexy in a brothel or in a saloon with a bullet in your guts and your beard in the sawdust."

"That's what you think. Listen, I've met widder women before, only this time I plan to wed one of them, a nice fat lady who'll keep me warm at night and give me plenty of shade in summer."

"It ain't gonna happen."

"You watch me. That is, if you can see that far from New York."

"You're a stubborn man, Gus."

"Yes, I am, one bullheaded ranny."

"Then I'm better off without you. Now, get the hell out of here."

"What about you, Luke?" Finley said.

"I'm going to check into another hotel and sleep till morning. Then I'll go see Vincenzu Grotte and tell him what happened tonight. Maybe we can still work out some kind of a deal about Erica Hall."

"Forget her, let her go," Finley said. "Come with me. Leave this place."

"That's not going to happen," Powell said. "Erica Hall took my eye and that's burned into my soul."

"I know it is, like she put it there with a branding iron," Finley said.

"No, damn her, with a curling iron."

Finley nodded. "Well, good luck, Luke. Could be we'll meet again under happier circumstances."

"Yeah, and good luck to you, Gus."

Finley was about to drift into the night when Powell stopped him. He reached into his pants pocket and pulled out a wad of bills and peeled off five twenties. Then, in one of those spontaneous gestures that had always brought him the loyalty of rough-hewn men, he shoved the money into Finley's hand. "That will help you with expenses while you're looking for your widder woman."

From that day on, Gus Finley never had a bad word to say about Luke Powell and there are those who claim that in his later years he regularly drank a toast to his "absent friend."

The Houston streetcars provided an around-the-clock service and it wasn't yet midnight when Gus Finley reached the Scriver livery, silently saddled his horse, and rode into the night and out of the history of the West.

When Red Ryan and Buttons Muldoon woke up to find the gunman had quietly retrieved his horse and skedaddled, they were horrified. Buttons declared that he and

Red could've been murdered in their beds and he blamed the lack of security on Tom Scriver and the two soldiers who'd been asleep in the stage . . . that is, until Red pointed out that the Muldoon snores had covered up any sounds Finley might have made.

CHAPTER TWENTY-NINE

Trying to conserve what little money they had left, Red Ryan and Buttons Muldoon had just returned from breakfast, a frugal meal of rubbery scrambled eggs and burned toast, when Tom Scriver walked out of the livery stable and told them it was their lucky day.

"Well, boys, it's your lucky day," Scriver said.

Surly, feeling acidic, Buttons said, "Son, we don't have lucky days, only the unlucky kind. What's his name? Gus Finley proved that last night."

"Wrong, wrong, wrong," Scriver said. He held up two pink tickets. "Guess what this is?"

"Tickets of some kind," Red said.

"Not just of any kind," Scriver said. "These are two tickets to tonight's show at the Diamond Theater. And guess what, you'll see Miss Erica Hall—remember her?—strip down to the altogether. It's the biggest news in town, and the man who gave me these tickets said her fan dance is reckoned to be vaudeville at its best."

"We remember Erica Hall," Red said. "You could say we almost got hung over her."

"We can't afford no tickets to a fan dance," Buttons said. "We ain't got a tail feather left."

"They're free! Why else would I say it's your lucky day?"

Buttons scowled. "Where did you steal them?"

"I didn't steal them. I got them from a cattle buyer who came in to get his horse. He says he'll be out of town for a week and can't use the tickets. He said I was a likely young feller and gave them to me."

"So how come you ain't using them?" Buttons said.

"Because I can't leave the barn at night and my pa won't be back in town until next Thursday."

"Let me see those," Red said. He took the tickets and said, "They look sure 'nuff genuine, Buttons. See there, it's printed 'Diamond Theater' right on the ticket."

"Of course, they're for the cheapest seats, up in the gods," Scriver said.

Buttons was immediately suspicious. "What does 'up in the gods' mean?"

"It means the upper balcony," Scriver said. "But you'll be able to see Miss Hall's dance right good, I'm sure." The kid looked wistful. "I'd like to see it myself."

Red said, "Well, Buttons, what do you say? Should we wash and shave and go to the theater tonight and sit among the gods?"

Buttons suddenly brightened. "Hey, maybe we could talk to her."

"Visit her backstage, you mean?" Scriver said. "Since you drove her here all the way from San Angelo, I'm sure she'll see you."

"Drove her and fit Apaches and badmen for her," Buttons said.

Scriver said, "There you go, women never forget stuff like that. My pa says when Ma was still alive, she never forgot anything."

"Well, what do you say, Buttons?" Red said.

"Seven o'clock sharp, mind," Scriver said.

"All right, sure, we'll do it," Buttons said. "And it will get us away from those damn soldier boys and the bad luck stage."

"Wait a minute, how do we get there?" Red said.

"Take a streetcar. The driver will set you right." Scriver's smile was infectious. "After tonight, everybody in the world will know where the Diamond Theater is located."

By five-thirty Red Ryan and Buttons Muldoon were washed, shaved, and shined, on account of Buttons's insistence that they'd have a better chance of getting a prime seat in the gods if they arrived early. Before they left, Red shoved his Colt into the waistband of his pants and covered it with his buckskin shirt.

"You planning on shooting somebody?" Buttons said.

"Nope. I just don't want to be fooled," Red said.

After exchanging streetcars three times, Red and Buttons stood outside the theater at six o'clock, the first to arrive. A billboard on a stand outside the main door touted twelve acts including a magician, acrobats, trained animals, a ventriloquist, a strongman, and singers and dancers. Erica Hall took top billing, described as "an Egyptian fan dancer to the crowned heads of Europe."

"I didn't know Miss Hall was an Egyptian," Buttons said.

"She's not, but folks love Egyptian stuff," Red said.

Buttons shrugged. "You could've fooled me."

Most students of the frontier agree that if Rosie Lee hadn't arrived at that moment in time, a small makeup case in her hand, events would have taken a different turn and the celebrated Erica Hall could've been the one to die that evening. In all probability, their assumption is the correct one.

Her high-heeled ankle boots clacked on the sidewalk and suddenly stopped. Rosie smiled and said, "I'd recognize that sailor coat anywhere. Why are you boys still in town?"

Red smiled and said, "Nice to meet you again. You look even prettier than I remembered, Miss Lee. Well, we're stuck here until the army says we can leave. And we can't leave until their passengers for Fort Concho arrive, so they've impounded the stage until then."

"I'm so sorry. So you've come to see the show?"

Before Buttons put his foot in it, Red said quickly, "Yes, we're here to see you and Miss Hall. We're really looking forward to it." A pause then, with emphasis, "Aren't we, Buttons?"

Buttons caught on immediately. "Yes, we sure are, young lady. You and Miss Hall."

Rosie smiled. "You probably didn't even know I was on the bill. You're here to see Erica and I don't mind a bit. She's worth watching, the way she makes those little fans flap. She and I are sharing a room at the Grand Hotel until I get established and she showed me a few of her dance moves."

"We hear she gets nekkid," Buttons said, earning a sidelong, irritated glance from Red.

"Yes, she does. Briefly," Rosie said. "You'll get a fleeting glimpse."

"We figured we could visit Miss Hall after the show," Buttons said. "I mean, since we're acquainted, an' all."

"Backstage in her dressing room, you mean?"

"Only if it's convenient for her," Red said.

"Well, you're very early for the show, and since this is her first performance Erica's probably already here. So why not pop in and say howdy now?"

"She wouldn't mind?" Buttons said. "I don't want to intrude."

"Her makeup takes a long time and I'm sure she'd be glad of a little company."

"But she might be . . . um . . ." Red began.

"Only in her robe?"

"Yeah . . . that," Red said.

"Mr. Ryan, nobody who performs in vaudeville is shy, believe me," Rosie said. "Have you ever seen a dozen dancing girls hurry to get onstage? They run around half-naked and don't care who takes a peek, male or female."

Red blinked away a vivid mental image and then said, "You're sure she won't mind us visiting? In a way we feel like kinfolk."

"Erica won't mind in the least. Just wish her luck and leave. Come with me."

Rosie Lee led the way around the side of the building to the stage door and Red and Buttons followed her inside. An elderly man with a big nose and ears and a pointed chin sat in an office just inside the door and Rosie said, "My name is Rosie Lee. I'm one of tonight's performers."

The man nodded. "I know. My name is Jacob, and I was here when Mr. Grotte hired you, Miss Lee. Go on inside."

"And these gentlemen are friends of Miss Hall, Jacob. They just want to wish her luck."

The old man's unfriendly eyes moved from Buttons to Red and back again. "A rough-looking pair and no mistake. Will you vouch for them?"

Buttons said, "My dear sir, we're employees of the Abe Patterson and Son Stage and Express Company. No one needs to vouch for us."

"Will you vouch for them, Miss Lee?" Jacob said.

"Yes, I'll vouch for them," Rosie said, smiling.

A shake of the head from the old man, then, "Theater folk have odd friends. I should be used to it by now. By the way, Miss Hall already has a gentleman caller, a man named the Great Stefano. I asked her about him, and she agreed to meet him."

"Yes, he's an expert knife thrower, but Mr. Grotte didn't hire him," Rosie said. "For a while he and Miss Hall performed at the same theater in Fort Smith. That's how they met."

"Well, since you vouch for these . . . gentlemen, I guess you can take them on inside, Miss Lee."

Rosie led the way along a dark corridor that opened up into the dressing rooms, a rectangular area with a low ceiling and numbered doors on all four sides. A sturdy wrought-iron staircase in a corner gave access to the stage and the entire space was lit by gas lamps.

"Give it another fifteen minutes and this place will be crowded," Rosie said. "At rehearsals this morning, you couldn't move down here. Best you give Erica your best wishes now. She's in dressing room Number One and she's very proud of it." She smiled. "I'm right here, Number Eighteen, that I'll share with a lady dog trainer." She stepped to the door. "Enjoy the show."

As Buttons and Red walked toward Erica Hall's room, Rosie Lee said, "Wait." She hurried toward them and then sang, "*I'm only a farmer's daughter, but I love him just the same* . . . How does that sound?"

"Good," Red said, shutting down any comment Buttons might make. "It sounds really nice."

"And look." She pulled down the neckline of her dress and said, "I'm going to wear it this low. Now, be truthful, am I showing enough breast? My corset pushes them up quite well, as you can see."

The words thick in his throat, Buttons stammered, "Oh yes, definitely enough. Yes . . . corset . . . push . . . ah, yes . . . What do you think, Red?"

"Oh yeah, yeah, just . . . just enough," Red said. "Definitely enough."

Rosie smiled. "Thank you, gentlemen. I'm so excited. And you've been so kind to me since we first met in San Angelo."

"And, young lady, you've been so very kind to us," Red said.

CHAPTER THIRTY

"We should've brought flowers," Buttons Muldoon whispered as he and Red Ryan stood outside Erica Hall's dressing room. "White roses."

"Where were we going to get white roses?" Red said.

"I don't know. Maybe . . ."

"Shh . . ." Suddenly Red was alarmed. "Listen."

The words were distinct . . . a woman in panic-stricken fear.

"No . . . don't . . . please . . . don't . . ."

Red and Buttons exchanged a look until a strange little yelping scream broke their gaze.

Buttons tried the door handle. "Locked," he said. Then, "Miss Hall, are you all right in there?"

From inside . . . "Help! For God's sake, help!"

Red pulled his Colt and said, "Stand back." He lifted his leg and crashed his booted foot into the flimsy door and it shattered, splintering from its hinges, and hung askew. Buttons tossed the door aside and Red charged into the room. He took in the situation at a glance.

The Great Stefano, a large and powerful man, had Erica Hall pinned to the wall, his left hand around her throat, a broad-bladed knife in his right hand, pressed against her belly. Blood trickled from the point. There had been a struggle and the woman's scarlet robe lay puddled on the floor. She was naked, a matching look of naked terror on her face.

Stefano, a man wearing a grotesque mask of insane hatred, turned and snarled, "Get back or I'll gut her right now."

"Drop the knife," Red said.

Stefano's hand tightened on Erica's throat, the knife pressing deep, drawing more blood.

Red knew he had only one shot. And it had to be an accurate, instant killer. The thought seared through his brain that it was impossible. Erica was way too close to her assailant.

Then Buttons moved.

He bent over, scooped up the robe from the floor, and tossed it at Stefano's face. The robe fluttered through the air like a crimson bat and the man swung his knife at it, slashing it aside.

Red fired. A hit.

The bullet slammed into Stefano's right shoulder and for a split second the man lowered his knife. Erica clamped both her hands around her assailant's wrists and tried to push them away. Stefano shook her off, roared his anger, and the knife came up fast.

Red fired again. His bullet plowed into Stefano's right side, smashing through ribs, entering deep, the .45 bullet destroying a lung. Even for such a strong man, it was a mortal wound and it instantly weakened him. Erica managed to push Stefano off her and Red fired again. A hit to the chest. Stefano staggered until his back slammed into the wall. Red shot him again and the man slowly slid to the floor, leaving a snail trail of blood on the wall behind him. The knife was still in Stefano's hand and with the last vestige of his strength he tried to throw it at Erica. But the blade fell from his dead fingers and clattered harmlessly between his legs.

Running footsteps and raised voices sounded outside and Rosie Lee was the first to run into the dressing room. She looked at the dead man and then at Erica, her eyes lingering on the wound at the left side of the woman's belly. She picked up Erica's robe, helped her into it, and then guided her to her chair. As Rosie dabbed away at Erica's trickle of blood with a makeup cloth, a few others, including Dave Weathers and the distraught doorman, crowded into the small room.

"What . . . what happened?" Weathers said.

"Stefano tried to kill me," Erica said. "He almost succeeded."

"Why?" Weathers said. "I don't understand."

"Stefano blamed me for him not getting hired," Erica said. Her voice was very calm, matter-of-fact. "He said I betrayed him and that Mr. Grotte took a set against him because of me." She looked at Red. "You saved my life."

Red couldn't read her eyes. They betrayed nothing . . . fear, anger, relief, gratitude, none of that . . . just two beautiful pebbles in a riverbed.

"He was obviously touched in the head," Red said. "It seems I shot a madman." Then saying something that had to be said, "Stefano showed grit at Jenks's station, made a play and killed his man. He might have saved us all that night."

"Mr. Ryan, don't blame yourself. Stefano was crazy

with jealousy," Rosie said. "He blamed Erica for all his troubles and I guess he just couldn't live with that." She looked at the man's bloody body and shook her head. "Poor man, poor deluded man."

A couple of minutes later Vincenzu Grotte arrived with a huge bouquet of red roses to find a dead man on the floor and his new star bleeding from a stomach wound.

"What happened here?" Grotte said. "By God, someone will hang for this."

Her voice emotionless, Erica said, "His name's Stefano. You didn't want his knife-throwing act, remember?"

"No, I don't remember," Grotte said. He said to Weathers, "Do you remember his act?"

"He was here with Miss Hall and a juggler," Weathers said. "But they didn't audition for you."

Grotte was suddenly aware of the flowers in his arms and handed them to Erica. "Here, these are for you."

"Stefano tried to kill me and Mr. Ryan shot him," Erica said. She dropped the flowers on her dresser without much enthusiasm.

"Who's Ryan?" Grotte said.

"That would be me," Red said.

Grotte's bloodshot eyes scalded Red from the scuffed toes of his boots to the top of his plug hat. "What the hell are you?"

Buttons answered that question. "Mr. Ryan and me are representatives of the Abe Patterson and Son Stage and Express Company. I'm a driver and he's my messenger and he's sober most of the time and had a good mother. That's what he is."

Without taking his eyes off Red, Grotte said to Weathers, "Call the police."

"I already have," the manager said.

"Erica, how bad are you hurt?" Grotte said. "Don't tell me I have to cancel tonight's performance."

"It's only a scratch," the woman said. "I can dance."

"Thank God for that," Grotte said. "We sold a lot of tickets. Mr. Weathers, remove the stiff and prop up this door. Miss Hall has to get ready for her debut. Let me see that wound." Erica opened her robe and Grotte took a look. "It's nothing. You can cover that up with makeup and nobody will ever see it." He grinned. "Use your fans a lot down there."

Weathers came back inside. "The police are on their way!"

"I have to go," Grotte said. "Erica, good luck. I'll see you after the show."

Chapter Thirty-One

The same grim police sergeant and the same four constables were not glad to see Red Ryan and Buttons Muldoon. In fact they were downright hostile.

"You two again," the sergeant said. "Is this your handiwork?"

"Yes, I shot him," Red said. "His name is Stefano and he was about to murder Miss Hall. He didn't give me any choice."

"Seems like all the men you ventilate don't give you any choice," the sergeant said. "Is that true?"

"No," Red said.

"You mean sometimes you have a choice?"

"No. It means that what you said isn't true."

"Sergeant, Mr. Ryan saved my life," Erica said. "Now can we get that body out of here? I'm due onstage in less than an hour."

The four constables dragged the body outside the door and Dave Weathers said, "I'll send for an undertaker."

"Do that," the sergeant said. "And unless the deceased has money in his pockets, you'll have to bury him at your own expense." He waved a hand in the direction of Red and Buttons. "Unless these two foot the bill."

"Now, see here, Mr. Ryan saved Miss Hall's life, as you just heard her say," Buttons said. "We're not responsible for burying him."

"You're responsible for killing him," the sergeant said. "He's all shot to pieces."

Buttons's anger, always simmering below the surface, bubbled over. "Sergeant, do you have a brain in your thick head? Didn't you listen to what I just said?"

"I heard what you said and who's to say that you and the lady are not in cahoots, that all three of you plotted to murder Mr. Stevens."

"Stefano," Buttons said. "Stefano, Stefano, you can't even get the name right."

"I didn't plot to kill anyone," Erica said. "Stefano came here to murder me."

"Why?" the sergeant said.

"Because he was angry that Mr. Grotte hired me and not him," Erica said.

"Vincenzu Grotte?"

"Yes. The owner of this theater. Do you know him?"

"I know of him," the sergeant said, his face impassive. "Are you and Grotte friends?"

"He's my employer."

"Nothing more?"

Erica's anger flared. "Sergeant, what are you imply-ing?"

"Ma'am, I'm implying nothing. I let City Marshal Erichson do all the implying."

"Are you arresting me for almost being murdered?"

"No, ma'am, not at this present time," the sergeant said.

"Red, we'd better go find our seats," Buttons said. "We don't want to miss the show."

"That's out of the question," the sergeant said. "You're coming with me to Caroline Street. I'm sure City Marshal Erichson will be glad to see you again."

"We've committed no crime and we're going nowhere with you," Buttons said.

"Do I have to resort to manacles again?" the sergeant said.

"Try that and you'll be sorry," Buttons said.

"Put the irons on both of them," the sergeant said.

"I won't wear manacles and be damned to you," Buttons said, his dukes up.

It was unfortunate for him that, like the last time, the same constable used the same nightstick to render him, as the *Houston Age Semiweekly* would later report, "hors de combat."

"You boys are killing me," City Marshal Alexander Erichson said. He looked glum, for all the world like an older version of Colonel Custer when he first realized he'd lost the Battle of the Little Bighorn.

"And your boys are killing me," Buttons Muldoon said. "Now I've got two bumps on my head."

"Just as well you have a thick skull, Mr. Muldoon. When will you learn that you can't assault the police?"

"When you stop hiring motherless blockheads?"

"You're not helping your case."

"Case? There is no case. Red Ryan saved Miss Hall's life. That's a natural fact, not a case."

Erichson sighed. "That indeed seems to be the truth of the matter. I believe Mr. Stefano went to the Diamond Theater with the sole intention of murdering Erica Hall. Miss Rosie Lee said he was very angry and she heard him say the day Miss Hall was hired that he'd soon take her down a peg or two. That sounds like a threat to me. When are you two leaving Houston?"

"As soon as the army lets us go," Red said.

"When will that be?"

"A couple of days, we hope."

"Can you two stay out of trouble for a couple of days?"

"Somehow it has a way of finding us," Red said.

"It's the cursed Gray Ghost to blame. The stage is haunted," Buttons said. "It didn't even allow us to see Erica Hall's dance."

"Yes, you told me about the stagecoach before," Erichson said. "Ah well, I suppose it will be better for all of us, including the city of Houston, when you finally leave."

"You're letting us go?" Red said.

"Given the testimony of Miss Hall and others, I see no reason to detain you. You want to hear something funny? Well, it's not funny, but it's interesting."

"Then let's hear it," Red said.

"Up El Paso way, I think it was the summer of '79, I saw a lynch mob hang a man for being a damned nuisance. That was the only charge against him, nothing else, and him with a wife and three snot-nosed kids."

"Is that a threat?" Red said.

"No . . . but it sure gives a man something to think about when he's knotting his necktie." The marshal smiled. "Don't be nuisances, boys. Enough is enough."

"We can leave now?" Buttons said.

"Yes, jehu, go with God. And don't forget to pay your fine on the way out. You know the drill."

"What fine?" Buttons said.

"A ten-dollar fine for assaulting a police officer."

"I didn't assault a police officer and I don't have ten dollars," Button said.

Erichson sighed again. "Then mail it from San Angelo. The clerk will give you the address. For pity's sake, don't return to Houston to pay it in person and become a damned nuisance again."

Buttons opened his mouth to say something but Red cut him off.

"I'll make sure Mr. Muldoon sends the money by tele-graphic transfer," Red said. "There's no need for him to come back to Houston.

"Thank God for that," City Marshal Erichson said.

CHAPTER THIRTY-TWO

After taking several curtain calls amid raucous do-it-again yells from male members of the audience, Erica Hall changed quickly and hurried out of the theater. Grotte had said he was uneasy about leaving the heroin in her hotel, so he'd pick up the drug and then come for her with his carriage, but she decided not to wait. By now, Rosie Lee must have been very upset, and Erica had to try to make her feel better. The girl's performance had been terrible, her voice weak, out of tune, and boos had cascaded down on her like a hailstorm. To make matters worse, she'd been sick all over the stage as she bolted for the wings.

Since Erica's was the final act, she'd had no chance to sit Rosie down and tell her it was all right, that every entertainer had at one time or another given a bad performance. She was probably now lying on the hotel room bed sobbing her heart out.

"I saw her leave, Miss Hall." Shaken by the Stefano incident, the old man called Jacob now guarded the side door like a hellhound. "She was crying and very disturbed," he said.

"I know. I heard the catcalls," Erica said. "It was heart-breaking." Then, "Jacob, will you get me a cab?"

"Sure thing, Miss Hall."

Jacob stepped outside, pushed his way through a handful of stage-door johnnies, and hailed a cab. Holding her admirers at bay, the old man helped Erica into the vehicle. "Where to, Miss Hall?"

"The Grand Hotel."

"To the Grand Hotel, cabbie," Jacob yelled, over a sudden rumble of thunder that crashed into the warm, humid night.

"Walk on," the cabbie said to his horse.

"Hurry, please," Erica said. "It's a matter of the greatest moment."

She had a premonition . . . but of what she didn't know.

Rosie Lee was dead.

The girl was sprawled on the floor on her back, her mouth rimmed with white heroin. Police would later say that Rosie Lee was a first-time user and obviously had no idea how to administer the drug . . . so she swallowed it in handfuls and washed it down with water. Death came very quickly.

An opened kilo bag lay next to the body and Erica's steamer trunk hung open.

She kneeled beside Rosie and whispered over and over again, "My God, oh my God, forgive me." She knew the catcalls at the Diamond had driven the girl to suicide, but it was the heroin, the heroin she stole, that had killed her.

Rosie's face was very pale and under the dusting of powder her lips had turned blue. Her eyes were wide open, scared, staring into eternity. She was young, barely twenty-two, but she did not leave a pretty corpse.

Devastated, feeling like a murderer, feeling like death itself, Erica Hall rose to her feet. She and Rosie had joked about the size of Erica's carpetbag, now she picked it up from the floor and tossed its contents onto the bed. Quickly, fearing that Grotte might get there before she did what she had to do, she took the bags of heroin from the steamer trunk, included the bag Rosie had opened, stuffed them into the carpetbag, and buckled it shut. With the uncut heroin, the bag weighed in excess of twenty pounds, but Erica was strong and found it easy to handle.

Erica took a last lingering look at Rosie Lee's body and immediately dashed away the tears from her eyes. She must remain stoic to do what had to be done.

She grabbed her purse, walked downstairs to the foyer, and immediately drew the attention of the suddenly wide-awake night clerk. "You're not leaving us, Miss Hall, are you?" he said. "It's storming out there."

Right on cue lightning flashed and a powerful thunderclap shook the building.

Erica Hall's beautiful face was expressionless, blank, like a Mona Lisa without the smile. "Is there a church nearby?" she said.

"What denomination?" the clerk said.

"Any denomination."

"It's raining. There's nothing within walking distance."

"I could get a cab."

"In this city during a thunderstorm? It's unlikely. Because of the streetcars there aren't many cabs."

"Then I'll walk."

Erica moved toward the door, but the clerk's voice stopped her. "Wait. There's what Mexicans call a church on the corner of this block. But white folks don't ever go there."

"I'll go there," said Erica.

"It's called the Temple of Santa Maria de Guadalupe." The clerk grinned. "If you can call an adobe shack with a tin roof in the middle of a muddy waste a temple."

"Does it have a priest?" Erica said.

"Yes, he's old and I see him walk past the hotel now and again. I hear his place will soon be demolished to make way for a cotton warehouse."

"What's his name?"

"I have no idea. Call him Padre, I guess. But I strongly suggest you wait for morning, Miss Hall. Begging your pardon, but what's the big rush?"

"I need to see a clergyman, that's all," Erica said.

Thunder banged and a lightning flash briefly shimmered in the foyer like the flicker of an unsteady lantern. The air smelled of ozone and the musty odor of the rain.

"Be careful, Miss Hall. It's not real safe out there this late for a lady alone," the clerk said. He was young and earnest, taking his job seriously.

Erica reached the doorway and then turned. "Miss Rosie Lee killed herself in my room earlier tonight. You may want to inform the police."

She opened the door and stepped into the storm.

The night clerk was already running up the stairs.

CHAPTER THIRTY-THREE

Erica Hall walked through the teeming, lightning-seared night to the Temple of Santa Maria de Guadalupe, a pretentious name for a stucco building, much in need of repair, with a hipped roof of rusty corrugated iron. It had a single door to the front and a small window at the rear behind the altar. A squat, timber bell tower had been added at some point, but it had no bell. The ramshackle building was isolated on a patch of muddy waste ground like a shipwreck that had been cast on a treacherous shore.

The door was unlocked and Erica pushed it open. Hinges creaked and the door opened only halfway before it jammed on the uneven threshold. Erica shoved the carpetbag inside and then turned sideways and slid through the entrance. The nave was as black as spilled ink but a flare of lightning illuminated the building for an instant, long enough to reveal a row of benches and an altar overhung by a large wooden cross. To the left of the altar an interior door hung ajar and the relentless rain rattled on the tin roof and the church smelled of incense and dry rot. A rustling in a corner of the building suggested rats.

Erica called into the darkness. "Is anybody here?" She let a full minute pass and then said, "Anybody?"

After a few moments a rectangle of dim yellow light appeared in the back doorway and a man's voice, weak with illness or age or both, said, "Who comes to my church?"

"Are you a clergyman?" Erica said.

"I am Father Martinez Rojas, a priest of Holy Mother Church."

"I must talk with you, Father, on a most singular matter."

"Could it not wait until morning?" Father Rojas said, mildly. He was a small, bent old man with a shock of white hair, and was wearing a threadbare, ankle-length nightshirt and rope sandals. He held a candlestick with a single candle, much melted, and gray smoke lifted from its bud of flame and tied knots in the listless air.

"No, it can't wait," Erica said. "It's a matter of the greatest moment."

"Then perhaps your being here is the will of God," the priest said. "We will talk in the sacristy. I have a kitchen, but it's small and the roof leaks."

Father Rojas led the way to a small room used to keep vestments, sacred vessels, and parish records. The priest placed the candle in the middle of a small, round table and bade Erica to sit in the only chair while he stood. The candle produced light and shade, highlighted the woman's high cheekbones and lustrous eyes, and made an oil painting of her beauty. The same faint light accentuated every craggy wrinkle and hollow of the old man's face, revealing much hardship and shared sorrow.

"Before we talk, a treat." Father Rojas smiled. He opened a wardrobe and from somewhere in its depths he produced a bottle and two glasses. "Tequila, a present from one of my parishioners. Would you care for some?"

"Very much so," Erica said. Her dress was soaking wet and the room was cold.

The priest poured the tequila and then said, "Are you of the Catholic faith?"

"I have no faith."

The old man smiled. "A subject for a future discussion, perhaps. Now, how can I help you?"

Erica took a sip from her glass and then pushed the carpetbag with her toe. "Father Rojas, in there are ten kilos of heroin powder and please don't ask me how I got it." She looked into the priest's face. "It's an addictive drug. Do you understand what that means?"

"Yes, like opium and morphine. I understand because I have seen them destroy lives, even among my own people."

"I want you to help me get rid of this drug."

"But why me?"

"Because I can't do it myself. I could take it down to the bayou and throw it in the water, but I'm afraid of being seen. Besides, I'd never find my way in the dark."

Father Rojas smiled. "I ask again . . . why me?"

"Because you're a clergyman and I can trust you."

"But why now? Why tonight?"

"Because tonight, a girl I knew and liked, used this heroin to kill herself. Father, there's no other way to put how I feel . . . I'm filled with remorse and my heart is broken."

Father Rojas crossed himself. "Then I will not break it further. I will not say that your friend is lost to God or that you have committed a great sin, because who am I to say what is in the mind of Our Savior?"

"I have another reason why the heroin must be destroyed tonight," Erica said. "Very soon a man will come here looking for it to use for his own purposes and that's why we've so very little time. There's not a moment to be lost."

Father Rojas caught the urgency in the woman's voice and said, "Behind the church is an area of swampland that the developers who want this land refer to as the Houston Mire, a great exaggeration. We can dispose of it there. I'll fetch a lantern."

By lantern light, in a torrential downpour, Erica Hall and Father Martinez Rojas fed the heroin, bag by bag, into the mud of the morass behind the church. The swamp eagerly devoured the deadly drug, and it was the work of just a few minutes to dispose of the powder and then the carpetbag that carried it.

When Erica Hall and Father Rojas returned to the church, there was still no sign of Vincenzu Grotte, but Erica knew the hotel night clerk would tell him where she was headed, and he could arrive anytime.

"Father, will you tell a lie for me?" she said. Question marks of wet hair hung over her forehead and her wet dress clung to her body like a second skin.

The priest smiled. "That very much depends on the lie."

"When a man comes here looking for me, will you tell him I'm gone? My life may depend on it."

"A venial sin at most," the priest said. "I'm sure the good Lord will understand. Yes, I'll tell this man you were here seeking shelter from the storm and that you left a while ago."

"Thank you, Father," Erica said. "I have one more thing to ask of you. May I stay the night here? I can sleep on a bench."

"I can surely do a little better than a bench," the priest said. "Adjoining the sacristy was a room that years ago I partitioned into two bedrooms, one for myself and one for the bishop when he visits. Well, the bishop has never visited, but the church ladies keep the bed made up on the chance that one day he will." Father Rojas threw up his hands in mock panic. "Oh, that sounds like a criticism of His Excellency the bishop, but it's not. He's a busy man and this is a small church."

"Then I'll be honored to sleep in the bishop's bed tonight," Erica said.

What she'd just said sounded so ludicrous and it made her laugh, a small laugh, to be sure, but Father Rojas took it as a sign that the woman's guilt-ravaged soul was capable of healing.

The bed was clean and comfortable and Erica Hall lay between the sheets naked, her clothing hanging on hooks, hopefully to dry a little. She'd destroyed the heroin and knew the dangers she faced. She'd no doubt that Grotte would kill her if he could, and he would have the backing of Antonio Matranga. Luke Powell was probably in Houston, hell-bent on revenge for the loss of his eye. She didn't know what story he'd put out to Matranga, but he'd tried to rape her and the curling iron came to her defense. Stealing the heroin had been a mistake and with poor Rosie Lee's terrible death she was now paying for it.

Vincenzu Grotte, Antonio Matranga, Luke Powell, she had powerful enemies aplenty in Houston, and no friends. Ask the police for protection? There would be too many questions asked and maybe one of them would be about what she'd done in Fort Smith. That one would be difficult to answer.

Then Erica had a thought.

There were two men that might help her . . . Red Ryan and Buttons Muldoon.

A rough-and-ready pair to be sure, but like many western men she'd met, they seemed to live by a simple code: take pride in your work, live each day with courage, and be prepared to do what has to be done. Red had already saved her life once and he might be willing to do it again.

Yes, that was it. She would try to reach them tomorrow. Erica finally slept with hope in her heart.

CHAPTER THIRTY-FOUR

When dawn broke and Houston awakened under a lemon-colored sky, Luke Powell left his hotel and ate an almond biscotti and drank coffee at a nearby café. He'd left his gun in his room, since he was certain he'd be searched before a meeting with Vincenzu Grotte. He was aware that his pants, shirt, vest, and boots showed the wear and tear of the prairie. His shabby clothing was a far cry from the broadcloth frock coats and spotless linen he'd worn in Fort Smith, and to someone like Grotte he must look like a rube from the sticks. But he was not. He was *siciliano*, still an associate of the capo dei capi Antonio Matranga, and he could meet Grotte on almost equal terms. His wardrobe could wait until Erica Hall was taken care of and the heroin safely in his possession.

But when he stepped off the streetcar and stood in front of Grotte's mansion, Powell's confidence eroded. It seemed that there was a face at every window watching his every move . . . watching and waiting.

Powell swallowed hard and knocked on the door. A few long moments passed and then Henry Trapp, big, unfriendly, and menacing, stood in the doorway. He looked

Powell up and down and said, "Mr. Grotte is breakfasting and must not be disturbed."

"It's urgent that I see him," Powell said.

"The very fact that you're here suggests it's urgent."

Trapp didn't look like he was going to budge from blocking the doorway and Powell grew desperate. "It's about Leoluca Vitale," he said.

"Is he dead?" Trapp said.

"No. He isn't dead. We lost him."

"Lost him? Do you mean mislaid him somewhere?"

"I mean he shot one of my men and then ran into the dark and we lost him."

Trapp's smile was slight, bordering on contempt. "Vitale ran from you?"

"Yes, he did. He ran from me."

"Bad news, Mr. Powell."

"I know."

"This is more bad news for Mr. Grotte. He will not be pleased."

"That's why I'm here. To tell him what happened."

"To give him your excuse."

"Something like that."

"Mr. Grotte is interested only in successes, not excuses."

"All right, the fault was mine. But I still need to see him."

"You better come in. Walk inside and stand in the foyer. I'll see if he wants to talk with you."

Trapp closed the door behind Powell and said, "Face me."

Powell did as the man asked.

"Now, spread your arms wide like you were about to be crucified."

"I'm not carrying a weapon."

"Spread your arms."

"This is humiliating."

"Losing Leoluca Vitale in the darkness was humiliating. This is the price of failure. Raise your arms."

Seeing no other option, Powell spread his arms and Trapp searched him thoroughly. "All right, wait here," the butler said. He smiled. "If I'd found even a barlow knife in your pocket, I would've shot you dead on the spot."

"Good to know," Powell said.

Trapp nodded. "It is indeed."

He returned a couple of minutes later and said, "Mr. Grotte will see you now. I warn you, Powell, he's not in the best of moods."

Vincenzu Grotte stood hip-leaning against a solid round mahogany table in his library, the bookshelves on all four walls heavy with thick volumes that he may or may not have read. He wore a dark-colored dressing gown in heavy silk with a padded shawl collar and the bulge in the right pocket betrayed the hideout gun he carried. Niles Piper took up his usual stand at the door, a Colt in a shoulder holster. He didn't look friendly and neither did Grotte.

"You lost Vitale," Grotte said. "That's what I've been told."

"Yes. He ran into the dark and it was misty last night, so he gave us the slip."

"And now he knows I betrayed him. Suddenly I'm a

target of probably the most dangerous triggerman in the Sicilian Mafia. How do you think that makes me feel?"

Powell didn't answer that.

"Where is Erica Hall?"

Powell's utter surprise showed. "I don't know. I thought you'd know."

"A man tried to kill her last night. There were coppers everywhere. And then after her turn onstage she fled the theater in a hurry."

"You tried her hotel?"

"What a foolish question. Of course I tried her hotel and found a dead woman in her room, a singer by the name of Rosie Lee. She got booed at the Diamond last night and then overdosed on heroin. Needless to say Erica Hall checked out in a thunderstorm carrying only a large carpetbag and left no forwarding address."

"She couldn't have gotten far," Powell said.

"I know she stopped at a Mex church and asked for shelter," Grotte said. "The priest said she'd been there for a while but had already gone."

"And you believed him?"

"Damn you, Powell, what kind of Catholic are you? The priest was Mexican, sure, but he was still an ordained holy father. He wasn't lying, if that's what you mean."

"Did he give any indication of where she went?"

"No. She left the church and walked into the night and I returned here under a damned thunderstorm that made me think of death and Judgment Day."

Powell said, "You searched her hotel room?"

"There was no sign of the heroin, only a stiff. The night clerk had summoned the police and I didn't care to linger."

"We have to find her," Powell said.

Grotte's voice was mocking. "We have to find her. Here's who you have to find . . . his name is Leoluca Vitale. Now, as triggermen go, I know you're not in his class, but step up, man, step up. *Capiche?* Go after him. Start at his hotel and dog his footsteps and then kill him." Grotte smiled. "Or I'll kill you." He turned his head, not taking his eyes off Powell. "Ain't that right, Niles?"

"Just as you say, boss," Piper said.

"What about the heroin?" Powell said.

"Forget about the heroin, and Erica Hall. I'll take care of it. She'll show up someplace and I'll be waiting."

"Vitale will have changed hotels by now," Powell said. "His trail will be cold."

"Then make like a Pinkerton detective and investigate," Grotte said. "I want the heroin, but I won't rest easy until Leoluca Vitale is dead, dead, dead."

"Maybe he'll come here," Powell said.

"Damn it, Powell, you were around Tony Matranga and you don't know how a soldier like Vitale works? Of course he'll come here, or to the Diamond, or to one of my other businesses around town, but he'll come, even if he has to follow me to the gates of hell he'll come. The only way to stop men like Vitale is to kill them. And when you've shot them, shoot them all over again. They might try to rise from the dead."

"I'm not used to these people," Powell said. "A hundred miles west of here, I'd catch Vitale in a saloon or a dance hall and tell him to go for his iron and then I'd outdraw and kill him. It would be up-front and open, man-to-man, no skulking around in shadows like here. How the hell can I flush Vitale from his hiding place if he won't come into the light and fight like a man?"

"Houston is no longer the frontier, Powell," Grotte said. "You've got to adapt to modern times, and maybe a one-eyed man sees better in the shadows. You've got one simple task, Luciano . . . see, I address you by your honorable Sicilian name . . . remove Leoluca Vitale from the face of the earth and do it quick." Grotte turned, "Mr. Piper, see this gentleman out."

"How long do I have?" Powell said.

"To live?" Grotte said.

"No, to find Vitale."

"Report back to me in two days and tell me he's dead."

"That's not long enough."

"Two days. And incidentally, that's how long you'll live if you don't find him and finish him off." Grotte waved a dismissive hand. "Now, get the hell out of here."

CHAPTER THIRTY-FIVE

Sitting in damp clothes in the church's makeshift kitchen, a small stove and a table with two chairs, Erica Hall shared Father Rojas's breakfast of coffee, chilaquiles, and refried beans provided by one of his parishioners, a plump matron he called Senora Lopez. She was obviously curious about Erica, the first white woman to set foot in the church in many years, maybe the first ever. But the priest offered no explanation and Senora Lopez held her tongue.

"The rain is stopped and the sun is shining," Father Rojas said. "Where will you go, Senorita Hall?"

"Best you don't know, Father," Erica said. "For your own sake." She tried her coffee, made with cinnamon and raw dark sugar, and found it surprisingly good. Then, "I'll get in touch with two men I know and ask for their protection."

"Are they good men?"

"Most of the time, I suppose they are. One of them, Red Ryan, has already saved my life."

"Ryan . . . an Irish-sounding name."

"His friend is called Muldoon, also an Irish name."

The priest nodded. "Then I will pray to Saint Brigid, the patron saint of fugitives, for you. She is one of Ireland's most famous saints, second only to holy Saint Patrick himself."

Erica smiled. "You know your Irish saints, Father Rojas."

"When I was a younger man, before I was ordained, I laid track for the Baltimore and Ohio Railroad and many of my fellow gandy dancers were Irishmen. Big, brawny muchachos they were, and very religious. They told me about their Saint Patrick and Saint Brigid, the nun who fed the poor and healed the sick, and many others beside." Father Rojas tilted his head to one side like an inquisitive bird. "Will you listen to a suggestion?"

"Of course. I'll listen to anything you say."

"Then make your way to Grand Central Station and buy a railroad ticket to anywhere. When you decide you're far enough away from Texas, step off the train and begin a new life."

"Father, I already thought about that, but I'd be looking over my shoulder for the rest of that new life, waiting for the bullet to end it. My troubles must be resolved right here in Houston. I can't and won't run away from them."

"My child, if you stay here, your troubles could be the death of you," Father Rojas said.

"I know that, Father," Erica said. "But a woman like me, the things I've done . . . Well, everyone lives but not everyone deserves to live."

"Pray to God to forgive the sins of your past. What's done is done, there's no going back to change things, to make them better. There's good in you, Senorita Hall, I can sense it. I think you've as much right to live as anyone else."

"And so had Rosie Lee. If I hadn't stolen the heroin and fled to Houston, she'd still be alive. I killed her just as surely as though I'd taken a gun and shot her."

"I will pray that you soon find peace within yourself," Father Rojas said.

A piece of tortilla was stuck to the corner of the priest's mouth and Erica smiled and brushed it away. "Thank you for all your help, Father Rojas," she said. "Now I have to be on my way."

"You'll seek out the Irishmen?"

"Yes, I will."

"How will you get there?"

"Hopefully I can hail a cabbie. All my luggage is at the Grand Hotel and I can't go back there."

"Senora Lopez's son is helping her put flowers on the altar. I can send him to bring a cab."

"That would be very kind of you, Father. I look a sight and would rather not stand in the street trying to flag down a cab."

The cab arrived ten minutes later and Erica kissed Father Rojas on the cheek and said, "Thank you for all your help. As long as I live, I'll never forget you."

"Nor I, you, Senorita," the priest said. "*Vaya con Dios.* I will pray for you."

CHAPTER THIRTY-SIX

The morning sun did nothing to lighten Buttons Muldoon's mood. He was livid and he gave army sergeant Gunther Brandt both barrels of his anger. "How much longer, you blockhead? I want my damned stage back." His voice dropped. "Even if it is accursed and has brought me nothing but bad luck."

"Then I have good news for you, Mr. Muldoon. You'll be free to leave tomorrow."

"Well, about time."

"Or the next day."

Buttons exploded. "Or the day after that, you knuckle-head! What are you trying to tell me?"

"These things take time," the sergeant said. "Paper-work, you know, and army regulations."

"How can bringing two women to a stage take time? The trip to Fort Concho takes time, changing teams takes time, but loading females into a stage takes no time at all."

"The army doctor is back on his feet and he'll examine the women today," Brandt said.

"Why was he off his feet?"

"A minor ailment. A touch of the croup, I believe."

"He didn't show up for work because of the croup?"

"I'm afraid so, Mr. Muldoon."

"I've been shot and showed up for work the next day."

"Well, let me assure you that the doctor is well again and he's as keen as mustard to get the job done. He'll examine those ladies and write up his report in triplicate in no time at all. And then . . ."

"You damned bonehead, this is ridiculous."

"And then you'll be free to go." Sergeant Brandt saluted. "And now I must be on my way. Busy, busy, busy, you know. A soldier's work is never done."

"Seems to me a soldier's work never starts," Buttons yelled. But he was talking to the sergeant's retreating back.

Red Ryan stepped out of the depot cabin and said, "Good morning. You look like the cat just ate your canary."

"Maybe we can leave tomorrow, or maybe the next day, the army says. That lunkhead sergeant says the doctor was down with the croup and couldn't examine the two women and write them up in triplicate."

"So when is the sawbones examining the soldiers' wives?" Red said.

"Today, if he don't come down with something else."

Tom Scriver walked out of the barn and said, "Coffee back there in the office."

"I could use some," Red said.

"Wait," Scriver said. "How would you boys like to earn a dollar?"

"Each?" Buttons said.

"Yeah, each."

"I'm game," Buttons said.

"Me, too," Red said. "What's the job?"

"Cleaning out the stalls. You wheelbarrow the dung to

the pile over there, ready for the out-of-town farmers and the in-town gardeners to come in and pick it up. The good news is that I have two wheelbarrows so you'll complete the job in no time at all."

"How come you ain't doing it?" Buttons said.

"I'm sparking a young lady across town and I'm meeting her for lunch. You wouldn't want me to go a-courting smelling like horse dung, would you?"

"No, you go meet your lady friend and we'll smell like horse dung," Buttons said.

"Crackerjack!" Scriver said, his young face alight. "I knew I could depend on you boys."

Red said, "That will be two dollars."

Buttons motioned in the direction of the livery. "How many stalls?"

"Just twenty and you might want to clean up the corral."

"The corral will be fifty cents extry," Buttons said. "That's a lot of work."

"All right, I'll go two-fifty, but then I'm done," Scriver said, frowning.

"Pay us," Red said.

The youth gave Red the money and then said, "You'll find that the stalls haven't been cleaned in some time, but I'm sure you boys will do a *bueno* job." He smiled. "Well, gotta go. I have a streetcar to catch."

After Scriver left, Buttons walked into the barn and walked back out again. "Have you seen them stalls?" he said. "What does that kid do all day?"

"Bad, huh?" Red said.

"Maybe the worst I've seen."

"How many horses in there?"

"Seven, all of them making more stuff to be shoveled."

"Coffee first," Red said. He pulled a Bull Durham sack from his shirt pocket and shook his head. "Damn, I'm running out of tobacco."

"Well, as soon as we get this job done, buy yourself a sack," Buttons said. "Now we're rich we can afford five cents."

Red rolled a quirly, lit up, and then said, "Coffee first. I can't shovel horse dung on an empty stomach."

Ignoring the two grinning young sentries, Buttons and Red pushed their third heaped wheelbarrow load to the dung pile when a cab pulled up and Erica Hall stepped out.

Maybe it was just a trick of the wind, but Buttons was sure the Gray Ghost whispered something, a warning maybe, at the sight of her.

As for Red, he ran his fingers through his unruly hair, replaced his derby hat, and wished he smelled better.

Chapter Thirty-Seven

Erica Hall's dazzling beauty was under siege. She was pale, dark shadows under her eyes, and her full lips looked bloodless. Her obvious fatigue had robbed her of vitality and she looked tired, beaten down. Gone was the elegant dancer who filled the stage like a golden flame, and in her place a woman who seemed close to the breaking point, teetering on the edge of the precipice. Her hair, normally brushed to a lustrous, amber cascade, hung around her shoulders limp and lank and lifeless and her clothes were damp, mud-stained, clinging to her body like a wrinkled skin.

Buttons Muldoon, as tactful as ever, said, "What in God's name happened to you?"

Without thinking, Erica unloaded what was uppermost in her mind. "Rosie Lee is dead. She committed suicide." Then, "Is there a place I could sit? I'm very tired."

Red was stunned, as was Buttons, but Red said, "Of course. Let me help you into the stage depot."

"You're very kind," Erica said.

She took Red's arm and he led her into the cabin. Inside there were two iron cots, a table and two chairs, and in one corner a potbellied stove. Red's Greener and two cartridge belts and holstered guns lay on the table and he removed them and dropped them onto a cot. The place smelled of horses, sweat, tobacco smoke, and gun oil.

"Can I get you a cup of coffee, Miss Hall?" Buttons said. "By the way, it's against the rules of the Abe Patterson and Son Stage and Express Company to allow non-employees to enter the depot. But I'm making an exception in your case."

"You've always been very caring of me, Mr. Muldoon, and I trust you'll continue to be in the future."

He didn't like the sound of that, but Buttons said, "Of course."

Red didn't like the sound of it, either, but left to get the coffee.

"Rosie Lee killed herself," Buttons Muldoon said sadly. "She was such a sweet little gal, it's hard to believe. Why? I mean, why?"

Erica Hall took a sip of coffee and carefully placed the cup on the table.

"She was booed off the stage on her debut, the same night Stefano tried to murder me," Erica said. "But the boos didn't kill her . . . I did."

That last was met with a thunderstruck silence and Erica's voice filled the void. "She stuffed a drug into her mouth, a drug called heroin. The drug was mine."

The woman studied the faces of the men. Buttons Muldoon looked dumbfounded as he tried to grapple with what she was saying. Red Ryan had only one visible reaction . . . bafflement.

But it was Red who spoke next. "Drugs . . . heroin . . . I don't understand."

"Me, neither," Buttons said.

"Opium is a drug and so is morphine," Erica said. "Heroin is a new drug and it's just as dangerous and addictive." She saw Red drawing a blank and said, "*Addictive* means that you want, crave, more and more of the drug and pretty soon you become its slave."

"Rosie Lee was addicted?" Red said.

"No. But I told her what heroin was and its effects and she knew it could kill her."

Buttons said, "Where did you get this drug . . . What's it called again?"

"Heroin. A rich and powerful man in New Orleans called Antonio Matranga hired me to sell his drugs in Fort Smith, at first opium and morphine and later the new drug, heroin. That's when I met Luke Powell. I'd had lovers before, including the great French composer Charles-Marie Widor, but none of them were like Luke. I thought him dangerous and exciting and soon we became lovers." Her face tightened. "May God forgive me."

"And then you put Powell's eye out," Buttons said.

"Because of Luke's unfaithfulness I'd ended our affair and he tried to rape me. The curling iron was the only weapon I had at hand."

"But how did you get the . . . heroin?" Red said, stumbling on the unfamiliar word.

"Luke Powell could've killed me that day, but he didn't," Erica said. "He was too concerned about trying to save his eye. We had ten kilos of heroin, about twenty-two pounds, and I stole it." She brushed a stray hair off her forehead and shook her head, then said, "I don't know why I did it. To get out of the kind of life I was living in

Fort Smith, maybe. Or more likely I took the heroin to turn it into money. At the time I didn't think about it. I just grabbed it and ran."

"How much money are you talking about?" Buttons said.

"About a hundred thousand dollars when it's cut. That means mixed with something else, like powdered milk."

Buttons whistled through his teeth. "A hundred thousand, that's not chicken feed."

"It doesn't matter now, the heroin is all gone." Erica said.

"Gone where?" Buttons said.

"Last night I took it to a Mexican priest, and then we threw it into a swamp. Now only the frogs are happy."

"Why did you do that?" Red said.

"Because after the drug killed Rosie Lee, I came to the realization that I was planning to peddle death. I knew then that I had to get rid of it. I'm being sorry here, penitent, not sanctimonious."

"Beggin' your pardon, Miss Hall, but why are you here at all?" Buttons said.

"I need your protection because my life is in danger. There are men who will try to kill me for destroying the heroin."

"What men?" Red Ryan said. "You mean Luke Powell and the outlaws he rides with?"

"Him, and others who call themselves respectable businessmen. Vincenzu Grotte, for one."

"The ranny that owns the Diamond Theater?"

"Yes. And another is Antonio Matranga in New Orleans, who owned the heroin in the first place. I worked for him in Fort Smith, selling opium and morphine."

Buttons said, "What kind of handles are those? Vin . . . Vin . . . hell, I can't even say it."

"They're the names of men who brought the Sicilian Mafia to this country," Erica said. "Luke Powell's real name is Luciano Tiodoro and he is one of them."

Buttons almost yelped his surprise. "You mean Luke Powell ain't Luke Powell?"

"No, he's not," Erica said.

"So his real name is Lu . . . Lu . . . what you said."

"Yes, it is."

"And what's this Sicilian Mafia?" Red said. "I've never heard of it."

"It's a powerful criminal organization that began in Italy and has since spread to other countries, including the United States."

"Organization," Red said, obviously pondering on the word. "You mean like the James and Younger gang and them?"

"Nothing like the James and Younger gang. The Mafia is hundreds of times more dangerous than Jesse James ever was and they hold a grudge and don't play by any rules except their own."

"Iffen you don't mind me sayin' so, Miss Hall, it seems a whole passel of folks want you dead," Buttons said. "And I'm not trying to scare you."

"I'm already scared and that's why I'm asking for your protection. Apart from Father Rojas, the Catholic priest I told you about, you're the only men I trust."

Buttons thought about that and then said, "Miss Hall, as a representative of the Abe Patterson and Son Stage and Express Company, I advise that you go to the police and tell them bluecoats what you've just told us. If they don't beat you up with clubs, they'll protect you."

"They're more likely to throw me in jail when they check into my past," Erica said. "All it would take is a wire to Fort Smith. And you don't know how the Mafia does business. Their tentacles reach everywhere. Believe me, there's a good chance I'd be found hanging in my cell."

Buttons shook his head. "Well, we're right sorry we can't help you, ma'am," he said. "Now, me and Red have a chore to finish, so if you will, please excuse us."

"Hold on," Red said. He glared at Buttons. "What's the matter with you? We can't throw Miss Hall to the wolves."

"What can we do?" Buttons said. "We're leaving tomorrow or the next day. That doesn't give us a whole lot of time for protecting."

"I'd like to stay here until you leave," Erica said. "I need time to get myself together and try to come to terms with my guilt."

"You can come with us," Red said. "You'll be safe in San Angelo."

"Of course, Red means if you have the fare," Buttons said.

"I'm staying right here," Erica said. "I won't run away from the dangers I face."

Red began, "Miss Hall . . ."

"Erica, please."

"Erica, you can't buck the odds you're up against. No one could."

"I can handle it," the woman said. "I'm not going to let fear tie me in knots, and I'm not going to run for my life."

"Your funeral," Buttons said.

"Erica, you're a mighty brave woman," Red said.

"No, I'm not. But I'll survive this, don't worry." Then, "Red, I noticed the sun is shining on a section of the corral fence—would you do something for me?"

Erica Hall, wrapped in a blanket, sat in the cabin while Buttons shoveled horse dung and Red Ryan walked to the corral with a bundle of damp clothes in his arm . . . a dress, a chemise, drawers, corset, and several petti-coats. Garment by garment, he hung the clothing over the corral fence to dry, much to the delight of the two young soldiers.

"Gettin' ready for the ball, are ye?"

"Did you fall in a lake, shotgun man?"

"Nice dress. Is it yours?"

Red Ryan gritted his teeth and said nothing. Erica Hall was a mighty demanding woman.

CHAPTER THIRTY-EIGHT

Sleepless, Leoluca Vitale spent the entire night standing at his hotel window looking out at the pounding thunderstorm that hammered rain on the city and scarred its sky with razors of lightning. Come the dawn, the storm had gone and Houston, swept clean by the downpour, gleamed in the morning sunlight. People already thronged the streets, pale clerks, millworkers, mostly young girls in drab dresses and white aprons and the odd top-hatted businessman with a gold watch chain and huge belly, all competing for sidewalk space with yelling, running street urchins who seemed to appear out of nowhere. The mule-drawn and the latest electric streetcars were full enough that adventuresome youths clung onto their sides and yelled pleasantries to the mill girls. The slowly awakening city was already noisy, a boisterous, clanging clamor that Vitale could hear in his hotel room.

In the course of his dark-of-night vigil, he'd come to a decision and made plans to even the score with Vincenzu Grotte. The man had betrayed him and plotted his death, and by connection, capo dei capi Antonio Matranga. He was aware that Grotte had two triggermen protecting him and it would be a difficult task. But he consoled himself with the knowledge that he'd once killed four men in a much trickier situation than this.

As he stood at the window and watched Houston come to life, Vitale remembered the scene as though it were yesterday and not two years ago . . .

The man's name was Jason Hubbard and he owned a general store in New Orleans, and according to the accounts of people who knew him he was fond of children, especially sweet-natured little girls, and he gave them stick candy to encourage frequent visits. One of those girls was eight-year-old Mattie Cavalli, too young and innocent to know that not all men are good, that some are evil.

The day Mattie disappeared she'd walked into Hubbard's store in the hope of candy and was never seen to leave. The New Orleans police investigated and suspicion fell on Hubbard, but three of his cronies swore that he'd been playing cards with them on the day Mattie disappeared. Privately, the police knew that Hubbard was the girl's killer, but against the bulwark of his pals' evidence nothing could be proved.

Then Antonio Matranga got involved.

Mattie was the daughter of the woman who cleaned his office and he'd met the lively little girl and liked her. Not only that, but the girl's father, a hardworking Italian, a skilled metalworker, had asked Matranga for the justice the law could not provide.

Through his police contacts, Matranga had studied the case and quickly became judge, jury, and executioner. He gave the hit to Leoluca Vitale.

"Don't wait, Leoluca, I want it done soon," Matranga said. "Look into his eyes when you eliminate Hubbard, let him know there's no mercy in you. Let him know he's dying. Child killers are cursed by God and I hate Hubbard's kind. The other three with him will die with him, *capiche?* Send them all to hell, Leoluca. Perhaps I ask too much of you. Perhaps I should give you help, someone to watch your back."

"I don't need help, capo," Vitale said. "I can handle it alone."

"After it's done lie low for a while, Leoluca," Matranga said. "Stay home for a week and drink wine and read your Bible. Make love to your lady friend. The police will nose around for a day or two and then give up very quickly. They want Hubbard dead as much as I do." He sighed. "Mattie Cavalli is now with the angels, but say a prayer for her now and then, Leoluca. Let God know we care."

Jason Hubbard was a boasting man and loud, and Leoluca Vitale frequented his store for several days to learn his habits. And then he struck gold. Hubbard told a customer that he was playing cards that night at his hideaway, a cabin built on vacant ground close to his house. "I call it the Boys Club," Hubbard said, "a place where we can cuss and drink and play cards away from nagging wives."

Vitale already knew where Hubbard's house was, in an upscale neighborhood on Royal Street, but during his daytime visit he'd paid much attention to the tar paper cabin a hundred yards away on a vacant lot. Two windows to the front and a single door. It was vulnerable. If he closed the door his shots would be muffled and it would be a while before the alarm was raised, time enough for him to disappear into the night. He walked to the cabin and tested the door. It was open and there was no lock. He looked around at the surrounding houses. Good. No one was paying him any interest. People must use the vacant lot as a shortcut to the parallel street all the time. Satisfied, Vitale returned to his own house by streetcar.

On his way he bought a flower for his buttonhole, in anticipation of the night's work, and he cleaned and oiled his self-cocking Colt. His lady friend prepared him a light meal of bruschetta and a glass of white wine. The girl never questioned Leoluca's comings and goings with his gun, so she kissed him on the cheek, wished him luck, and promised to say a rosary to Saint Julian the Hospitaller for him.

The bright day had turned to dusk and as shadows formed across well-tended lawns oil lamps burned in Jason Hubbard's house and in other dwellings along the street. But what interested Leoluca Vitale were the two rectangles of amber light in the distance . . . the lair of the card-playing child murderer and the men who'd lied for him.

He crossed the open ground unseen, cloaked by the growing darkness, and slowed his pace as he neared the cabin, quieting his footfalls. He stopped opposite the door, drew his revolver, and took a deep breath.

Now!

Vitale grabbed the knob, opened the door wide, and immediately closed it behind him. Four pairs of startled eyes locked on his, and Hubbard said, "What the hell do you want?" He wore a green eyeshade, a nice touch.

Leoluca Vitale said nothing. He'd been taught by experienced soldiers that professional triggermen don't powwow. They shoot.

He put a round into the middle of Hubbard's chest and then swung his gun on the other three.

BOOMBOOMBOOM

Three shots sounded as one. All were center-chest hits designed to fatally damage the heart, lungs, esophagus, ribs, and major blood vessels. In other words, to drop a man where he stood . . . or sat. To Vitale's surprise, the only man who still lived was Jason Hubbard. He had blood in his mouth, his eyes full of terror, and he was trying to talk, making a strangled, "Gaa . . . gaa . . . gaa . . ." sound. Leoluca silenced the man with a stiletto thrust to the throat that killed him.

There was little time to be lost and quickly Vitale got to work.

He propped up the dead men in their chairs and shoved playing cards into their cold hands. In an unspoken tribute to Wild Bill Hickok, the great folk hero who'd died nine years before, Vitale rummaged through the cards and placed two aces and two eights into Hubbard's fingers. He then straightened the green visor on the man's head, looked around at his handiwork, and stepped out of the cabin.

Men were calling to one another in the gloom, formless shadows moving warily toward the cabin. Leoluca Vitale skillfully faded into the darkness and became one with the night.

* * *

All that was two years ago, enough time for it to become a memory recalled as a daydream. Leoluca Vitale turned from the window and left his hotel room in search of coffee and croissants.

It was not good for the digestion to kill men on an empty stomach.

CHAPTER THIRTY-NINE

Luke Powell had seen enough of Houston to last him a lifetime.

Whitey Quinn and Bill Cline gone, shot in the back by a pair of stagecoach-driving rubes. Now more than ever he needed Whitey's fast gun at his side because Powell was afraid, afraid of both Vincenzu Grotte and Antonio Matranga, not the men themselves but of what they represented. The Mafia was a brutal organization with a long reach that wouldn't hesitate to kill someone, anyone, who broke their laws. They'd kill not only the offender, but his wife, children, grandchildren, and his close friends. Nothing could stop them, they'd keep coming and coming at you and never stop.

But Powell felt some consolation in the fact that the Mafia capos were city animals. They flourished in the darkness of the sewers, dealing in drugs, prostitution, and extortion and never allowed a light to shine on their activities.

Like Vitale, Powell had moved into a room in a cheap hotel and when the thunderstorm that drenched the city was at its height, he'd been visited by the scared prostitute in the next room, who pounded on his door.

She was small, blond, and thin, dressed in a threadbare yellow robe over a nightgown and she said she hadn't come to sell it.

"I'm just scared of thunder, mister, and I don't want to be in my room alone," she said.

Her name was Harriette Cooke, she was twenty-five, and she said she'd been whoring since she was sixteen. And she brought with her a bottle of cheap gin.

"There are people who are scared of thunder," Powell said, after he'd invited her into his room. "Everybody is scared of something."

Harriette sat on the bed and drank from the gin bottle. Every time thunder banged, she jumped and made the bed screech. "What are you scared of, mister?" she said.

"Not much," Powell said. "I don't scare easily."

"I bet you're scared of losing your other eye."

"You'd win that bet."

"Tell me something. Have you ever had a conversation with a whore? I mean, a real serious conversation about life and its meaning?"

"No. I like whores who don't talk. How in God's name can a man have a serious conversation with a two-dollar whore like you? What would we discuss? The cracks on the ceiling?"

Thunder crashed and the girl jumped and Powell saved the bottle that fell from her hand. He tried the gin and grimaced. "That tastes vile, like gray swamp water."

"It's cheap," Harriette said, taking back the bottle. Her face was warm from the booze. "You're not a nice man, are you?"

"Some of the time I'm nice. I'm not nice to whores and horses. I don't particularly like either."

"How did you lose your eye?"

"A woman did it."

"A whore?"

"A fan dancer."

"What's that?"

"She dances naked and covers herself with two fans."

"I'd like to do that."

"You're too skinny for fan dancing. You need something to cover up."

Thunder roared and lightning flickered in the room.

"Do you smoke?" Powell said.

"I like smoking cigarettes like the Texas cowboys do."

"I'll roll you one. Help settle your nerves." After a while he held out a paper and said, "Here, lick that."

Powell built two quirlics and gave one to the girl. He thumbed a lucifer into flame and lit her cigarette and then his own.

From behind a blue cloud of smoke, Harriette said, "Do you think I'm pretty?"

"No."

"Whores don't have to be pretty."

"It's been my experience that the pretty ones get more business."

"Yeah, that's the case. I wonder if you can see the storm out your window. All I could see out of mine was a brick wall."

Powell looked out the window. "I can see rain on the street. It looks like falling steel needles. Come see if you want."

Harriette stepped to the window, just as lightning flashed, silvering the whole night sky for just an instant.

"No, I don't like that," she said, and sat on the bed again. "I don't like looking at that."

"It frightens you."

"It make me feel small and insignificant."

"You are small and insignificant. You're just a whore, nothing else."

"I think I'll get married one day."

"Who would marry you?"

"I don't know. Somebody."

"Good luck."

"My brother Lonnie ain't scared of thunder. He ain't scared of anything. And my brother Key ain't, either."

"Brave brothers," Powell said. He wondered at himself for conversing with a whore, a thing he'd just said he'd never do. "Are they lawmen?"

The girl laughed. "Hell no. They just got out of Yuma after doing a three for armed robbery with violence. Lonnie ain't much of a letter writer, so I wrote to Key and told them both to come down here to Houston where I could help them get settled."

"Is that why you're—damn, listen to that thunder—is that why you're working the line, to support your brothers?"

"Mister, I don't work the line, at least not yet. As long as I got my own teeth, I'm an independent, and I ain't selling it for Lonnie and Key, either. Are you crazy? What did they ever do for me? But they're still my brothers and I try to help them the best I can."

An idea began to form in Powell's head, still hazy but worth exploring.

"Lonnie and Key, can they ride horses and shoot?" he said.

Harriette smiled. Lightning again shimmered in the room. "Can they ride and shoot? Mister, we was raised in the Appalachian Mountains of Tennessee and them boys could ride a horse before they could walk. By his tenth birthday Key could shoot a squirrel out of a pine tree at a hundred yards. Pa kept poorly, so Lonnie and Key kept him and Ma and eleven young 'uns fed."

Now Powell's idea took shape.

"Where are your brothers?" he said, smoke trickling from his nostrils. "Are they here in Houston?"

"Yeah, right now they're living in a flophouse in Scott Street and finding out that the streets of Houston ain't paved with gold."

"Can you bring them here?" Powell said.

Harriette looked at him suspiciously. "Why?"

"I want to offer them a job riding for me. I'll provide the horses and guns."

"Key says him and Lonnie are through trying to rob banks, if that's what you have in mind."

"Nothing like that. I just need someone to watch my back."

"Key can do that. Lonnie ain't too bright, but Key tells him what to do and he does it. When do you want them here?"

"Tomorrow morning after the storm has passed."

"Mister, I have to sleep sometime."

"Sleep here in my bed," Powell said. "I'll keep you safe from the thunder."

"I need to pay for the streetcars," Harriette said. "Expenses, you know."

"When I meet your brothers, I'll give you ten dollars."

"Hell, mister, for ten dollars I'll bring you the whole Cooke family," the girl said.

The following morning, about the same time as Erica Hall gave Red Ryan her damp clothes to dry and across town Leoluca Vitale enjoyed a croissant with his coffee, Luke Powell met the Cooke brothers. He was mightily pleased. They looked like men he could use.

CHAPTER FORTY

Red Ryan dutifully ran the gauntlet of soldierly jeers as he gathered up Erica Hall's sun-dried clothes and carried them back to the cabin. She dressed and stepped outside, just in time to see Red and Buttons Muldoon push their last wheelbarrow loads of horse dung to the pile.

The woman's duds looked a little wrinkly and she'd finger-combed her still-damp hair, but Red thought her breathtakingly beautiful and even Buttons, in a thoroughly bad mood, smiled at her.

"I'm taking you boys out for dinner this evening," she said. "But nowhere too expensive, unfortunately."

"There's a place just down the road a ways," Red said. "The food's quite good and it's cheap."

"Is that all right with you, Mr. Muldoon?" Erica said.

"It is, unless a certain square-headed army sergeant tells me I can leave Houston."

"Is that why there are two sentries on guard?" Erica said.

"Yeah, the army impounded the Gray Ghost until such times as they complete the paperwork on two soldiers' wives headed to Fort Concho. Blockheads!"

"And, depending on when you leave, I'll be your third passenger, Mr. Muldoon," Erica said.

"Beggin' your pardon, ma'am," Buttons said, "but the Abe Patterson and Son Stage and Express Company requires that passengers pay full fare in advance. It's in the rules."

"I have enough to cover my fare," Erica said. She suddenly felt the need to explain, especially to Red Ryan, who had the most open, guileless face she'd ever seen on a man. "Vincenzu Grotte, the owner of the Diamond Theater, gave me an advance on my dancing pay."

"Why?" Red said.

"He just did."

"Generous of him," Red said.

"He wasn't being generous. He and I were planning to share the proceeds from the sale of the heroin." Her beautiful eyes misted. "Oh, how I regret that now."

Red and Buttons exchanged a look that Erica caught.

"I'm not proud of what I did," she said. "And I'll live with the guilt of Rosie Lee's death for the rest of my life."

"Don't carry that burden around," Red said. "It's way too heavy."

"If I'd not stolen the heroin, Rosie would still be alive."

"She was booed off a stage," Red said. "She'd have found another way to kill herself."

"Maybe. But I'll never know."

Buttons, who never in his career actually touched a passenger, surprised Red when he put his arm around Erica's shoulders. "Life goes on," he said.

"I suppose it does," Erica said.

"Here's a story," Buttons said. "One time when I was seventeen years old, I rode shotgun for the Frank Davis stage line up Lincoln way in the New Mexico Territory. This was years before that Bill Bonney kid ran wild up there. Anyway, to make a long story short, we were a couple of hours out of Lincoln when we were attacked by Apaches. There were only three of them, trying their luck. I let one of them have it with a double load of buck and the other two ran away. Turns out that the Apache I killed looked to be about ten or eleven years old, just a boy. Well, that kid's face lived with me for a long time before I forgot it . . . and I'd forgotten it up until now. The point is, I finally let it go, and that's what you have to do, Miss Hall. You've grieved for Rosie Lee, now put that book back on the shelf, no need to keep reading it over and over again."

"I'll try," Erica said. "I'll really try."

"Buttons," Red said, smiling, "you're a philosopher."

"No, I'm not, I drive a stagecoach. But what I know, I know."

"I'm putting you and Red in terrible danger," Erica said.

"You mean Powell?" Red said.

"Yes, him and Grotte. I have a feeling, call it woman's intuition, that for better or worse this thing will be resolved soon."

"We could leave for San Angelo sooner than soon," Buttons said.

"If that's the case, I won't be with you."

"Why?" Red said.

"If I run away, the men who want me dead would only follow me."

"Then pay your fare to San Angelo and do it now," Red said.

"I told you, I won't run."

"And I don't expect you to. Erica, once you pay your fare, you become a passenger of the Abe Patterson and Son Stage and Express Company and are under our protection."

"That's in the rules," Buttons said.

"I've asked for your protection, but only up to a point," Erica said. "I don't want either of you men to lose his life saving mine. I stole drugs to sell them, I whored myself to Vincenzu Grotte, and I'm holding myself responsible for Rosie Lee's death. I'm just not worth it."

"Pay your fare," Red said.

"I thought Grotte was a gentleman," Erica said.

"The devil is always a gentleman," Red said.

"Luke Powell makes no pretensions of being other than what he is, a born criminal and killer."

"Then we know what we're dealing with," Red said.

"I think he's not as dangerous as Grotte. Luke will come at me head-on. Grotte will find other, more devious means to end my life, but it will be done in the shadows. That's how Mafia revenge works. I heard what Antonio Matranga's boys did in Fort Smith to a small-time heroin dealer who'd cheated on him. The newspapers said that his wife woke up beside her husband and his head was on the mantel."

Red Ryan's face tightened. "I won't stand by and let anyone, Powell, Grotte, or what's his name? Matranga, walk into this stage depot and do you harm."

"Red, you don't owe me a thing," Erica said.

"No, he don't," Buttons said. "But he loves to help a lady in distress. Under them buckskins is a knight in shining armor."

"And what about you, Mr. Muldoon?"

For a moment Buttons thought about the complexities of Miss Hall's situation and then said, "Ma'am, I just don't know. But you sure got a skunk by the tail. I reckon I'll tag along and see how the pickle squirts."

"Mr. Muldoon, in the meantime I'd like to pay my fare to San Angelo in advance," Erica said.

CHAPTER FORTY-ONE

At the same time as Erica Hall spoke with Buttons and Red, Leoluca Vitale, with a hunter's patience, stood in the shade of a hickory sidewalk tree and watched the house of Vincenzu Grotte. For an hour traffic came and went, streetcars, brewer's drays, hansom cabs, and all kinds of delivery carts, the lifeblood of the city flowing through its arteries. Chenevert Street was in an upscale residential area and there was little foot traffic.

Then, shortly after noon, Vitale saw what he'd been hoping for. The carriage house doors opened at number 85 and Grotte's coach and pair emerged and turned smartly into the street. Grotte was no doubt leaving to check on his varied businesses and would probably be gone for some time. That suited Vitale's plan perfectly.

Dodging traffic, he crossed the road and when he reached the sidewalk he stopped and looked around him. There was no one in sight and it didn't really matter. To the casual observer Vitale would look like a middling-rank warehouse clerk out for a stroll or, more likely, carrying a message to a business owner. He reached behind him under his high-buttoned sack coat and drew his stiletto, its long slender blade and sharp point made for sticking, not slashing. Holding the knife close to his pants leg he opened the gate and then walked toward the house. Its painted Greek pillars looked like marble in the sun and the curtains were drawn in all the front windows against the glare. Vitale was a student of human nature, an excellent course of study when you need to eliminate a man with a minimum of fuss and bother.

For the execution he planned, the door was the key.

When she opens her door to a knock, a timid old lady will open it just a crack, barely wide enough to admit a breeze. But a big burly man, armed, like Henry Trapp, will throw the door open wide, confident that there's nothing on the other side he can't handle. But a gunshot was out of the question in that quiet neighborhood. It had to be the knife . . . and Vitale would have only one chance to get it right . . . a quick thrust that must be on target.

Even an accomplished triggerman can get nervous, and Vitale swallowed hard before he used the brass knocker on the door. Time ticked past. Nothing. No answer. Vitale tried again. This time the door swung open almost immediately and Trapp, tall and broad and tough, stood there like an oak, as though he planned to never let anyone enter. For a fraction of a second the eyes of the two men met. Clashed. And Vitale thrust. At close-quarters fighting and in a skilled hand, there is no more deadly weapon than the knife. Driven with all the force he could muster, Vitale's slender blade sank deep into Trapp's chest and reached his heart. Shocked by the unexpected attack, Trapp staggered back and Vitale went after him. To the right of the doorway, on a small, ornate table was a Colt Peacemaker, and Trapp, losing blood, a bucket of blood, tried to reach the gun but Vitale got there first. He didn't stab Trapp again because the man was dying on his feet and incapable of hurting him, but the blood presented a problem. When he returned, Grotte would likely enter the way he left, by a side door that led to the carriage house. But if he came in the front, blood around the front door would alarm him and his gun-toting groom.

Trapp went to his knees, and Vitale said, "Damn you, stop bleeding. Just die."

"You're trash, Vitale," Trapp said. The last three words he ever said.

When his heart stopped pumping so did the blood.

Vitale wiped off his blade on a window curtain, slid the knife back in its sheath, and explored the house. He found that there was a side door that led to the carriage house and horse stalls. It was likely that Niles Piper would let his boss off there. Nothing was certain and Vitale knew he was taking some big chances, but the need for payback vengeance ran too strong in him to quit now. He had no idea when Grotte would return, so he had to act quickly.

There was what seemed to be a dining room on the right side of the house opposite the side door, outfitted with a long rectangular table that was surrounded by chairs. It was perfect.

Trapp's blood had drenched his front but his back was not as gory. And again, that fit Vitale's plan. He grabbed the man under the arms and dragged him to the dining room. Trapp was a big man and a deadweight and Vitale needed all the strength he could muster to get the body onto a chair, its back facing the door. He propped up the corpse, elbows on the table, and then went to what looked like Grotte's parlor. There were cigars in a box and several decanters and glasses on a tray on a table. Vitale lit a cigar, selected bourbon, and carried the decanter and a glass to the dining room. He placed the decanter and glass to the left of Trapp's body, where it could easily be seen by Grotte, and his preparations were complete. He stepped into the huge kitchen, where there was a water pump, and washed his hands and used a scrubbing brush to get rid of as much blood as he could from his coat.

Leoluca Vitale walked back to the dining room and poured himself a glass of whiskey. "You don't mind, do you?" he said to Trapp. The dead man's eyes were wide open, but he was staring into eternity, not Vitale. He took a sip. "I didn't think so." He finished the whiskey and replaced the glass on the table. "Now, don't you go anywhere," he said to the corpse.

Vitale stubbed out his cigar in an ashtray in the middle of the dining table and then took what architects called the grand staircase. He stood in the shadows of the first landing and behind him a grandfather clock ticked away time, the only sound in the entire house. The dead are very still, very quiet. For Vitale, now was a time for patience. In his business to lose patience was to lose the kill. He'd learned that early in his career.

Time wore on, and the ticktock of the clock acknowledged the passing of each second. A rat rustled in a corner and Vitale thought that Grotte should've got himself a cat. Well, too late for that now.

BONG . . . BONG . . . BONG . . .

The grandfather clock chimed three. Where was Grotte? The unsettling thought occurred to Vitale that the man could be overnighting somewhere. If that was the case, all his work had been for nothing.

Vitale stood at the banister rail and looked around the house. From what he could see, the place was well built, solid, expensive. More to the point, he believed it was probably soundproof, at least enough to quieten pistol shots into a series of pops. Vitale smiled. Champagne corks popped all the time in that neighborhood and there would be no cause for alarm.

Then a noise from outside that did ring Vitale's alarm bells, the clatter and clang of horses followed by the thump-thump of the opening carriage house doors.

A full minute ticked by and then the soft clip-clop of led horses and carriage wheels trundled past the side door.

Very much on edge now, that keenly felt surge of excitement that Leoluca Vitale craved, he drew his gun and moved out of the shadows and stood at the top of the stairs.

Now long minutes of silence . . . three . . . four . . .

Then suddenly down below Vitale, the side door opened, croaking like a frog for oil. Then Grotte's voice. "Niles, come inside and have a drink and tell me about the pair of grays Logan's livery have for sale. Are they worth buying?"

Piper's voice in return. "Grays can smell bad, capo. A lot of people don't like them and that's why Race Logan is selling them cheap. But they're good carriage horses."

"He's selling then how cheap? No, don't answer that. Come inside. No, wait." Grotte stopped in his tracks and his voice raised said, "Why is my butler sitting down in the middle of the day drinking my booze?" He sniffed the air. "And smoking my cigars?"

"I don't know," Piper said. "Do you want me to ask him?"

"No, I'll ask him. Mr. Trapp," Grotte yelled, "we need to talk about why I shouldn't fire you on the spot."

Quickly Vitale reached a decision. Both men were standing targets. Shoot Piper first, the man with the gun. There was always a chance that Grotte might be armed, but it was unlikely.

Before he saw Trapp, Vincenzu Grotte had reached the bottom of the staircase and Piper was close behind him. The groom wore a thigh-length black coat with a velvet collar, breeches, and riding boots and carried a top hat. His gun was unhandy.

Vitale said, "Piper, up here."

The groom turned, following the voice, and saw Vitale on the stairs, his Colt in his hand. In that instant Niles Piper knew he was a dead man. His face drained of color and he attempted to make a play, his hand reaching under his coat. But he never completed the movement. Firing at a downward angle, Vitale's bullet crashed into the top of Piper's head at the hairline and killed him instantly.

Grotte was aghast.

He watched Piper fall and stood rooted to the spot for a long moment. And then he screamed in terror. "Holy mother of God, don't kill poor Vincenzu." He fell on his knees and joined his hands. "Mercy, I beg mercy for Vincenzu."

Vitale walked briskly down the stairs and said, "Give you mercy when you'd none for me? That seems hardly fair."

"That was not of my doing. It was all Luke Powell."

"You're a liar."

"I'm telling the truth. Powell wanted you out of the way so he could claim the heroin."

"Where is the heroin?"

"I don't know."

"Does the woman still have it?"

"Maybe. I don't know."

"Where is she?"

"I don't know."

"You don't know much, do you?"

"She may have left Houston."

"You know where she is. I can see it in your eyes."

"I swear to God, I don't know where she is."

"Give me a reason not to kill you."

"I want a man like you working for me, Leoluca. I need you to watch my back."

"Give me the Diamond Theater. Sign it over to me."

"Sure, sure, anything you say. It's yours. It's all yours."

"When do we do the paperwork? There's always paperwork."

"Right now. And then I'll show it to my lawyer so it's all nice and legal. You can come and get it the day after tomorrow."

Vitale smiled. "What a devious little slug you are, Grotte."

"I mean it. The theater is yours."

"I don't want your damned theater. All I needed to know is what you think your life is worth."

"Everything, Leoluca, my life is worth everything I've got and it's all yours. This house, everything, is yours if you spare Vincenzu."

"I was sent here to bring back the heroin, nothing else."

"And I'll find it for you, Leoluca. I promise," Grotte said. "Just give me a couple of days."

"No. I'm going back to New Orleans. I don't think the heroin is still in Houston."

"I think it is. I'll get it for you. Like I said, I just need a few days. Don't point that gun at my head, Leoluca. We can reach an agreement, you and me."

"Your time is over, Grotte," Vitale said. "You're done."

The roar of the gun cut off Grotte's scream. Shot in the middle of his forehead he toppled forward, just a few feet from Piper.

Vitale walked to the front of the house and opened the door. He looked outside and the street was still the same, people and vehicles coming and going, no alarmed or curious faces around the gate. Life went on and what happened at number 85 had been neither seen nor heard.

This had been a vengeance kill and hardly professional, but capo dei capi Matranga would understand. The Sicilian code of *vinnitta*, revenge taken for an insult, injury, or other wrong, was strong in him.

CHAPTER FORTY-TWO

The evening light changed as though seen through cloudy glass, smoky gray, waiting on the coming night to abolish it completely. The street that ran parallel to the Scriver livery was busy as workers headed for home, jamming the railcars, crowding the sidewalks, walking wide of the lamplighters on their ladders igniting gas mantles, diffusing a bluish light. The teeming city rebelled against the darkness, an inconvenient anachronism to be abolished just as mercilessly as the Western Frontier that had become increasingly embarrassing in this new age of steam, coal, and iron.

Imagine, then, young Tom Scriver's surprise when three men walked into his place looking like they'd just stepped out of the pages of a dime novel. Luke Powell, the one with the eye patch, he recognized from before, but not the two with him. Both were tall, gangly men, dressed in shabby coats and pants that matched in color, dark gray, and were a size too small. Both wore stained, collarless shirts, scuffed shoes, apparently without socks, and flat caps of unknown origin. Their huge hands stuck out from their sleeves like grappling irons and both had wide shoulders, thick necks, and heavy, jutting jaws. But what struck Scriver most was their eyes, black, lusterless, looking out on the world with complete disinterest, as though they didn't give a damn what happened to them or happened to others. The young man pegged them as half-trained wild animals, ready to do Powell's or anyone else's bidding.

"Tom, isn't it?" Powell said.

"Yes, sir," Scriver said. "Have you come for your horse?"

"Yeah, and the other two that belonged to Whitey Quinn and Bill Cline. And I'll want their guns as well."

Scriver smiled, eager to please. "Yes, sir, I'll do it right away."

"Wait," Powell said. "I see the stage is still there with its army escort. Where are Muldoon and Ryan?"

"Ah, Miss Hall took them to dinner. They just left if you wish to dine with them."

"Erica Hall is here?"

"Yes, sir, she's leaving for San Angelo on the Patterson stage in a day or two."

"Where is her luggage?"

"She doesn't have any. I don't know what happened to all her luggage, I really don't."

Powell's brain was working, but the inescapable conclusion was that this wasn't the time or place for a showdown. Catch them somewhere on the trail to San Angelo where there was no one to see or hear.

"Listen up," Powell said. "When Muldoon and Ryan get back here, tell them Luke Powell said, 'No hard feelings.' You got that? I have no hard feelings about Whitey and Quinn."

"I'll tell them."

"And tell them I'm headed for Waco to buy some cattle. You got that?"

"Yes, sir. You're headed for Waco to buy cattle."

"Right, now, bring out the horses, saddles, and guns. My associates Lonnie and Key will help."

Harriette Cooke hadn't lied, her brothers were at ease around horses. They strapped on the belt guns, clumsily, as though they'd never done such a thing before, but they handled the Winchesters like experienced rifle shooters.

Powell watched this and said to Scriver, "Lonnie and Key are as thick as planks, but they're good with cattle."

"They don't look like cowboys to me," Scriver said.

"Looks can be deceiving," Powell said. "How much do I owe you?"

Scriver toted up the bill and Powell called him a damned robber but paid anyway.

He swung into the saddle, looked down at the young man, and said, "What are you going to tell Muldoon and Ryan?"

"That you're headed for Waco to buy cattle."

"And the rest?"

"Oh, and no hard feelings."

Powell nodded, then touched the brim of his hat and said, "See you around, kid."

"Good luck with the cattle, Mr. Powell," Scriver said.

The three men rode from the livery yard into the waning day and out of Tom Scriver's life.

All the city's gas lamps were now lit, row upon row of white orbs in the distance, and the bustling streetcars remained busy.

CHAPTER FORTY-THREE

"That's what he said? He's headed for Waco?" Buttons Muldoon said.

"Yes, and he said he'd no hard feelings and I was to tell you so," Tom Scriver said.

Red Ryan used the nail of a pinkie finger to dislodge a shred of steak wedged between his teeth and that done said, "I don't believe him. He's up to something, you can bet the farm on that."

Erica Hall said, "It's quite simple, Red. Luke would rather kill me out on the prairie than here in Houston."

"Yeah, too much law in Houston, as I know from experience," Buttons said.

"Then better you stay here, Erica," Red said. "You'll be safer in town."

"No. Luke would only turn round and come back for me," the woman said.

She seemed tired and had eaten very little supper and Red was concerned about her.

"Well, me and Buttons can protect you once you're in the stage," he said. "I got a Greener scattergun that says,

Powell, keep your distance or I'll blow a hole in you a foot wide."

Erica smiled. "That's sure a talky shotgun."

"You bet," Red said. "Look into Miss Greener's black eyes and she talks volumes."

"Well?" Buttons said.

"Well what?" Red said.

"Where do we go from here?"

"We go to San Angelo."

"And Miss Hall?"

"It's her decision."

"I'll think about it," Erica said. "Right now with everything that's happened I'm not thinking straight."

Buttons said. "Well, Miss Hall, study on it and let us know by and by. The good news is that your fare is refundable anytime before the stage leaves the depot."

"In the meantime I think I'll lie down," Erica said. "I'm dreadfully tired and I'm again forcing you gentlemen out of your beds."

"We'll take our blankets and sleep in the coach with the soldiers," Red said.

"And if the Gray Ghost kills us all in the night, burn it," Buttons said. "Look at it just sitting there, listening to every word I say."

Tom Scriver had been talking to a passing policeman in a blue uniform and helmet who'd just walked into the yard. The man was obviously excited and gesticulated constantly with his hands. Now Scriver walked over and said, his young face grim, "Miss Hall, I've got bad news for you. It all came out earlier this evening and now the whole town is talking about it."

Erica sounded alarmed. "What is it?"

"Be brave, Miss Hall. A woman who cooks at the death house most nights found the bodies and she ran into the street screaming, 'Murder! Murder!'"

"Damn it all, who's been murdered?" Buttons said.

Scriver looked sympathetically at Erica and said, "I'm so sorry, Miss Hall, but it's Vincenzu Grotte, the owner of the Diamond Theater, him and two other men. According to the policeman I was talking with, City Marshal Erichson says it looks like a robbery gone wrong and he suspects the local criminal element is to blame. You'll be glad to hear that he promises arrests soon."

"I'm sorry to hear about Mr. Grotte's death," Erica said in a small voice, playing her part.

"I bet that whoever inherits the theater will keep you on, Miss Hall," Scriver said. "That will be crackerjack."

"Yes, it would be . . . wonderful . . . if that happened."

The young man leaned closer and his voice dropped to a whisper. "The policeman's name is Dan O'Hara and he drops by now and then for a cup of coffee. He tells me things, you know, and he says that all three men were shot, but City Marshal Erichson believes a gang of amateurs were involved and they panicked when they were discovered robbing the house." He placed a hand on Erica's shoulder. "Don't worry, the police will find those responsible very soon."

"Yes, very soon," Erica said. "That's good."

"I heard Mr. Grotte was very generous to the poor and needy and that he went out of his way to help people," Scriver said. "It's always the good ones that are the first to die, isn't it?"

"Yes, it is," Erica said. "Now, if you'll excuse me, I think I'll retire to bed."

"Certainly, by all means," Scriver said. "I know this news must've come as a terrible shock."

"Yes, yes, it did," Erica said. "A terrible shock."

Scriver watched her enter the depot cabin and then said to Buttons and Red, "She's a very brave lady. She took that bad news without a whimper."

"Yes, she is, very brave," Red said.

"I hope the new owner, whoever he is, keeps her on at the Diamond."

"I'm sure he will," Red said.

"You don't see fan dancers every day," Scriver said. "Poor Miss Hall, she's so very talented and I hate to see her hurt this way. She looked absolutely devastated."

"Filled with grief," Buttons said.

"Heartbroken," Red said.

"Ah well, she'll get over it," Scriver said. "By the way, you did a good job with the stalls."

"You're welcome," Buttons said. "We're experts at shoveling dung."

Scriver nodded. "Well, as I said, an excellent job. And now I've got some bookkeeping to get done."

"Good news for Erica," Red said after Scriver left.

"Now she's only got Powell to worry about," Buttons said.

"You mean, we've only got Powell to worry about."

"He's out there in the prairie somewhere."

"Biding his time, I reckon."

"He said, 'No hard feelings.'"

"Do you believe him?"

"No."

"Neither do I," Red said.

CHAPTER FORTY-FOUR

Red Ryan woke cramped and stiff in the Gray Ghost and looked out the window at another gray ghost . . . the listless mist that draped the entire livery, thick and opaque enough to blot out the depot cabin and horse corral. Beside him, Buttons Muldoon snored softly, his chin on his chest, his hat on his knees. Opposite, the two young cavalry troopers were still sound asleep. For some reason known only to God and the army, they both carried sabers, huge, curved scimitars that got tangled in Red's feet most of the night and woke him half a dozen times.

He reached inside Buttons's coat, took his watch from a vest pocket, and checked the time. It was five-thirty in the morning. Red replaced the watch, carefully untangled himself from the sabers again, and stepped out of the stage. He walked through the mist to the sidewalk and looked down the street in the direction of the cheap restaurant.

Visibility was down to a few yards, and hazy at that, but the streetcars still ran, most still drawn by long-suffering mules, and people were already on the gaslit sidewalks. In the distance, carried by some trick of the mist, Red heard the clanking of a locomotive as it pulled into the station, an aggressive warning from a massive machine of fire, steam, and iron that it was ringing out the death knell of the stagecoach.

Oddly depressed, Red walked to the stable in search of coffee and Tom Scriver didn't disappoint him. The young man was up early feeding the horses and Buttons's hungry team in the corral was already raising a fuss.

"It's in the usual place," Scriver said. "I just made it fresh."

"Much obliged," Red said.

He poured himself coffee, stepped outside with his cup, and built and lit a cigarette. The smoke from the quirly drifted into the mist and became invisible.

"Is that coffee?" Buttons stepped through a gray curtain and said, "I didn't sleep a wink, wondering if the Ghost was gonna do for me."

"Well, I got news for you, Buttons, you're alive and well," Red said.

"Damned stage whispered to me all night."

"What did it say?"

"I don't know."

"Didn't it whisper in American?"

"No, in some other heathen tongue."

"Too bad."

"What's too bad?"

"That you couldn't understand what the Gray Ghost was saying to you."

"I don't want to hear what it says to me."

Red nodded. "That's just as well. Better you don't know about some things."

"You think that square-head will show up today?"

"What square-head?"

"The army sergeant. What's his name?"

"Gunther Brandt," Red said.

"Yeah, him. What kind of handle is that for a man?"

"The kind of handle that belongs to a man who can spring us out of here," Red said. "Now, get yourself some coffee and improve your mood."

"The only thing that will improve my mood is getting out of Houston forever."

Buttons stomped into the stable . . . and thirty minutes later Sergeant Brandt, looking like he'd had eight hours' sleep and eaten a good breakfast, showed up with two plump women in tow, a young private carrying their carpetbags.

"Good news," Brandt said. "The women are all ready to go, champing at the bit, you might say."

"And so am I," Buttons Muldoon said, his face still sour. "And champing at the bit I do say."

"Sugar cookie?"

One of the women held out a large, brown paper sack with grease stains on the bottom.

"Maybe later, dear lady," Buttons said, always polite to womenfolk.

"Then you only have to ask," the woman said. "I'm Mrs. Maggie Hannah, the wife of Corporal John Hannah, and this is Mrs. Opal McDermott and she's married to Corporal Henry McDermott. Our husbands serve in K Company of the 19th Infantry at Fort Concho and I'm sure you've met them . . . Mr. . . . . ah?"

"Patrick Muldoon, ma'am. And this gent here wearing the funny hat is Red Ryan, my messenger."

Red touched the brim of his derby and said, "Pleased to meet you, ladies. We'll make your trip to San Angelo as comfortable as possible."

"And in turn I'll give you a shining testimonial to Corporal Hannah," Mrs. Hannah said. "He'll be very pleased."

"And likewise with Corporal McDermott," Mrs. McDermott said. "He, too, will be pleased as punch."

The women were two peas in a pod, both plump, round-faced with rosy cheeks and bright blue eyes, and both wore their hair tied back in severe buns. Fine fabrics and bright colors were unaffordable luxuries for lower-class women and their cotton dresses were drab, much worn, and probably purchased second- or thirdhand in a used-clothing store. But what the soldiers' wives lacked in style, they made up for in their honest smiles and cheerful demeanor and both Buttons and Red liked them instinctively.

But as far as Buttons was concerned his good will did not extend to the army.

"You can leave now, Sergeant Brandt," he said. "And take your soldier boys with you."

Softening that last, Red said, "And good luck with your recruiting drive."

"Thank you," Brandt said. "So far, I've signed up half a dozen lively lads."

"Seems to me, the youth of Houston isn't exactly flocking to the colors," Buttons said, his dislike of Sergeant Brandt unshakable.

"There will be more," the soldier said. "Perhaps you'd like to join up, Mr. Muldoon?"

"And pigs will fly," Buttons said.

"Ah, too bad," Brandt said. "I'm sure we could make a soldier out of you." He smiled at the women. "Now I'll leave you in the hands of Mr. Muldoon. I'm sure he'll look after you."

"Sugar cookie?"

"Why, thank you, Mrs. Hannah," the sergeant said, putting his hand in the bag. He took a bite of a cookie and chewed. "Excellent. First-class."

"It's the butter in them, you know," Mrs. Hannah said.

Both Mrs. Hannah and Mrs. McDermott were very concerned about Erica Hall's thinness and overall health.

"And you do look tired, you poor thing," Mrs. Hannah said. "As Corporal Hannah always says, a thin woman is not a healthy woman. Have a sugar cookie."

"I feel just fine," Erica said. "Really I do." She bit into the cookie and said, chewing, "Oh, very nice indeed."

"And you're so pretty," Mrs. McDermott said. "But a few more pounds would plump up those cheeks. At Fort Duncan, our previous post, when Corporal McDermott's important duties wore him down and he lost weight, I fattened him up with apple dumplings and custard. Do you like apple dumplings and custard, Miss Hall?"

"I don't know," Erica said. "I don't think I've ever tried them."

"Then there's your answer. When we get to Fort Concho, I'll make apple dumplings for you. Don't worry, Mrs. Hannah and me will soon fatten you up."

"What are you, Miss Hall?" Mrs. Hannah said. "Are you in service? A lady's maid perhaps?"

Erica smiled. "No, I'm a fan dancer."

"And what's that, my dear?" Mrs. Hannah said.

"I dance naked on stage with fans," Erica said.

"Oh," Mrs. Hannah said.

And Mrs. McDermott said, her voice breaking, "How nice for you."

Buttons Muldoon and Tom Scriver hitched up the team. The army wives' luggage was placed onboard along with the two women and Erica Hall, and the Gray Ghost was ready for the road.

Buttons didn't showboat out of the livery, mainly because he hated the Ghost and the Houston streets were too crowded with traffic. The Abe Patterson stage made its sedate way out of the city and into the open prairie.

With the featureless horizon miles ahead of him, long grass on all sides, and the sun high in the blue arch of the sky, Buttons's mood improved. But only just. Driving the Gray Ghost was always a chore.

"It pulls to the right, I tell you," he said to Red. "It's upsetting the team."

"The team looks just fine to me," Red said.

"You're a messenger. What do you know?" Buttons said.

"I know a hoss when I see one, a big animal with a long tail. And right now I see six of them in front of me that look as though they're out for a Sunday jaunt in the park."

"All right, feel that? Did you feel that lurch to the right?"

"No, I didn't."

"It's trying to turn over. If we make it to San Angelo alive it will be a miracle."

Red looked around him. The wind rippling the grass was oddly soothing, like watching waves rush toward a lee shore, and away from the city the air smelled fresh and clean and was easy to breathe.

"Nothing in sight but grass," Red said.

"You worried about Luke Powell, Red?" Buttons said.

"Not worried. Concerned, maybe, but not worried."

"If he comes after Erica Hall it won't be over open prairie where we can see him for miles."

"Not if he comes, but when he comes. But you're right, he won't ride straight at us."

"I reckon he'll be waiting for us at one of the stations. Jenks's or Potts's or maybe another," Buttons said. "That off leader is dawdling again." Buttons did something clever with the reins and yelled, "Git up, you." Then to Red, "We headed for a gunfight?"

"I hope not."

"Spell it out, Red. Are we headed for a gunfight?"

"Powell is a one-eyed man because of Erica Hall. He wants her dead, or blinded."

"Well?"

"Well what?"

"Do we draw down on him to protect her? She means nothing to us."

"She's a passenger."

"I bet Powell is sore because we done for two of his boys," Buttons said.

"Yup. And that's a good reason to kill us."

"And maybe that's why he hired on them two other rannies Scriver told us about."

"That would be my guess."

"Then back to my question. Are we headed for a gunfight?"

"Buttons, I don't think we can avoid it," Red said. "If

Powell kills Miss Hall, he's also got to kill us and the army ladies. That's just too many witnesses."

"I don't like it, but I'll study on that," Buttons said.

"Then again, he might just try to take her," Red said.

"She's a fare-paying passenger under the protection of the Abe Patterson and Son Stage and Express Company," Buttons said.

"Then we don't let him take her," Red said.

Buttons nodded, his face grim. "That's right, we don't let him take her."

CHAPTER FORTY-FIVE

About the same time the Patterson stage pulled out of the Scriver depot, Leoluca Vitale was on an early-morning train to New Orleans. He arrived in the city just after dark and pondered his next move. He could wait until morning and report to Antonio Matranga then, or head for the Garden District and the capo dei capi's villa. Matranga had a crime empire to run and worked long hours and would probably still be at his desk.

"Get it over with, Leoluca," Vitale told himself. "Confess your failure and promise him you'll do better next time. And tell him you triggered that no-good louse Vincenzu Grotte. As a Sicilian, it was a vengeance killing that Matranga will understand. The other killings were of no account and needn't be mentioned."

Vitale decided that was the best plan. A streetcar ran right past Matranga's villa and he could be there in less than fifteen minutes.

It was a Saturday night and New Orleans was a town that knew how to party. The blazing streets were bustling, noisy, the people full of life and energy, the bars and restaurants crammed with activity and excitement. Leoluca Vitale was glad to be home.

There was light in every window of the Matranga villa and that boded well. It meant that the capo dei capi was at home, perhaps entertaining. Vitale used the brass knocker and after a few moments the door opened and a butler dressed in a black tailcoat and spotless white linen stood in the doorway.

"Leoluca Vitale to see capo Matranga, and I apologize for the late hour," Vitale said.

The butler looked down his nose and said, "Wait there. I'll see if Mr. Matranga is available."

The door closed again and Vitale stood on the doorstep and watched the New Orleans Garden District go by him on the street. The night was clear, without mist, and everywhere Vitale looked there were gas and some electric lights. He thought the city must have at least ten thousand streetlamps turning night into, if not day, at least dusk.

The door opened and the butler said, "Mr. Matranga will see you. Please come in."

Vitale stepped into a large foyer, its ceiling and walls covered in paintings of naked nymphs and satyrs frolicking in Elysian woods, and the butler said, "Are you armed, Mr. Vitale?"

"Yes." He raised his small carpetbag. "I just got off the train from Houston."

The butler laid his hand on a table that stood against a wall. "Please leave your weapon and luggage there. They will be quite safe."

Vitale did as he was told, divested himself of his Colt and bag, and followed the butler upstairs to Matranga's office. The man knocked on the door and from inside came the command to enter.

Antonio Matranga sat at his desk in full evening wear and a cigar burned in an ashtray in front of him.

"Please take a seat, Mr. Vitale," he said. "I can't give you long. As you see I will dine with my family soon." Matranga picked up the cigar and waved it, blue smoke curling. "You bring me good news, I trust?"

Now Vitale knew he had to tread carefully. "I'm afraid not, capo."

Matranga's face changed, tightened. "Where is the heroin?"

"I don't know. The secret of its location was known only to Vincenzu Grotte."

"Did you apply some pressure, make him see the error of his ways?"

"Yes, I did."

"And?"

"And he tried to have me killed."

"He what!" An exclamation, not a question.

"He sent three men to my hotel with orders to kill me."

Matranga looked grave. "This is very serious, very serious indeed." He stared at the ceiling for a few moments as though seeking inspiration there and then said, "You obviously survived the assassination attempt, and you were right to return to New Orleans. I will deal with Mr. Grotte in my own fashion."

"There's no need for that, capo," Vitale said. "I dealt with him myself."

"Did I hear you right?"

"Yes. I killed him."

Matranga jolted forward on his desk, his eyes wild.

"You killed him? Without my permission? Without a meeting of my associates where such things are discussed and decisions made?"

"Did I do wrong, capo?" Vitale said.

"Our organization has rules, rules that we all live by, some of them very old. You have broken one of those rules and it is a very grievous thing. A capo, any capo, even one as inconsequential as Vincenzu Grotte, cannot be executed without the approval of his peers and then, as the capo dei capi, the decision is ultimately mine. You took that right away from me as though I didn't matter. Am I so ill thought of that my authority no longer matters?"

"I'm sorry, capo," Vitale said. "I meant no disrespect."

"I will think deeply about this," Matranga said. "I will seek advice, listen to others, hear what they have to say. Perhaps some of the younger men will tell me that I grow old, that my authority is no longer respected, my counsel no longer heeded. Others, with gray hair, will say that the killing of Vincenzu Grotte has shamed me and I must act to restore my good reputation and honor our code. All this is what might be said to me, but I don't really know and that is why I must find out what road to take. Go home, Leoluca, contemplate on what you have done, and say a rosary for me that I find good guidance."

"Capo, no one knows that I killed Grotte," Vitale said. He was desperate now, clutching at straws. "We can put out the word in Houston that the police triggered him, fearful that their illegal dealings with a known criminal were about to be revealed. There is nothing to connect us to his death, nothing at all."

"Only you, Leoluca. You are the link. And no matter who we blame, it is you who broke the rule, and now you wish to break another, the one that commands us to have nothing at all to do with the police." Matranga carefully placed his cigar in the ashtray and kneaded his temples. "Now I have a headache, and, if the truth be told, a heartache. You were a trusted associate and a good soldier, Leoluca, and now you've thrown all that away for petty vengeance. Now, go home. Wait for my word on this matter."

"Capo, I'll do better in the future," Vitale said.

Matranga nodded but said nothing.

After Vitale left, Matranga rang for the butler and told him he needed to speak with Giacomo La Rosa. When the man arrived, Matranga said. "Giacomo, I have a job for you. Tomorrow is fine. It's Leoluca Vitale."

La Rosa looked stunned. He started to speak and Matranga cut him off.

"Yes, I know it's a surprise. It's more than that, it's a tragedy, but he has broken our rules and shamed me and that I cannot forgive. It would perhaps be better for all of us if he took his own life. Be nice, Giacomo, talk to him, show him the error of his ways and tell him the life of his pretty lady friend will be spared if he cooperates and kills himself. And if he refuses? Then you know what to do. Make it a clean kill, Giacomo. For old times' sake don't make Leoluca suffer."

He sighed, passing his hand across his eyes.

"How is your own family, Giacomo? I was told little Laura is sick."

"Much better, capo," La Rosa said. My wife took her to the priest and she was cured."

"Oh, good, I'm relieved to hear that."

"We'll speak again tomorrow then. Good night, Giacomo."

Antonio Matranga sighed again.

Leoluca Vitale. What a misfortune. What a waste.

* * *

Two days later a young man's body, never identified, was found in the Bayou St. John, just a little north of the French Quarter. The death was ruled a suicide by a gunshot wound to the head.

CHAPTER FORTY-SIX

"Yeah, a one-eyed man who put his name out as Luke Powell was here," station master Art Jenks said. "Him and two others."

"How long ago?" Buttons Muldoon asked.

"Real early this morning. They had coffee and ate biscuits and salt pork and then some supplies. Powell gave me two dollars."

"Did they say where they were headed?" Red Ryan asked.

"North, that's all I know." Jenks's eyes went to Erica Hall. "A bit quieter around here since the last time you visited, ma'am."

"That wouldn't be difficult," Erica said. "As I recall, you wanted to sell me for fifty dollars."

"Well, you and the other young lady," Jenks said. "Is she staying in Houston?"

"Yes," Erica said.

Jenks was about to say something more but Buttons cut him off. "That's the team I left here the last time I changed horses. You've had nobody since?"

"If you're talking about stagecoaches, not a one. Makes

me think I'll need to close the old place down before much longer."

"Maybe if you improved your food the stages would stop," Opal McDermott said, making a face.

"Your biscuits are soggy and the salt pork is turned," Maggie Hannah said.

"It's a disgrace," Mrs. McDermott said. "Corporal Mc Dermott would take you to task over your biscuits and goodness knows what he'd say about the pork."

"Food don't keep out here, ma'am, and it's hard to come by," Jenks said. "For a while I kept pigs, but that didn't last. No forage for pigs around these parts."

"Well, that's too bad," Mrs. McDermott said. "But you must really try to improve the quality of your food."

"The horses come first, ma'am, and that's where all the money goes," Jenks said. "But recently that money is drying up. There was a time when I'd get two, three stages a week, now I'm lucky if I get that many in a six-month. The railroads have done for us and they're about to put me out of business."

"There will always be stages," Buttons said. "How are folks gonna get to places when the railroads ain't there? Mark my words, a hundred years from now and stage-coaches will still be the best way to travel across rough, open country. And that's a natural fact."

"You may be right, jehu," Jenks said. "But all them coaches just ain't coming in my direction."

Red Ryan said, "Jenks, them two with Luke Powell, how do you figure them?"

"Rubes. But they're not just off the farm. And they ain't too bright."

"How do they stack up as gunhands?"

"Maybe good with a rifle, but they didn't look comfortable wearing a gun rig. Take you, shotgun man, you look as though you were born with an iron on your hip. But not them boys. It's hard to describe, but it seems to me their gun belts just didn't fit them right, as though they were fretting them in some way."

"They looked uncomfortable wearing a gun?" Red said.

"Yeah, you got your boots on the right feet, shotgun man. They looked mighty uncomfortable. Now, as I said, they may be handy with a rifle, because they managed them Winchesters like they'd used them a passel of times before."

Buttons said, "Looks as though Powell's found himself a couple of riflemen."

"I'd say that's the case," Jenks said. "Them boys didn't look like much, but they could be marksmen."

"So he doesn't intend to make it close," Buttons said. "He'd rather pick us off at a distance."

"Seems like," Red said.

The army wives had been listening intently to that exchange and Mrs. Hannah said, "Mr. Muldoon, are you expecting trouble?"

"It sure sounds like it, " Mrs. McDermott said. "Now I'm all aflutter. Mrs. Hannah, am I flushed?"

"Ladies, dear ladies, there's no trouble me and Mr. Ryan can't handle," Buttons said. "Just compose yourselves with the knowledge that you're in safe hands."

"I do wish Corporal Hannah was here," Mrs. Hannah said.

"And Corporal McDermott," Mrs. McDermott said.

And together, "We wish both of them was here."

"We'll arrive safely in San Angelo without any trouble, I assure you," Red said.

But trouble was waiting in the wings and when it came, it was from a totally unanticipated source.

CHAPTER FORTY-SEVEN

Johnny Alford had robbed that coach before, killed the driver and messenger, and ended up with pocket change. "What do you think, boys?" he asked the two with him, John Walls and Aaron Savage, a couple of killers out of Pickens County in the Chickasaw Nation country of the Oklahoma Territory. Two years before they threw in with Johnny Alford, they'd fled the Nation after murdering a Chickasaw elder for his horse and the few dollars in his poke.

Hidden in a stand of oak and mesquite, John Walls had a telescope to his eye and after studying the oncoming gray stage for a few moments, he said, "Well, it ain't on a mail run, coming up from the south like that."

"Maybe it's carrying gold or bonds from a Houston bank," Savage said.

"To where?" Alford said, a young man with hard eyes and a thin, steel trap of a mouth. Historians, usually unwilling to explore the nature of evil, do concede that there was no good in Johnny Alford and a great deal of viciousness, depravity, and villainy, traits he shared with Walls and Savage.

"Most likely San Angelo," Savage said. "They could even be carrying an army payroll for Fort Concho."

Walls used his telescope again. "I think there are passengers," he said. Then, after a few moments, "Yeah, passengers with luggage. Definitely."

"It might be worth our while," Alford said. "Pick up a few dollars."

"What do we do about the driver and messenger?" Walls said.

"What we always do." Alford pulled his bandana up over the bottom of his face. "Kill them."

"Idiots!" Buttons Muldoon yelled.

He dropped the ribbons, drew his gun, and fired. Beside him Red Ryan's scattergun roared. John Walls bent over in the saddle, cradling a wound, and drew rein on his horse. Whether he was hit with bullet or buckshot, now was not the time to find out. Alford and Savage split up, charging to the right and left of the stage. They both fired, their horses at a run. Both bullets zinged over the stage, missing Buttons and Red by at least a foot. Then they were past, but now within the range of the Winchester Red had swapped for the shotgun. He turned, leaned over the top of the stage, took aim, and fired. A hit. A man wearing a shirt of washed-out blue reeled, slowly slid from the saddle, and thumped onto the ground.

Buttons stood in the box and yelled, "Idiots!" His Colt hammered at the surviving road agent, but the man decided enough was enough and fogged it out of there. Red helped him on his way with a couple of shots from his rifle.

Buttons reined in the team and then turned to Red, his face incredulous. "Do you believe that?"

"Do you mean the bandanas? Strange, that."

"Yeah, it was strange. If the idiots hadn't covered their faces they could've got a lot closer and shot first. I mean, they could've been Rangers, and I wouldn't have fired. But when they tried to disguise themselves, they removed all doubt that they were road agents. Idiots."

"Let's go see if either of the idiots we shot is still alive," Red said.

Only one man was still alive but he was in a bad way, still sitting his horse. As Red walked closer to the wounded man he levered a round into the Winchester's chamber. "Don't!" the man yelled. "Mister, I'm all shot to pieces."

"Then git down from there," Red said. "Slowly now. Let me see both your hands."

John Walls half fell out of the saddle, landed on both feet, but was unable to stand. He sank to the ground and his horse tossed its head and nervously sidestepped away from him.

"Who are you?" Red said.

"Name's John Walls. I saw Aaron Savage cut and run, so the man you shot must be Johnny Alford. Too bad, he was a mighty smart man."

"But stupid enough to wear a bandana over his face," Red said. "That identified you as road agents."

There was blood on Walls's mouth and his face was ashen. "We robbed that gray stage afore," he said. "The bandanas worked the last time. The driver and messenger saw us and threw up their hands right quick." The man coughed up blood and then managed, "You two don't scare easy."

"Damn right," Red said. "And then you shot them."

"Yeah. That was Johnny's idea. Leave no witnesses."

"You killed better men than yourselves," Red said. "Phineas Doyle and Dewey Wilcox died for no reason. The Abbot stage was coming back after a mail run."

"We didn't know that," Walls said.

"You know it now," Red said.

"Yeah, and I'll take it to hell with me," Walls said.

Buttons stood beside Red and looked down at the wounded man. "You're all shot up," he said. "Best you try to come to terms with your Creator."

"Too late for that," Walls said. "Too late for everything. Go away and let me die."

Mrs. McDermott was in a terrible state of nerves and her round, homely face was burning. Mrs. Hannah, looking concerned, waved a small pocket handkerchief in the woman's general direction, trying vainly to generate some air.

Mrs. McDermott looked down at Walls and whispered, "Is he . . ."

"Dead?" Buttons said. He took a knee beside the man and studied him closely. "Yup, he's gone, ma'am. It looks to me that Red's scattergun just about blew out his lungs before my bullet hit him. I'm surprised he lasted this long."

"Oh . . . oh . . ." Mrs. McDermott said. "I feel faint and I've come over all a-tremble."

"I wish Corporal Hannah was here," Mrs. Hannah said. "He'd know what to do."

Erica Hall put her arm around Mrs. McDermott's waist and said, "Let me help you back to the stage."

"You're so kind," the woman said. "I know I'm being a

burden to everyone. It's my nerves, you know." Then to
Mrs. Hannah, "Maggie, where's the brandy flask?"

"It's in my purse inside the coach, dear. I'll get it
for you."

"Just a sip will help calm me," Mrs. McDermott said.

"And a sip or two will help me as well," Mrs. Hannah
said.

CHAPTER FORTY-EIGHT

"Victor Potts will buy the horses and traps," Buttons Muldoon said. "Maybe we can turn a profit on this trip after all."

The road agents' horses were tethered to the back of the coach, the saddles on the roof of the stage. The bodies of Johnny Alford and John Walls lay on the prairie and the coyotes and gray wolves would be their undertakers.

The day was hot, the sun high, but the air was clear, free of dust, and a farsighted man could see for miles across the open prairie. The team was performing well, but Buttons kept up a tirade on the faults of the Gray Ghost, now claiming that the stage would not stay on a straight line but pulled badly to the right.

"It hates me," he said. "That's why it's acting up so bad."

"I don't feel anything," Red said. He looked behind him. "The wheel tracks are as straight as a fire poker."

"That's because you don't see too good, Red," Buttons said. "You need a driver's eyes to see stuff like that. There! Feel it? It's pulling right and upsetting the leaders."

"Maybe it wants to go somewhere," Red said.

"Go where?"

"Somewhere. Is there a ghost town around these parts?"

"Not that I know of," Buttons said. He thought for a few moments and then said, "No, wait, maybe there is. A week before he died, I recollect Phineas Doyle, God rest him, say that real recent a big wind blew him off course on this very trail, and him and Dewey Wilcox, may he rest in peace, ended up in a ghost town and it was like to booger the living daylights out of them."

"Seems unlikely, way out here. Why would anyone build a town miles from anywhere?"

"I don't know, but there's no accounting for folks. When they set their minds to it, they can do some mighty peculiar things." Buttons's fingers made an adjustment on the reins, and then he said, "Now, here's a thing . . . Phineas said that every door in that town had a red cross painted on it and all the doors was locked . . . from the outside, keys still in the locks."

"What did Phineas figure had happened?" Red said.

"Plague town."

"What kind of plague?"

"Cholera, probably. They had a contaminated water mill and it can happen anywhere at any time."

"How many people?"

"Who knows. Phineas said they locked the victims in their homes so they wouldn't spread the disease."

"And they just let them die?"

"Seems like. Phineas and Dewey looked in a few windows and saw people who'd been dead for a long time. They were all dried up and their skins had turned black."

"Was there anybody alive?"

"Not a living soul. Some had died and the rest had cleared out."

Red looked around him and then said, "I don't see anything that looks like a ghost town or any other kind of town."

"Phineas said the dust storm was so bad that he turned his team's tails to the wind and it blew them a right smart piece."

"How far?"

"I don't know. He never told me how long it took him to get back on the route to Houston."

"I'll keep looking," Red said. "It's a clear day, so maybe we'll see it in the distance."

"And we'll keep it at a distance. I don't want anything to do with a plague town. Phineas said the ghosts of the dead walk the streets and if you're not careful, they'll follow you home and stand around your bed at night."

"Maybe you're right," Red said. "We should leave that ghost town alone."

"And you ain't heard the kicker yet," Buttons said, staring straight ahead, his face grim.

"And what's that?"

"Guess what stage Phineas was driving."

"I know what you're about to tell me and I don't want to hear it."

"Guess."

"No, I won't say it."

"It was this one. The Gray Ghost."

"Buttons, tell me this is another of your big windies."

"No big windy. It was this stage. And it's pulling like crazy. I think it wants to go back there to that town."

"I don't believe it."

"Believe it. If I let the team have its head, I guarantee the Gray Ghost would drive it in the direction of the cholera town."

"Well, keep a tight grip on them ribbons," Red said. "We don't want to do any sightseeing today."

"You believe the story Phineas told about the town, though, huh?" Buttons said.

"Maybe. I don't know."

"When we get back to the old Long John Abbot depot, I want to show you something."

"What is it?"

"A long piece of wood, say four foot long and six inches deep. Phineas brought it back from the ghost town."

"A part of one of those locked-up houses, I guess."

"No, it stood on the edge of town. It was the burg's name," Buttons said.

"And what was it?"

"Painted on the sign were the words 'Last Hope.' Makes you think, huh?"

"Yeah, that's kind of sad," Red said. His eyes swept the far horizon ahead of him, looking for ghost towns.

"And you know what's strange?" Buttons said.

"Phineas said the buildings were old, the wood crumbling, and all the paintwork faded to almost nothing, but the sign with the town's name one it was as fresh as the day it was painted. Dewey took it with him and it still looks like new."

"I don't think I want to see that sign, Buttons," Red said. "And I never want to see that town, either."

"Why not?"

"Well, considering what happened to Dewey Wilcox, it seems to me that taking the sign brought him bad luck."

"No, Red, it wasn't the sign that brought him bad luck. It was this stage," Buttons said.

CHAPTER FORTY-NINE

L uke Powell's empty eye socket ached and squatting
by a small mesquite fire in the middle of the night
with two inbred idiots did nothing for his mood. Lonnie
and Key Cooke knew nothing and talked about nothing.
Earlier their sole conversation had been . . . "This coffee
is hot, Key."

"Then blow on it, Lonnie."

"It's still hot, Key."

"Blow on it some more, Lonnie."

"Ah, that's better, Key."

"Good, Lonnie."

Powell had tried to turn the talk to women, their charms
and beauty and the great whores he had known.

Lonnie hee-hawed, Key giggled, but they'd nothing to
add. Lonnie said that one time he'd seen Betsy Chalmers's
almost-naked butt at the swimming hole and Key said that
Maryanne Dover had let him touch her chest, but they
were ten years old at the time.

Powell's attempt at a discourse on desirable females
died right there.

The biscuits he'd bought at Jenks's station had been

eaten and the remaining coffee in the small, soot-blackened pot was all they had. Powell wanted a good cigar and a glass of bourbon but he had neither. He also wanted Whitey Quinn and Bill Cline, but they were gone. He'd have to make do with what he had, and that wasn't much.

"When we enter the stage station, you boys know what to do," Powell said.

"Yes, sir," Key Cooke said.

"Tell me."

"We grab the pretty woman."

Powell sighed and shook his head.

"No, you don't. I'll do that, understand?"

"Oh, I remember, we shoot the stage driver and the shotgun guard," Lonnie, marginally smarter than Key, said.

"Right. You shoot the driver and the messenger and then I grab Erica Hall and then we all ride away." Powell smiled. "You rubes never had a pretty woman before, huh? Well, you'll soon have one to play with."

The Cooke brothers giggled, slapped at each other, and crowed like roosters, and the thought occurred to Powell that if he shot them both he'd be doing the world a favor.

"Watch the messenger real close," Powell said. "His name is Red Ryan and he's fast on the draw. You'll need to shoot him before he has time to make a play, *capiche?*"

"What does that word mean?" Key said, his vacant face screwed up in puzzlement.

"*Capiche?* It means 'understand' in Italian," Powell said.

"Who are them eye-talians?" Key said. "Do they live in Texas?"

"No, they don't. They're nobody. Forget I said it."

"Hey Lonnie, eye-talians," Key said. "Ain't that a funny name?"

"Ain't it, though," Lonnie said.

Both men slapped at each other again and laughed . . . and laughed . . . and Luke Powell began to have doubts that the Cooke boys could handle Red Ryan and that tough driver of his. He consoled himself with the thought that when the lead started flying, they'd come up to scratch. Powell had only one chance of getting his hands on Erica Hall and he needed the Cooke brothers as cannon fodder.

"Your sister told me that you boys did three years in Yuma," he said.

"Yeah, we did," Lonnie said, suddenly serious. "Me and Key was in the snake den twice and both times that place near killed us."

"What was the snake den?" Powell said, only half-interested.

"We was put there because the warden called us problem prisoners," Key said.

"What was it?" Powell said again.

"It was a cell dynamited out of solid rock and it only measured ten feet by ten feet," Key said. "And it was pitch-black all the time unless the sun was directly over-head. There was no cot and we slept in shackles on the bare ground. Some men died in there, bitten by side-winders that crawled inside. Rattlesnakes killed a lot of cons. We got grub once a day and that was the only time we saw a living soul. The snake pit was made to break a man's spirit, but it didn't break me and Lonnie. No, sir, when we got out after ten days, we spit in the guards' eyes and took the beating we got without crying out. The guards used to get mad when me and Lonnie told them that when our pa got drunk, he beat us a lot worse than they did."

"You're lucky you got out of Yuma alive," Powell said.

"We sure don't want to go back," Key said. "Lonnie, what did the warden say we were?"

"Mentally deficient," Lonnie said. "And he said if we ever came back, we'd go right into the crazy hole."

"Another cell?" Powell said.

"Yeah, but only four feet by five feet and a tall man couldn't sit up in it," Key said. "If they put a sane man in there, he came out crazy. And the warden said that would happen to us, didn't he, Lonnie?"

"Yeah, he said that, and he meant it."

Powell smiled. "What did you boys do to get sent to Yuma in the first place?"

"We don't like talking about it," Key said.

"No offense, I hope," Powell said.

"We didn't do good," Lonnie said. "Ah, go ahead and tell him, Key."

Key took a deep breath and then, his words tangled in a sigh, "Well, we was working on a ranch up in the Mogollon Rim in the Arizona Territory."

"You were cowboys?" Powell said, surprised.

"No, we just helped around the ranch, keeping the barns and corrals clean, fetching water for the cook, and running errands and that kind of thing," Key said. "Then came the day when Lonnie heard the rancher, he was a man named Gillette, say he was going into town to deposit money he'd earned on the sale of a hundred head of cattle."

"Well, me and Key were pretty tired of ranch work, so we decided to rob him," Lonnie said. "The hands were out on the range, so we took a couple of horses and a rifle and went after Mr. Gillette. When we caught up with him, we told him to hand over the money . . ."

"And he just laughed at us," Key said.

"So we pulled him off the buckboard and Lonnie grabbed the money sack, and then a bad thing happened," Lonnie said.

"Tell it," Powell said, interested despite himself.

"Well, a bunch of cowboys from another ranch rode up on us and held us at gunpoint," Lonnie said. "There was a big sycamore close by and they dragged us there to hang us. But Mr. Gillette stopped them and handed us over to the law and the judge gave us three years in Yuma."

"And what have you been doing since you got out?" Powell said.

"Odd jobs here and there," Key said. "And stealing stuff, chickens and melons and whatever else we can find that ain't nailed down."

"Well, after I get my hands on Erica Hall, I'll give you a hundred dollars each and you can keep the horses and guns," Powell said. "How does that set with you?"

"It sets with us just fine, Mr. Powell," Lonnie said, grinning. "That will give us a new start in life and maybe me and Key can go into the bank-robbing business."

Powell clapped his hands and said, "There you go! A quick way to make a fortune. Go after life like it's something to rope in a hurry before it gets away and I'll read about the Cooke brothers in all the newspapers. I got a feeling you boys will be more famous than Jesse and Frank."

That pleased Lonnie and Key and they laughed and slapped each other around.

Powell smiled. *Have fun while you can, boys. By this time tomorrow you'll be dead.*

CHAPTER FIFTY

"I see them," Buttons Muldoon said. "Staying just ahead of us out of rifle range."

"Do you think it's Powell and his boys?" Red Ryan said.

"It's got to be," Buttons said. "He's watching us."

"Watching and waiting," Red said. "But for what?"

"I guess we'll know when it happens," Buttons said.

The sky was ribboned with scarlet and jade and the morning air was sweet with the smell of grass and sage. On all sides of the stage the prairie rolled away to the horizons, rippling in the wind like a vast and endless sea on an infinitely large alien planet.

Erica Hall stuck her head out the window and yelled above the rumble of the wheels across some uneven ground. "Red, that's Luke Powell ahead of us."

Red leaned over in his seat and said, "I know."

"I watched him," Erica said. "He came up from behind and then rode wide until he was ahead of us. I know how he sits a horse."

"Me and Buttons figured it was him," Red said. "I

reckon he'll play his hand soon, maybe at the Potts stage station." Then, "How are the ladies holding up?"

There was a pause and Erica said, "As well as can be expected."

"How are you?" Red yelled.

Another pause, then, "As well as can be expected."

"I heard most of that," Buttons said. He was grouchy again. "Damn it, Red, I learned something this morning. If you're gonna get up before breakfast, eat breakfast first."

"That don't apply to stage drivers," Red said. "You didn't get up this morning, you were right where you're at come sunup."

"I reckon Powell will be waiting at Potts's station," Buttons said. "I don't want Victor Potts or his family to get hurt."

"We could just drive past," Red said. "It's not Potts's fight."

"Then Powell will wait at another station and we'll drive past, and another and we'll drive past and so on and so on until my team drops dead from exhaustion and the Gray Ghost sniggers. No, we've got to face him at the Potts place."

"We're headed for a gunfight," Red said. "Does that occur to you?"

"Yeah, it occurs to me, but Powell has us cornered and there's no other way," Buttons said.

"We could always just give him what he wants."

"Erica Hall, you mean?"

"Who else?"

"Could you live with yourself afterward? Would you ever be at ease in the company of men?"

"No, to both questions."

"I thought so," Buttons said.

Then Erica Hall's voice from inside the coach. "Mr. Muldoon!"

"Ask her what she wants, Red," Buttons said.

Red leaned over on his seat, his head near the window. "Erica, what do you want?"

"Tell Mr. Muldoon to stop," the woman said. "We need to talk."

"About what?" Red asked. He shook his head. "Argh . . . I just got a mouthful of dust."

"Just tell Mr. Muldoon to stop," Erica said. "It's very important."

"I'll tell him," Red said, coughing up dust. "But I don't think he'll stop. Stages never do between stations."

"If he doesn't, I'll open the door and jump out," Erica yelled.

"I heard her beller," Buttons said. He drew rein on the team. "Go see what she wants, Red."

Red climbed down, holding his rifle. The stage was stopped, a good time for Powell to make his play. Up in the box, Buttons held the Greener, like Red, taking no chances.

Red walked to the door just as Erica Hall stepped out of the stage. She said nothing until she walked to the front so Buttons could hear.

"Mr. Muldoon, I want to be left here," she said. "The stage can go on without me."

"That would break the Abe Patterson and Son Stage and Express Company rules, Miss Hall," Buttons said. "Now, get back inside. We have to be on our way."

"Mr. Muldoon, Luke Powell and his men will be

waiting for you at the next station or the one after that," Erica said. "I won't have you and Red Ryan die because of me. I'm not worth such a sacrifice and I don't think I've ever been worth it. I sell drugs and dance naked for men and because of me a girl killed herself, for God's sake."

"You no longer sell drugs and you've got to stop blaming yourself for Rosie Lee's death," Red said.

"I supplied the means," Erica said. "I can't get around that."

"And it signifies nothing," Red said. "Rosie Lee killed herself because she was running away from a problem she didn't want to face. It was cowardice, and a coward will always find a way. If it wasn't heroin, she'd have found something else."

"Do you really think that?" Erica said.

"I don't think that, I know that," Red said.

"I wish I had your certainty," Erica said.

"Give it time, it will rub off on you."

"I hope so."

"Now, will you please get back in the stage. It's against the policy of the Abe Patterson and Son Stage and Express Company to abandon a passenger on the prairie."

"Unless he's telling lewd jokes to a lady or otherwise making himself obnoxious," Buttons said. "I've only done it once in my career and I don't ever want to do it again."

"But . . . I can save your lives," Erica said.

"At the cost of your own," Red said.

"And what of Luke Powell? Won't he kill me anyway?"

"Oh, don't say that, dear." Mrs. Mc Dermott laid a hand on Erica's shoulder. "We won't let anyone harm you. Isn't that so, Mrs. Hannah?"

Mrs. Hannah said, "There's something strange going on here, Mrs. McDermott. And Mr. Ryan, since we're all passengers on the same stage I think you should tell us about it. If Corporal Hannah was here, he'd demand an accounting and in no uncertain manner. He can be very strict in these matters."

Red considered that for a few moments and then said, "There's a man by the name of Luke Powell who wants to kill Miss Hall."

"But why?" Mrs. McDermott said, and Mrs. Hannah's perplexed face asked the same question.

"Because he tried to rape me and I put one of his eyes out with a curling iron," Erica said.

"Oh my," Mrs. McDermott said, shocked. Mrs. Hannah was stunned.

"I also stole a large quantity of a drug from him," Erica said. "It's called heroin and it's addictive like opium and morphine and I planned to sell it and make myself a lot of money."

"And where is this man, this Powell creature?" Mrs. Hannah said.

"On the trail just ahead of us," Red said. "I figure he'll be waiting for us at Potts's station where we change horses, and that's about an hour away."

"If Corporal Hannah and Corporal McDermott were here, they'd take care of Mr. Powell right quick," Mrs. Hannah said.

"But they're not here, dear," Mrs. McDermott said. "So we'll just have to make do." She took Erica's hand. "Get back into the stage, young lady. Mrs. Hannah and I will not let you come to any harm. If I must, I'll give Mr.

Powell a piece of my mind he won't soon forget. Rape indeed. He's worse than an Apache savage."

"And for goodness' sake let bygones be bygones," Mrs. Hannah said. "There's no use crying over spilt milk. We can't go back and undo what we've done."

"Or think we've done," Mrs. McDermott said. "Now, into the coach with you, young lady. What you need is a sip of brandy and a sugar cookie."

"You're both so very kind," Erica said. "But . . ."

"No buts," Mrs. McDermott said sharply. "We're not going to leave you alone on the prairie to be eaten by wild animals. Now, into the coach, instanter."

"Better do as she says, Erica," Red Ryan said. "Or we'll be here all day."

The woman touched his chest with the fingertips of her right hand and said, "Red, I'm sorry. I'm sorry for everything." Then she turned and stepped into the stage and Red heard Mrs. McDermott say, "Don't cry, child. Everything is going to be all right."

Red climbed into the box and Buttons cracked his whip and urged the team into a distance-eating canter. "What you said about Rosie Lee killing herself an' all, was real good. I didn't know you were such a philosopher."

"I don't know where the words came from," Red said. "I was desperate, I guess."

"Well, they was good words, but they didn't really work," Buttons said.

"Erica Hall will either get over Rosie Lee or carry her

to the grave," Red said. "I don't know which will be the case."

"Maybe she'll carry the guilt for only as long as it takes us to reach Potts's station," Buttons said.

"You're a comfort," Red said.

"Well, we're headed for a gunfight, not a prayer meeting. Lead flies, bad things happen."

"Maybe Powell will just go away."

"If I wasn't driving this stage, I'd say that's a possibility. But it's the Gray Ghost so that ain't gonna happen."

"I can't see him ahead of us."

"He's probably at the station already." Buttons shook his head. "Hard times coming down."

They drove in silence for the best part of an hour and then Buttons said, "Here's a question I've been pondering of late. See if you can answer it."

"Fire away," Red said.

"Who discovered that dropping eggshells in the coffee keeps it shy of bitterness? I mean, why would anyone do that in the first place, put crushed eggshells in the coffeepot?"

"Like you said, we're driving into a gunfight and you ask a fool question like that?" Red said.

"If I'm gonna die, I'll go to the grave more willing if I know the answer to that question."

"Well, I reckon the first range cook had a chicken that dropped them eggshells in the pot by accident and then Cookie discovered that the coffee wasn't near as bitter."

"And who was he?"

"I don't know. He probably worked for Moses or one

of those old guys you read about in the Bible. They were always out on the range tending their flocks."

"They herded sheep."

"Yeah, and some cattle. A mixed herd, I reckon." Red looked at Buttons. "Does that answer your question?"

"No. I only asked it to take your mind off gunfighting because Potts's station is right ahead of us," Buttons said.

CHAPTER FIFTY-ONE

Luke Powell and Lonnie and Key Cooke watered their horses at the corral trough and then led them back to the cabin. Victor Potts, busy in his smithy, was used to travelers stopping by for coffee or grub and paid them little heed. His sons, Joshua and Ephraim, were away from the station quail hunting and played no part in the violent events that followed.

Powell and the others stepped into the cabin as Potts's wife, Martha, was busy in the adjoining, windowless bedroom. She stuck her head out the door and said, "Coffee's freshly made and there's bacon and beans in the pot. I'll be right with you."

"That's for us!" Key Cooke said. "Bacon and beans is our favorite. Back home in the Tennessee hills we ate a lot of that, but sometimes with salt pork and wild onions."

Martha pushed a fat, white pillow into its case and said, "Good, I hope you brought an appetite."

"We sure did, ma'am," Lonnie said, grinning. "And by the smell coming from that there pot, you're a fine cook."

Luke Powell's anger flared. "You two! You came here

to grab a woman and kill the men with her, not to fill your bellies. Keep your mind on the job."

"What did you say?" Martha said. "We just got over a scrape with Apaches and we don't want any more trouble here."

"And there won't be, if you keep your trap shut and do as I say," Powell said. He looked trail-worn, dusty, and dirty, and the canvas patch over his eye gave him a sinister, piratical look.

Martha Potts didn't want trouble but she realized it had landed right on her doorstep.

"I'm the only woman here and I'm pretty worn out," she said.

"I've no interest in you," Powell said. "The woman I want is coming in on the Patterson stage."

"What is she to you, this woman?" Martha said.

Powell's fingers strayed to his eye patch. "She gave me this. That's what she is to me."

"Is she your wife?"

"No. Her name's Erica Hall and she's a thief and a common whore who dances naked for men. Who would have her for a wife?"

Martha was alarmed. "What do you intend to do to her?"

Powell's eye was tinged with a glint of evil, but his voice was quiet, conversational, as though he and Martha Potts were having a friendly chat. "Among other things, I intend to blind her. I'll take both her eyes for mine."

"No, you're not doing that to a woman under my roof," Martha said. "That's barbaric, mister."

Powell smiled. "I won't do it here. I'll take her to a quiet place where no one can hear her scream."

"That's a terrible thing to say or even think," Martha

Potts said. She stepped toward the door. "I'm going to get my husband."

"And when he walks through that door, I'll shoot him dead," Powell said. "Now, you stay right where you're at, lady, or I'll drop you, too, understand?"

It was then, behind Powell's back, that Lonnie and Key Cooke exchanged uneasy glances. The situation was escalating beyond their control and neither had the intelligence to get a grip on it.

"You'll never get away with this, not in a hundred years," Martha said. "There will be people on the Patterson stage and they will not tolerate your abuse of a woman."

"I don't give a damn what people can't tolerate," Powell said. "I'll let my gun do the arguing and then I'll take Miss Erica Hall for a little ride."

"You're mad, insane," Martha said. She pointed a finger at the Cooke brothers. "And you're dragging these poor rubes along with you to hell."

"You know what you're doing, don't you, boys?" Powell said. "It's worth killing a few folks for a hundred dollars and a horse, ain't it?"

The Cooke brothers didn't answer, didn't holler and slap each other around, and Powell began to wonder if he'd made a mistake. He knew he'd hired idiots, but he didn't know they were idiots with a conscience.

"Keep those rifles handy, boys," he said, hoping for the best. "When he comes in, the messenger may open the door. His name is Red Ryan and I want him dead. You got that?"

"We got it," Lonnie said. "Ain't we got it, Key?"

"We sure have," Key said.

And Powell felt a surge of confidence. The brothers

didn't have the sense God gave a grasshopper, but when the time came, it seemed they'd use those Winchesters.

Outside, Victor Potts's hammer rang on hot iron and the cabin was warm, close, and gloomy, the light of day having not yet found the windows. Wood crackled in the stove and the beans bubbled softly and beside them the coffee in the pot got stronger. Under her sunburned skin Martha Potts's face had drained of color and the Cooke brothers stared fixedly at the cabin door like a couple of hound dogs on guard. Powell stood relaxed and easy. He knew that Ryan was the gun, and he was confident he could take him. He'd killed Whitey, but that was probably a shot in the back. Powell was always mindful that he was faster than Whitey, but he'd kept that knowledge to himself. Red Ryan, the San Angelo shootist, would very soon discover just how fast he was. And that brought a satisfied smile to Powell's lips.

"Stage is coming in," Martha Potts said.

"I hear it," Powell said.

His smile grew. At last he was within minutes of getting his hands on Erica Hall.

CHAPTER FIFTY-TWO

"Their horses are tied outside the station cabin," Buttons Muldoon said.

"I see them," Red said.

"How do we play it, Red?" Buttons said.

He was on edge. Red could hear it in his voice.

"We do what we always do," Red said. "You unload me and the passengers and then you drive to the corral and change your team."

"And leave you three against one. I don't like those odds and I'm going in with you."

"You'll only get in the way, old fellow," Red said.

"I never got in the way before."

"You never came up against Luke Powell before. Remember all the stories we heard around the mercantile stove about how fast he was?"

"No, that wasn't Powell. That was some other feller."

"It was Powell they talked about, claimed he was faster than Wes Hardin. I remember it."

"That was from rannies who didn't know him. Stories passed from mouth to mouth have a way of growing and all of them windies. The wolf is always bigger in the dark, and all those boys were in the dark about Powell."

Buttons pulled the team to a halt. They were about fifty yards from the station and after the following dust cloud rolled on top of them, he turned to Red and said, "Tell me now or do I drive right past the Potts place?"

Red brushed dust from his shoulders and said, "Tell you what?"

"Whether or not you want me backing you when you meet Powell."

"It's my fight," Red said.

"Hell, no, it isn't. It's our fight. I work for the Patterson stage as well, you know."

"You've had my back before," Red said.

"A number of times. Took a bullet for you once."

"Buttons, it grazed your shoulder."

"I still took the bullet. If you recollect, Banjo Bob Warner fired that bullet and I figure he was faster than Powell."

"I doubt it," Red said.

Erica Hall stuck her head out of the window and said, "Why have we stopped?"

"Just sorting out Buttons," Red said.

"You're the one needs sorted out, figuring you can go up against Powell and two other gunmen. This is one you can't go alone, Red. I'll be right by your side."

"Is that your last word on the subject?"

"It is. My mind's made up."

"All right, Mr. Muldoon, let's get it done."

Buttons stopped the stage outside the cabin and Red climbed down to assist the passengers, first the soldiers' wives and then Erica Hall.

"He's here," she said. "I can sense his closeness like I would a ghost in my closet."

"I won't let him harm you," Red said.

Tiredness and strain had subtracted from Erica's classic beauty and now fear took its toll. Since the day she'd first arrived in Houston it seemed as though she'd aged a dozen years, all of them hard. But her body remained the same, still slim and beautiful in her torn, muddy, and weathered dress.

She stood very close to Red, turned her face up to his, and said, "Promise me one thing."

"Sure, I promise."

"Please don't die for me today."

"We've been through this before, Erica. I'll do whatever has to be done."

The woman opened her mouth to speak, but Mrs. McDermott and Mrs. Hannah cut her off. "Well, young man, are we going inside?" Mrs. McDermott said.

"Yes, right now," Red said.

"About time," Mrs. Hannah said.

Most people walk through a door, sneakier folks sidle, and drunks stagger.

But Mrs. McDermott and Mrs. Hannah charged through the door with all the gusto of two forty-gun frigates under full sail. Even Luke Powell took a step back when they entered.

"La, la, la," Mrs. McDermott said. "Now, here's a welcoming committee."

Mrs. Hannah said, "Well, I've never seen the like." She rounded on the Cooke brothers. "What are you boys doing with those rifles? Are you planning to shoot somebody?"

Powell's eyes were on the door, but his words were aimed at Mrs. McDermott. "Stay out of this, lady. It's got nothing to do with you."

"It has everything to do with us," Mrs. Hannah said. She stepped to Lonnie. "Are you two brothers?"

"Yes, ma'am," Lonnie said.

"Then it's disgraceful that you're lying in wait with rifles to attack a defenseless woman as soon as she walks in the door. Did you have a good mother?"

"Yes, ma'am, we did," Lonnie said. "Didn't we, Key?"

"Yeah, we did an' she always smelled nice of lavender water."

"Then she'd be ashamed of you. I'm not your mother and I'm ashamed of you, and so is Mrs. McDermott."

"Indeed I am, and if Corporal McDermott was here, he would box your ears. Now, put those rifles away and behave yourselves instanter!"

"Don't do what she says, do what I say," Powell yelled. "Now, get ready. I'll give you the word when to shoot."

"Did you listen to me, young man?" Mrs. Hannah said. "Or did my chiding fall on deaf ears?"

Lonnie and Key were raised in the Tennessee hills and had been too young to fight in the War Between the States. Nor were they born to the feud. They'd used squirrel rifles to shoot their grub but had never pulled the trigger on another human being. Luke Powell had excited them, made them feel important, significant, comparing them to Frank and Jesse, but now the time had come to gunfight other significant men they'd neither the belly for it nor the will. This wasn't like stealing chickens where the only risk was an ass peppered with rock salt, this was the real thing. They'd have to kill or be killed during a few moments of hell-firing mayhem and neither of those options appealed to them.

Key said, "I don't want to shoot anybody, ma'am."

"Neither do I," Lonnie said. "We could be sent back to Yuma."

"Or hung in Yuma," Mrs. Hannah said.

Powell's volcanic anger flared. "Numbskulls! Idiots! Use those rifles or I'll shoot you both dead and those two interfering women along with you."

"You're a horrid, horrid man," Mrs. McDermott said, scowling.

And then the door opened . . .

CHAPTER FIFTY-THREE

To this day there are those who say that Erica Hall insisted she be the first to enter the Potts cabin and take the first bullet if Powell fired, but that is untrue. Red Ryan stepped inside first, followed by Erica and then Buttons Muldoon. And there was no welcoming gunfire, at least not then.

Luke Powell immediately reacted to seeing Erica. "You!" he said, cramming all his pent-up hatred into a single word.

"What do I say to you, Luke?" the woman said. "How are you doing? Or it's nice to see you again?"

"You look like hell," Powell said.

"Because I've been through hell," Erica said.

Powell shook his head. "Lady, your hell hasn't begun yet. An eye for an eye, remember." He took a single step to the side. His Colt was holstered a little high, slightly forward, and handy. "You're out of this, Ryan," he said. "And you, too, driving man. I only want the woman."

Red shook his head. "Miss Hall is under my protection. You can't have her, not today or any other day."

"I've got three guns here that say I can take her," Powell

said. "Besides, why play hero, Ryan? What's in it for you? You can find a prettier woman to share your bed. Erica Hall means a lot to me, but to you she's nothing, just another two-bit whore."

At that moment Victor Potts walked through the open door and said, "Buttons . . ." Then he stopped in his tracks, taking in at a glance what looked like a gun standoff. "What's going on here?" he said.

"Never you mind what's going on here," Powell said. "Get over there and stand by your wife. I'll tell you when you can leave." Without turning his head, he said, "Lonnie, keep your rifle on him. If he makes any fancy moves, kill him."

Both Lonnie and Key sensed the danger of the man in the buckskin shirt, plug hat, and low-slung Colt. He had an air of quiet confidence about him and by comparison Luke Powell seemed a loud, blustering bully. There had been a lot of talk in Yuma about drawfighters, the likes of John Wesley Hardin and Wild Bill Longley, and here, standing relaxed and easy, was one of them. His name was Ryan, and they'd never heard him spoken of in Yuma, but he'd be almighty sudden. Lonnie and Key—in a few years they and their ilk would be known as hillbillies— no longer had a stomach for Luke Powell's fight. Would their Winchesters have made any difference in what followed? Most historians say no, that Red and Buttons acting together would likely have prevailed. But all agree it would've been a close-run thing.

Powell stared hard at Erica Hall and then said, "Come over here."

The woman said, "All right, Luke, I'll come with you. I don't want men dying because of me."

"Then get over here beside me like I told you," Powell said.

Erica stepped beside the man and he roughly pulled her against him. His lips found hers and he kissed her, savagely, grinding his mouth hard against hers, an act of love used as a weapon. Erica cried out, struggled, and broke free. A trickle of blood ran from the corner of her mouth.

"That's only a taste of what's to come," Powell said. He grabbed Erica by the upper arm and said, "We're leaving. Clear the way there."

"Leave her alone."

Three words from Red Ryan's lips, flat, unemotional, sounding so strange that Buttons Muldoon looked at him as though he'd never heard his voice before.

Powell pushed Erica away from him and then, his face ugly with hate, he grinned and said, "I've been looking forward to this." His hand inched closer to his holstered gun. Then, surprising everyone present, he yelled, "Cooke boys, kill him!"

Lonnie and Key hugged their rifles close and made no other move.

"Powell, it looks like it's just you and me," Red said. "Erica, stand clear of him."

The man's face had changed. Now Powell looked uncertain. He hadn't planned for this to end up in a drawfight between himself and Ryan. A quietness fell and grew into a profound silence. Only the simmering bean pot made a small sound.

"Powell, drop it or draw it," Red said. "I don't have all day."

"Listen up, all of you," Powell said. "After I kill Ryan,

I'm taking the woman and I'll gun anyone who stands in my way."

Red said, "Powell, don't just stand there running your mouth, make your play and get to your work."

"Here, Ryan, catch!" Powell yelled, grinning. He drew as he said it, very fast, very smooth, very professional . . . way faster than Red Ryan.

But Powell was the one to die. He staggered toward Red and his twitching trigger finger fired three shots into the wood floor of the cabin before he dropped like a felled cottonwood, as dead as he was ever going to be.

A perfectly round hole had appeared on Powell's left temple. The wound didn't bleed much, but the .41 caliber bullet had blown his brains out.

Erica Hall stood very still, her face expressionless, the Remington derringer in her hand trickling a thin wisp of smoke. Her open purse lay at her feet.

For a second or two time stood still in the Potts cabin before Mrs. McDermott and Mrs. Hannah stepped to Powell's body. They looked down at the dead man for a few moments, crossed themselves, and then took rosaries from the voluminous pockets of their skirts and began to pray together.

"Luke Powell doesn't deserve that," Buttons said.

Mrs. Hannah's fingers stilled on her beads and she said, "The good Lord decides who deserves and who doesn't, Mr. Muldoon."

Martha Potts took the derringer from Erica Hall's un-protesting hand and dropped it into her purse. She led the woman to a chair and had her sit down. Using a wet cloth she wiped the blood from Erica's mouth and chin and said, "I'll get you some coffee and whiskey."

"You're most kind," Erica said. She seemed distant and very pale except where Powell's stubble had scraped her mouth and left it bruised and red.

Victor Potts corralled Buttons and said, "Help me drag out the body."

"We'll let his boys do that," Buttons said. "Hey, you two hayseeds, come here!"

Lonnie and Key Cooke leaned their rifles against the wall and answered Buttons's summons. He pointed to the dead man and said, "Take that out of here. You can help Mr. Potts bury it later."

Lonnie looked into Buttons's eyes and said, "We didn't want to shoot anybody."

"Just as well, or you'd both be dead by now," Buttons said.

"He promised us . . . somehow he looks smaller lying there."

"What did he promise you?"

"A hundred dollars and a horse."

"Look in his pockets," Buttons said. "See what you find."

Lonnie did as he was told and came up with a handful of notes.

"Count it," Buttons said. "If you know how to do your ciphers."

"Ma teached me them and the multiplication tables," Lonnie said. He counted the notes and said, "Two hundred and fifty-one dollars."

"Right, you take two hundred for you and your brother and you give the other fifty-one to Mr. Potts to pay for your boss's burial. Now, as soon as you get this body settled, you and . . ."

"Key," Lonnie said.

"Right, you and Key get the horses and ride the hell out of here before Red Ryan takes it into his mind to gun you both. He can be downright ornery when a feller beats him on the draw. Victor, I got two road agents' horses tied up behind the stage."

"Dead road agents?"

"Yeah, the best kind. I'd be obliged if you'd buy them from me."

"In San Angelo you'd get a better price than I can give you."

"No, I don't want to do that. Abe Patterson would claim them for sure. He's mean enough to steal eggs out of a widder woman's basket and crafty enough to hide the shells on a neighbor's porch."

"I'll take a look at the horses and tell you how high I can go," Potts said. "Now, let's get this body out of here. It's upsetting the womenfolk."

"Wait. I've got a piece of advice to say to this pair of hicks. Forget the outlaw profession, because you're putting your saddle on the wrong hoss. You boys just don't have the belly for it."

"I guess we know that now," Lonnie said. "I reckon me and Key will try to get a job on the railroads."

"You got just what the railroads are looking for, weak minds and strong backs. Speak to the section foreman and he'll welcome you with open arms. And them's words of wisdom."

"Right, let's get this dead man out of here and planted," Potts said.

CHAPTER FIFTY-FOUR

While Buttons Muldoon left with Potts to change the team, Red Ryan sat beside Erica Hall. Slim and suddenly looking frail, she was bookended by the ample forms of Mrs. McDermott and Mrs. Hannah, and Martha Potts, looking concerned, was hovering close.

"She's drinking whiskey and coffee, poor thing," Martha said.

"And so are we," Mrs. McDermott said. "Mrs. Hannah and I got a terrible shock when the gun fired." Her plump hands fluttered. "Not that we're blaming Miss Hall. Never let it be said that I'd even think such a thing. If Corporal McDermott ever found out that I placed blame he'd beat me with a stick."

"And likewise with Corporal Hannah," Mrs. Hannah said. She placed a hand on top of Erica's and said, "My dear, you did what you had to do."

"And saved my life," Red said. "Luke Powell had me cold. He was fast on the draw, the fastest I've ever seen."

"It was up to me, not you, Red," Erica said. Her voice was weak, strained, as though she forced each word. "I'll never again look over my shoulder and expect Luke Powell to be there."

"No, you won't," Red said. "Now you can live your life without fear."

"And that's a good thing," Mrs. Hannah said. "You can be a dancer again."

"Or even a lady's maid," Mrs. McDermott said. "I can just see you in a white half apron and a nice, lacy cap on your head."

Erica's smile was slight. "That's a fine idea, Mrs. McDermott. I think that if I danced again, I'd feel as though I was dancing on Rosie Lee's grave." She saw the woman's face draw a blank and said, "She was a girl I knew, a singer. She's dead now."

"I'm sorry to hear that, dear," Mrs. McDermott said. "Were you very close?"

"No, not really," Erica said. "We were never huggy friends, but I liked her."

"We all liked her. She was so full of life," Red said. And then to Erica, "Where will you go after San Angelo? Have you any plans?"

"I don't have a plan apart from living life one day at a time," Erica said. "Maybe I could find a job doing something. Working in a hat shop would be a welcome change of pace."

"Buttons and me will help you all we can," Red said. "You only have to ask."

"And so will I help, my dear," Mrs. McDermott said. "Corporal McDermott is not without influence in San Angelo. I'm sure of that."

Mrs. Hannah said, "The trouble is that I don't know if the town will survive after the army abandons Fort Concho in a couple of months, though I'm sure Corporal Hannah will keep us informed."

"San Angelo is right in the heart of the Texas ranching country," Red said. "It will survive just fine. It might be a good place to settle, Erica."

"It's worth thinking about," the woman said. She smiled. "Me living in a small cow town . . . It's hard to believe."

"You'll be fine so long as you believe in yourself," Red said.

"Now, there's something to think about," Erica said. "Me living in a small cow town believing in myself." Her laugh was music to Red's ears. "I'm looking, but I still can't see it."

"It's on the horizon," Red said. "You just need to look hard enough."

"When we're in San Angelo, even after everything that's happened, can I still count on you as a friend?"

"Of course you can," Red said. "I'll always stand by you."

"And so will we," Mrs. McDermott said. "Won't we, Mrs. Hannah?"

"Indeed we will, and so will Corporal Hannah."

"And Corporal McDermott," Mrs. McDermott said.

"Looks like you'll have lots of friends in San Angelo," Red said. "And I haven't yet counted in Buttons Muldoon."

CHAPTER FIFTY-FIVE

Buttons Muldoon needed both hands on the reins as the Gray Ghost traversed a patch of some rough, broken ground that marred a stretch of wagon road. "In my shirt pocket there's money, take it," he said.

"What is it?" Red Ryan said.

"Your share of the horses. I sold them to Victor Potts."

Red reached into Buttons's pocket and removed the folded bills. "Fifty dollars," he said.

"And that includes both saddles and Powell's horse that Potts claimed for himself since he'd buried its owner," Buttons said. "Daylight robbery is what it was." He shook his head. "Daylight robbery."

"You'd have done better in San Angelo," Red said.

"And let Abe Patterson confiscate the money? Not a chance."

Red smiled. "There's larceny in your soul, Buttons."

"Damn right there is," Buttons said.

They drove in silence for a while and Buttons said, "What do you think of Miss Hall?"

"In what regard?" Red said.

"Will she settle in San Angelo?"

"I really don't think so. Some towns aren't big enough to hold a woman like her."

"She saved your life."

"I know. I told her that."

"What did she say?"

"What you'd expect her to say . . . 'You're welcome.'"

"She reached into her purse, let the purse fall, and her stingy gun was right there and ready. I saw that with my own eyes."

"Yeah, it was slick," Red said. "Just as well, Powell would've gunned me for sure."

"He was fast."

"Best I've seen. I told Erica we'd be her friends when we reach San Angelo."

"What did she say?"

"She was happy."

"I've never seen her happy."

"She'll be happier now that Luke Powell is dead."

"The wheelers don't like this coach, that's why they're pulling so good," Buttons said. "They're trying to run away from it."

"Mrs. McDermott says she should get a situation as a lady's maid."

"Who?"

"Erica. Miss Hall."

"There are no ladies in San Angelo."

"I don't think she wants to be a lady's maid anyway."

"What does she want?"

"I don't know. Peace of mind, I guess. She says she'll never dance again because it would be like dancing on Rosie Lee's grave."

"She can't get over that, can she?"

"I don't think so."

"She shot Luke Powell and it didn't seem to bother her."

"That was different."

"How different?"

"Rosie Lee was a friend. Powell was a bitter enemy who wanted to torture and blind her."

"Yeah, I can see the difference. She needs clothes."

"Huh?"

"She's wearing a ragged, muddy dress. If she wants a job she'll have to look better. She needs clothes."

"Then we'll buy her some."

"We'll give her some money and she can buy her own. What do we know about women's fixin's?"

Red smiled. "You'd give Miss Hall money, Buttons?"

"Yeah, a little to see her through."

"You've changed your tune about her."

"Of course I have. Think about it. If she hadn't plugged Powell I'd be down a messenger."

"I figure Abe would soon find you another shotgun guard."

"Yeah, but not one as useless as you," Buttons said, grinning.

"You know how to hurt a man."

"I know messengers don't have feelings. That's why they're given the shotgun. Their emotions don't get in the way."

"This messenger has feelings and emotions, that's why I feel so involved with Erica Hall."

"Do you love her?"

"No, I don't. I think her past would keep getting in

the way. I'd want my wife to be happy. Erica will never be happy again."

"Too bad. She's a beautiful woman."

"Not right now. But she'll be beautiful again. You know what I think?"

"No, but you're going to tell me."

"Her mind is darker, but I think maybe her soul is brighter. What do you think?"

"I think you sound like a preacher."

"There's hope for Erica. I think she'll find herself and get on with her life. Maybe she'll marry a right nice feller and have a home and kids."

"Well, you got her future all charted out, Red. You should tell her."

"Maybe I will . . . someday," Red said.

"A station coming up and I'll be glad to change this team. They don't like the Gray Ghost any more than I do."

CHAPTER FIFTY-SIX

Something was brewing in San Angelo and neither Buttons Muldoon nor Red Ryan liked the look of it.

"Who are those fellers?" Buttons said. "Look, there's a dozen of them. A bunch of vigilantes, do you think?"

"Could be," Red said. "I'm sure they're meaning to tell us right quick."

The Gray Ghost's side lamps were still lit as the morning light started to chase away the night shadows and the new day was coming in clean. Or was it?

Two riders broke off from the rest and Buttons drew rein as they approached the stage. Buttons recognized both of them, Sheriff John Coffin and his deputy Tom Flagler. "Now what?" he said.

"I reckon Coffin is about to tell us," Red said.

The sheriff rode around to where Buttons sat and said, "Howdy, boys."

"Good morning, Sheriff," Red said. "What's happening?"

"Bad news from the fort," Coffin said. "Mighty bad news."

"What's amiss?" Buttons said.

"Cholera, that's what's amiss. It started in the Mescalero camp and spread to the fort. Seven dead already, all Indians, but Major Kane says several soldiers ain't expected to live and there will be a lot more dead before the epidemic is over. Now the worry is that the cholera will spread to San Angelo and that's why we've quarantined the fort. You can go in, but you sure as hell can't come out again."

Mrs. McDermott opened the stage door and stepped outside. She heard what the sheriff said and was beside herself with worry. "Sheriff, my husband, Corporal McDermott, is stationed at the fort."

"And mine, Corporal Hannah," Mrs. Hannah said, stepping beside Mrs. McDermott. She was just as distraught, her rosy cheeks very red in her suddenly ashen face.

"Major Kane is doing all he can," Coffin said. "But he's only got one orderly and they've had practically no sleep in the last three days." He shook his head. "Right now between the sick Apaches and the soldiers, it must be hell in Fort Concho."

The Mescalero camped near Fort Concho consisted of a dozen families, blanket Indians, landless, penniless, helpless, and hopeless. Many were already sick—most of them were, before the cholera struck—malnutrition and neglect making them prone to any disease. Once they were infected, the cholera spread like wildfire.

"Sheriff, who is enforcing the quarantine?" Mrs. McDermott said. "I must be allowed to enter the fort to see to my husband. He may be sick."

"And that goes for me, too, Sheriff," Mrs. Hannah said.

"The army is enforcing the quarantine at the fort, a vigilante committee here in San Angelo," Coffin said. Then, his expression deadly serious, "Ma'am, you don't want to go into Fort Concho, not now."

"I must," Mrs. McDermott said.

"And I must as well," Mrs. Hannah said.

"We'll assist the post doctor any way we can. Isn't that right, Mrs. Hannah?"

"Yes, we can see that the doctor and his orderly get some sleep," Mrs. Hannah said. "We'll care for the soldiers and our husbands."

Sheriff Coffin shook his head. "Ladies, I've seen cholera and it's a terrible pestilence. Caring for its victims is a dirty, dangerous business and you could soon be numbered with the dead. For pity's sake, remain in San Angelo until the outbreak is over."

"No, Sheriff, we must be beside our husbands," Mrs. McDermott said. "Myself and Mrs. Hannah are in agreement on that."

"Indeed we are," Mrs. Hannah said.

"Then I will say no more," Coffin said. "Buttons, you may proceed to the Patterson depot. As for you women, God help you."

"You're late back, and you look like you've been through it, Mr. Muldoon. And you, too, Mr. Ryan," Abe Patterson said.

"You could say that," Red Ryan said.

"Do you want to tell me about it?" Abe said.

"Maybe later," Buttons said. "It will be long in the telling."

Abe read his driver's drawn face and fixed stare and reached the obvious conclusion. "Then later it is," he said.

He opened a desk drawer and came up with two gold coins. With a flourish he laid one in front of Buttons and then Red. "A double eagle each, as I promised. There's bounty for you! And I have more good news." He got no answer and said, "Don't you want to hear it?"

"Sure, boss, lay it on us," Buttons said.

"I heard through the grapevine that a rail link will soon be laid between San Angelo and El Paso, so I've decided to use only the Abbot southern routes as far as Houston and New Orleans. Easy runs, boys, easy runs, and plenty of passengers. What do you think of that?"

"That's good," Buttons said. "The Houston run is a real pleasure."

"I thought you'd like that," Abe said. "You'll have one more mail run and that will be our last stage to El Paso." He looked for enthusiasm, saw only tired faces, sighed, and said, "You leave at first light tomorrow morning, so get a good night's sleep. Now, if you'll excuse me, I have work to do."

Buttons and Red stepped out of the depot and saw Erica Hall and the army wives talking on the street. Mrs. Hannah and Mrs. McDermott held their carpetbags.

"I guess they're worried about their husbands," Buttons said.

"Seems like," Red said. "Cholera is a hell of a thing."

Buttons touched his hat and said, "How are you ladies?"

"Very concerned for our husbands," Mrs. McDermott said. "But once we got talking to the sentries and they sent for the doctor, Major Kane accepted us as volunteers, thank the good Lord."

"Volunteers for what?" Buttons said.

"We're entering the fort to care for the sick soldiers and the poor sick and dying savages," Mrs. Hannah said. "The doctor says he's very glad to have us and that we arrived at just the right time as the epidemic seems to be hitting its peak."

"Isn't that dangerous?" Buttons said.

"Pah! No more dangerous than traveling on the Patterson stage," Mrs. McDermott said. "Now we must go. Are you ready, Erica?"

Erica Hall nodded. "Yes, I'm ready. I hope we can make a difference."

"We will make a difference, my dear. I know once we roll up our sleeves and get to work, we will."

Red Ryan said, "Erica . . . why you? I mean, I don't understand. You could become infected."

"I know, but it's a risk I'm willing to take."

"Are you coming, my dear?" Mrs. McDermott said.

"Yes," Erica said. "I'll be right there." She stood on tiptoes and kissed Red on the cheek. "You're a fine man, Red Ryan," she said. "Thank you for everything."

As she walked away with the army wives, Red called out, "Erica . . . what do you hope to find?"

"Redemption," Erica Hall said.

Early the next morning Red Ryan and Buttons Muldoon, still stuck with the Gray Ghost, harnessed up the team and went into the depot for the mail sacks. When they came back outside, they watched the stage move from the corral and then stop at the depot.

"Did you set the brake?" Red said.

"Of course I did."

"Well, it's off now," Red said. Then after a few moments, "Buttons, what did you see up in the box just now?"

"Nothing!" Buttons said, too quickly. "What did you see?"

"Not a damn thing," Red Ryan said.

CHAPTER ONE

Dewey Mackenzie hadn't seen what prompted the slap. But he'd heard the sharp crack of it landing and then, when he looked around, he saw all too plain what was about to happen next—the cocked fist of the hombre who'd been on the receiving end drawing back and getting ready to lash out in response.

Problem was, the target for this intended punch was a young, pretty gal. That was something Mac could hardly allow. Not if he could help it.

He knew better than to stick his nose in other folks' business, especially when it was taking place in a public establishment in a town where he was a freshly arrived stranger. But he also knew there were exceptions to every rule, and a grown man getting ready to slam his fist into a woman, even if she hadn't been such a doggone pretty one, surely fell into that category.

So, before the slapped cowpoke hurled his fist forward, Mac reached out, clamping the man's wrist in a tight grip, and gave the arm a hard yank in the opposite direction.

Not quite six feet in height and still with a trace of boy-ishness to his clean-shaven features, in spite of being darkened and sharply etched by days in the sun and wind, Mac had a naturally muscular build, made even harder and more solid by the work he'd been doing during all those hours out in the elements. When he grabbed hold of something—or someone—it stayed grabbed hold of until he chose to let go.

The cowpoke—a lanky specimen, average in height and build, thirty or so, with furry reddish sideburns running down either side of his narrow face—was pulled off balance and staggered. Turning half around, he faced Mac with a look of surprise and rage and demanded, "What are you doing?"

Mac met and held the man's glare for two or three tense heartbeats, then shoved his arm down and away before answering, "What I'm doing, mister, is saving you from making a big mistake."

The activity and murmur of voices that had been taking place throughout the rest of the cramped, low-ceilinged, moderately crowded Irish Jig Saloon now ground to a halt. The portly old gent playing a squeeze box over in one corner stopped, too, and his instrument went quiet after gasping out a final sour note. All eyes came to rest on Mac and the man with the furry sideburns. The slap from the barmaid had drawn only minimal interest. But this confrontation, to the eyes of the onlookers, apparently had the makings of something not to be missed.

Furry Sideburns turned the rest of the way around to face Mac, both of his hands now balling into fists. Lips peeled back to show gritted teeth, he said, "Well, maybe you think you fixed one mistake, you stinking meddler, but I guarantee you made an even bigger one for yourself!"

One of the other two men still seated at the table Furry Sideburns had risen up from said, "Go get him, Jerry Lee!"

Jerry Lee raised his fists and began waving them in small circles, like he thought he was some kind of boxer. "Since you ain't packing no gun, Mr. Nosy, I'm gonna have to teach you a lesson the hard way. And when I'm done, I'll leave enough of you to be able to look up and *still* see me give that snooty gal what she's got coming, too!"

Mac adjusted his weight, hands hanging loose and ready at his sides, and stood waiting. In truth, he *was* packing a gun—an old Smith & Wesson Model 3, .44 caliber, that he kept tucked in the waistband of his trousers rather than in a side holster. A gift from his late father, which, at present, was hidden by the short-waisted jacket he was wearing.

All things considered, that was just as well. While Mac had grown fairly proficient with the gun in recent years, he was never eager to reach for it and this occasion hardly seemed to warrant doing so. At least not yet.

From behind the bar, the elderly apron who was barely tall enough for his scrawny neck and liver-spotted bald head to poke above the level of the hardwood did his best to sound authoritative.

"You gents knock it off. Either that, or take it outside," he hollered. "You know what Farrell will do if he walks in on this!"

Hearing the warning, Jerry Lee snarled, "You keep your beak out of this, Shorty—and to blazes with Farrell!"

And then he charged at Mac.

Mac had been waiting for that. Instead of holding still for the other man's rush, he agilely stepped aside and at the same time swept an empty chair from the unoccupied card table he'd been standing next to directly into the path of the oncoming Jerry Lee. The latter immediately barked his shins on the sturdy chair, resulting in him issuing a painful yelp, and then got his legs tangled up in it as his wild swing at Mac pulled him forward and off balance. Jerry Lee belly-flopped across the toppled chair, taking hard jabs from the sharp wooden edges to his stomach and ribs before rolling off into an awkward sprawl on the sawdust-littered floor.

Some onlookers winced at this painful collapse. A few others chuckled at the ungainliness of it.

Jerry Lee roared in pain and heightened rage as he scrambled to get to his hands and knees so he could then rise to a standing position. But before he could do that, Mac took a hurried step around behind him, braced himself, then leaned over to haul Jerry Lee up to his knees. From there, Mac quickly slipped his left arm under the cowboy's chin, clamping the throat in the crook of his arm.

At the same time, he once again locked Jerry Lee's right wrist in the grip of his own right hand, then wrenched the arm back and up between the struggling cowpoke's shoulder blades.

"All right now, Jerry Lee," Mac rasped with his mouth close to the man's ear, "I think you'd better calm down before somebody gets hurt."

"There's hurtin' to be done, right enough," Jerry Lee managed to squawk out, even with the lock on his throat. "And you're the one gonna be gettin' a hard dose of it!"

"That's the wrong answer, you stubborn galoot," Mac told him. He squeezed the throat tighter and cranked the arm up even higher. "Now you'd best think about changing your mind and doing it quick; otherwise I might decide to start ramming your head against the side of that bar over yonder until you're ready to take a different notion about things."

Jerry Lee tried to issue another angry retort, but this time all that came out was a gurgling sound and some spit bubbles leaking from the corners of his mouth.

"Don't worry, Jerry Lee—we got your back!"

These words, accompanied by the sound of chair legs suddenly scraping on the floor and the clump of boot heels also in hurried movement, caused Mac to look around. Sure enough, the two men who'd been seated at the table with Jerry Lee were shoving to their feet and starting to surge forward.

Mac didn't wait for them to get very far on their intended rescue mission. He immediately hauled Jerry Lee the rest of the way up, whirled him around, and gave him a hard shove that sent him staggering with windmilling arms straight into his two pals.

One of the would-be rescuers, a plumpish number with a round face, oversized nose, and eyes set too close under shaggy black brows, was directly in the path of the propelled Jerry Lee. He put his hands up, as if to catch his friend, but Jerry Lee's momentum was too much to stop. Round Face was staggered in reverse until the back of his legs hit the edge of the chair seat he'd just vacated, forcing him to suddenly sit down again with Jerry Lee more or less flopping onto his lap.

While this was taking place, the remaining hombre from the table—lean and catlike, with heavy-lidded eyes, a surly curl to his mouth, and slicked-back black hair complete with another set of thick sideburns—momentarily froze. But then, when he broke into motion once again, it came in a long forward stride with his right hand reaching down to hover claw-like over the black-handled Colt riding in a tie-down holster on his right hip.

Mac swore under his breath. It looked like avoiding gunplay wasn't going to be possible after all.

Yet even as the fingers of his own right hand were getting ready to dive under the flap of his jacket, the pretty barmaid who'd played a part in setting this whole works in motion suddenly stepped forward to help bring it to a halt. She did this by raising the partially poured pitcher of beer she had evidently just delivered to the table and crashing it down on the back of Surly Mouth's head before his fingers had a chance to close on the grips of his Colt.

CHAPTER TWO

Just as Surly Mouth was crumpling to the floor, a dark-haired, middle-aged man dressed in a corduroy jacket worn over a brocade vest came striding purposefully through the Irish Jig's front door. As he pushed apart the batwings and passed between them, his expression was open, amiable. But a single sweep of his eyes, making an appraisal of the scene he was entering into, quickly brought a scowl to his countenance.

"What in blazes is going on here?" he demanded to know.

Then his gaze came to rest on Jerry Lee, struggling to shove up out of Round Face's lap, and beyond that clumsily flailing pair the sprawled form of Surly Mouth. The scowl intensified. "You three chowderheads . . . again. I might have known."

"Now you hold on a doggone minute, Farrell," huffed Jerry Lee, finally getting untangled from Round Face and standing upright. "You ain't gonna lay this on us, not this time. No, sir. We was the ones *attacked*, and all we was doing was defending ourselves."

"*You* were attacked?" Skepticism rang sharp in Farrell's tone. "By who?"

"By that high-minded wildcat of a barmaid you hired, that's who." Jerry Lee thrust a finger in the direction of the pretty, beer pitcher–wielding blonde standing on the other side of the table. "First, she hauled off and walloped me across the face for no good reason. Then, as you can see, she took that beer pitcher and banged it down on the back of poor Edsel's head! And if that wasn't enough, this slippery stranger"—a jab of his thumb to indicate Mac— "stuck his nose in and nailed me with a sucker punch from behind!"

Farrell listened, the look on his face remaining every bit as skeptical as his tone had been. "A lick of truth in any of that, Becky?" he asked the blonde as soon as Jerry Lee's spiel ended.

Becky thrust out her chin defiantly and answered. "You bet there is. Yes, I slapped that pig Jerry Lee's face. And yes, I also clobbered Edsel with this beer pitcher when he was going for his gun to use on that unarmed stranger. The stranger, by the way, never sucker-punched Jerry Lee. He just grabbed his arm and gave him a shove after Jerry Lee was getting ready to club me with his fist for slapping him. Would you like to know the reason for the slap that started it all?"

"I think I can make a pretty good guess," Farrell said through clenched teeth.

"You can't hold that against a fella," Jerry Lee was quick to protest. "Any gal who takes a job parading herself around in a saloon is bound to get grabbed a little bit. And don't tell me she don't know it from the start. She not only has to know it, truth to tell she's probably wanting—"

"Shut your dirty mouth!" Farrell cut him off, taking a step forward.

Jerry Lee backpedaled so hurriedly he almost tripped and landed in Round Face's lap again. He held up one hand, palm out. "Now you hold off with that blasted Irish temper of yours, Farrell! That ain't no way to treat steady, paying customers, is it?"

"Whether it is or isn't no longer applies to you three," Farrell told him, his voice strained by the anger he was barely managing to hold in check. "Effective immediately, you are no longer customers here. None of you are welcome in this establishment ever again. Now, collect your change from the table, pick up your friend off the floor, and the lot of you clear out before I take a bung starter from behind the bar and hurry your sorry butts along!"

"You'll be sorry if you try to keep us run out," warned Jerry Lee. "Oscar Harcourt is bound to hear of it, and I can guarantee he won't like it one bit!"

Farrell replied, "You let me worry about that. Tell Oscar to come around any time he wants—I'll be glad to tell him the same thing. In the meantime, clear out of my sight before I lose my patience with you!"

In just a handful of minutes, the three were slinking out the door, Jerry Lee and Round Face dragging their partner with his arms hung over their shoulders. In the doorway, Jerry Lee paused for a moment, casting a baleful glance over his shoulder as if he intended to say something more. But then, facing Farrell's glare, he thought better of it and went ahead on out.

Once the trio was gone, Farrell turned and again swept the room with his eyes. Swinging one arm in a broad gesture, he announced, "Show's over, gents. Go on about your business, nothing more to see here. Especially not from those three louts . . . who won't be returning, I assure you."

The other patrons scattered around the room returned obligingly to the conversations, card games, and, in a couple of cases, solitary drinking that had been occupying them before the ruckus broke out. A nod from Farrell also started the accordion player squeezing out his music once more.

With the strains of a lilting Irish tune drifting through the air, Farrell then turned his attention to Mac, who had been standing quietly by, watching and listening. Becky, the pretty blond barmaid, set down her beer pitcher and drifted over to stand with them.

Farrell's expression was again quite amiable, a touch of a smile even curving his wide, expressive mouth. "Now then," he said, his eyes dancing back and forth between Mac and Becky, "are the pair of you done wreaking havoc in my otherwise peaceful establishment, at least for the balance of the evening?"

Becky's mouth dropped open. "Eamon! You know better than that. I just got done telling you—"

Farrell held up a hand, stopping her. "Of course you did," he said with a chuckle. "I was just teasing you a bit. You think I don't know that any trouble involving those three scoundrels surely wasn't your fault? My only regret is that you feel the need to be here at all, where exposure to their kind of trash is bound to—"

Now it was Becky who cut him off. "We've been all through that. I need this job, and you know all the reasons why. You agreed to give me the chance and you also know that I've done well at it. I was fully aware from the beginning there would be a certain amount of rough conduct and I'm able to handle most of it without ever causing a scene. But tonight, that sleazy Jerry Lee and his pawing hands . . ."

"You don't have to go into any further detail," Farrell told her. "In fact, if you tell me too much more, I may have to go hunt down that piece of vermin and finish what our new friend here"—a flick of his eyes to Mac—"was luckily on hand to deliver a piece of."

"Number one, I don't want you hunting down Jerry Lee and making things worse," said Becky. Then, bringing her lovely blue eyes also to rest on Mac, she added, "But number two, I certainly am grateful that this stranger *was* on hand to do what he did. Hadn't been for him, I hate to think what Jerry Lee's fist was getting ready to do to me."

Eyes probing into Mac's, Farrell said, "You can certainly add my gratitude to the list. But before going any further, I think it's time to dispense with this 'stranger' business. Will you be so kind as to share your name with us, sir?"

With an easy nod, Mac replied, "It's Mackenzie. Dewey Mackenzie. Most folks just call me Mac."

Farrell promptly extended his hand. "Mac it is, then. I, in turn, am Eamon Farrell. In case you haven't already figured it out, I am the owner and proprietor of our modest surroundings, the Irish Jig Saloon."

As the two men shook, Farrell tilted his head toward Becky, adding, "And this fair princess, to whose rescue you came, is Becky Lewis."

"Pleased to meet the both of you," Mac said, releasing Farrell's hand and pinching his hat to Becky. "Far as that rescue business, no need to make more of it than it was. Mostly, I just happened to be in the right place at the right time. Ain't my way to butt into other folks' affairs, but standing by and letting a man take a punch at a woman . . . well, that ain't my way neither."

"I'd say it sounds like you have some pretty good ways," declared Farrell.

"And I say, again, how very grateful I am that you happened to be in the right place at the right time," said Becky.

Mac felt himself blushing some at her focus on him. Up close, she was even prettier than he'd first realized. Not more than a couple years past twenty, with finely chiseled facial features and those striking blue eyes, all framed by pale gold hair falling loosely to her shoulders. Clad in a simple white blouse and a flaring maroon skirt that reached to midcalf, she was no more than five-two in height, trim but sturdy looking, and very appealingly curved in all the right places.

"Inasmuch as you are present here in a saloon, Mac, I presume you came inclined toward having a drink," Farrell allowed. "That being the case, I'd be honored to buy you one and invite you to join me at one of the tables."

"Sounds good to me," Mac told him. "A cold beer is what I had in mind when I came in."

"You two have a seat," Becky said. "I'll bring a pitcher."

"That's not necessary," Farrell countered. "You need to head for home. It's getting on toward evening and you have a ways to go before darkness settles in."

Becky shook her head. "Nonsense. I've ridden the trail between here and home dozens of times. I could do it with my eyes closed, plus my horse knows the way as well as I do. Besides, before I go I've still got a mess to clean up where I wasted that half-full pitcher of beer on the head of Edsel Purdy."

"All things considered, it was far from wasted," Farrell corrected her. Then, sighing fatalistically, he rolled his eyes over at Mac and said, "But I recognize when an argument is hopeless. Let's have a seat, Mac, and I'll join you in putting away some of that beer after the young lady fetches us a pitcher, as she insists on doing."

Connect with U(s)

Visit us online at
KensingtonBooks.com
to read more from your favorite authors, see books
by series, view reading group guides, and more.

Join us on social media

for sneak peeks, chances to win books and prize packs,
and to share your thoughts with other readers.

facebook.com/kensingtonpublishing
twitter.com/kensingtonbooks

Tell us what you think!

To share your thoughts, submit a review,
or sign up for our eNewsletters, please visit:
KensingtonBooks.com/TellUs.